Praise for Devon Monk's
A CUP OF NORMAL

"A delicious sampling of her short fiction, including four stories original to this volume . . . Featuring quirky, well-developed protagonists whose decisions have significant moral consequences, these stories also show a strong sense of place. Sometimes funny, sometimes dark, often both, they are varied in form and invariably rewarding." —*Publisher's Weekly*

"Re-reading Devon Monk's short stories reminds me once again of what a terrific writer she is. I'm proud to have published her first story and look forward to publishing many more. She's got a long and bright career ahead of her!" —Shawna McCarthy, editor of *Realms of Fantasy*

"Here are stories to unsettle and disturb you. Whether it's Medusa in love, vampire heat, a spidery Christmas, shattered bowls of dreams or machine conspiracies, there are scenes that will continue to lurk in dark corners of your mind. Beautifully written. Enjoy the ride."
—James C. Glass, author of *The Viper of Portello*

"*A Cup of Normal* showcases the breadth and variety of Devon Monk's imagination. From science fiction to epic fantasy, and everything in between, Monk demonstrates a flexibility of style and concept that surprises, entertains, and touches the heart in equal measure."
—Marie Brennan, author of *Midnight Never Come*

"There may be the word "normal" in the title of Devon's collection, but the stories are touching, personal narratives of the extraordinary. Reading Monk's work is like going to your neighborhood supermarket only to find that everything on the shelves is magical. She has the exceptional gift of making the reader both comfortable and amazed at the same time."
—James Van Pelt, author of *Summer of the Apocalypse*

"Devon Monk's collection of stories is a series of little gems, some sparkling and bright, some dark and foreboding. Delightfully written and richly imagined, the reader will be charmed by such diverse tales as the monster in "Dusi" who finally finds her true love, and alarmed by stories like "X-Day," a very black Christmas indeed. From Greek mythology to the battlefields of Vietnam to a slightly twisted take on contemporary life, these sweet, weird, sometimes romantic stories always engender the sense of wonder for which the genre is famous."
of *Mozart's Blood*

Also by Devon Monk

Magic to the Bone
Magic in the Blood
Magic in the Shadows
Magic on the Storm
Magic at the Gate (forthcoming)
Magic on the Hunt (forthcoming)

Dead Iron, The Age of Steam (forthcoming)

A CUP OF NORMAL

A CUP OF NORMAL

DEVON MONK

FAIRWOOD PRESS
Bonney Lake, WA

A CUP OF NORMAL

A Fairwood Press Book
September 2010
Copyright © 2010 by Devon Monk

Fairwood Press
21528 104th Street Court East
Bonney Lake, WA 98391
www.fairwoodpress.com

Cover illustration by Michaela Eaves
Cover Design by Nicole Thomson
Book Design by Patrick Swenson

ISBN13: 978-0-9820730-9-4
First Fairwood Press Edition: September 2010
Printed in the United States of America

For My Family, Dreamers One and All

COPYRIGHTS

CONTENTS

INTRODUCTION
Patrick Swenson

Devon Monk isn't normal.

She wants you to think she is, but she's not. I mean look at the title of this collection. *A Cup of Normal*? Ha, who does she think she's kidding? Just follow the spill from the front cover to the back cover: dragons, robots, ogres, spiders, pixies, and ducks. Ducks? Oh yeah, nice try, Devon. Attempting to use ordinary, normal ducks in a story to distract us from the threads of real magic in this collection.

Devon Monk weaves a fine yarn. I mean, she uses yarn to knit a great story. I mean she knits great *Transformers* hats, Locoroco toys, and book bags. (She's an avid knitter, and if you haven't yet checked out her projects on her website gallery, you *must*.) The thing is, Devon Monk just knows how to put things together. In the case of this collection, I'm talking about fabulous, wonderful, inventive stories. She lets them slide into the dark where despair dwells, and after they've settled there for a while, she allows them to emerge into the light so she can show us all where hope lives.

As her publisher and editor for this project, I asked who she might want to write an introduction, but instead of giving me names, she veered from normalcy and pointed at *me*. Well, I'm honored to write it, and I have good *reasons* to do so. I bought one of her earliest stories for *Talebones*, the magazine I edited for fourteen years. That story was "Oldblade," and it was the first of four stories to appear in the magazine. Three of those stories are in this collection. The story that *isn't* in here (one of my favorites of hers, *period*, by the way) isn't in here for a very, very good reason, and you may all be lucky enough to understand why some day.

She might correct me later, but I believe I first met Devon at Orycon in Portland, Oregon. I used to throw room parties there, in the early years of *Talebones*, and I'm sure she must have dropped by. If not at the party, then we ran into each other somewhere around the con. Regardless, I was introduced to her, and was immediately struck by her warmth and sincerity, her friendliness, and, of course, her amazing ability to strike up conversations with her friends and fans.

This might be why her stories work so well. She knows how to talk to readers. Like a mother reading to a child, she knows how to tell bedtime stories to calm us and prepare us for sleep, yet with equal skill she can whisper scary ghost stories so menacing that the sanctuary of our campfire seems far from safe. That's because she makes great use of her own world, threading her own interests into her tales. Many of the stories have something to do with knitting or weaving or mending, yet none of them are even remotely the same. Those stories (and *all* these stories) are as unique as Devon's own knitted toys and clothes and pouches and bags and Cthulhu chapstick holders. Yeah, that's what I said. Unique, and far from *normal*.

You're going to read some amazing work in this collection, including stories never before published. Just wait until you take in some of Devon's ideas about Christmas. Definitely not normal. I have too many favorite stories to mention here, but if you really want to see what Devon can do with words, skip to the last story and give "When the Train Calls Lonely" a read and tell me you aren't changed by it. Or the delightful "Dusi," that begins the collection: this isn't the Medusa I remember from when I was a kid. "Falling with Wings" is a story Devon wrote as a part of a challenge with fellow writers, yet it turned out to be a positively stunning love story. It takes place on a garbage world. Go figure. That's not normal, is it?

It's not normal what Devon can do, spinning these complex tales, so you might as well give in and drink from the cup. Just see what happens.

Oh, and remember my comment about Devon distracting us with ducks in this book?

They're not normal either.

Perhaps my first urban fantasy, this story was written and published before urban fantasy had that name. I want to give Shawna McCarthy of Realms of Fantasy *the credit for pointing out the ending was much too short, and then giving me a second chance to submit it to her. This was the first published story that made me hope I could be a writer one day.*

DUSI

My last lover was a hero. A beautiful, chisel-jawed, shining-smile, bulky-pec'd man who dumped me cold for the first Queen of Forever that batted lashes his way. Let me say this straight right now: I didn't expect him to stay with me — not for eternity. But when he came washing up on my shore, bruised and swollen and half-starved, we made a deal.

I'd take care of the multi-headed sea monster he'd gotten himself into trouble with and he'd stay on my island for the summer. In exchange for a little body heat, I'd dance for him.

Believe me, being supple-spined made for some spectacular dance positions.

But Perseus had all the moves. Tough as a sailor, charming as a midnight poet, and that smile. . . .

I, the good little monster, slogged through the cold salt water to face down his foe. I, the good little monster, got a knock to the head trying to lock the serpent into stone and I, the good little monster practically froze to death right then and there.

Would it have killed him to thank me? When I finally came to and made my way back to civilization, all I heard was: "Perseus cut off Medusa's head, Perseus used it for a shield, Perseus saved the swooning beauty." The lout hooked up with some queen, spread a bunch of rumors about decapitating me and using my head, *my head* to bring down the sea serpent. He left me, head intact and heart broken, behind.

Not even a farewell, Medusa, my almost love. Over the years, I've begun to wonder if he had it planned all along. Make the monster fall in love, send her out to fight while he puts a move on the queen, and pray the monster doesn't surface until the wedding wine has gone to dregs.

I should have turned him to stone when I had the chance —before I fell in love.

A knock at my door broke my reverie. I crossed the living room, bare feet scuffing carpet and shooting static across my scalp. The snakes on my head swayed like they were high on hair spray. I swatted at them with one hand and looked through the peephole.

A dark-haired man stood against Seattle's unbreakable gray. His skin was brown, almost black in contrast with his loose white cotton shirt. Wide shouldered, he was taller than I and strong-boned. Handsome. I did not look in his eyes, but I suspected they would be gray, or blue.

My heart raced and the snakes hissed. I do not believe in reincarnation or any of those other quaint attempts at eternal life. But when he smiled, I saw again the cliff, smelled again the salt breezes brushing my skin. A ship rounded the cove, sail swollen with wind, and the man on deck smiled at me.

The man outside my door picked up one of my rabbit statues from the flowerbed. He turned it over in his hand, stroking the stone fur and set it back down. He frowned and knocked on the door again.

"I don't mean to intrude," he called, "but I've been watching Jenny take your statues into town. Are there any left for sale?"

My mind told me to say no. He had all the makings of a hero, including an accent I could not place. But I needed the money. Being immortal doesn't guarantee unlimited riches. My statues sell best during tourist season and the last warmth of summer had faded away weeks ago, taking the tourists, and my income, with it.

I crossed the room to the mantle and put on my mirrored sunglasses. The reflective lenses wouldn't help much; it was me looking into other people's eyes, not other people looking into mine that caused all the trouble. But if I were very careful, we wouldn't make eye contact. The man would buy a statue, I'd have some money to pay Jenny to pick up my groceries, and I could go back to drifting through my memories.

"Come in."

The snakes hung quietly at my shoulders, brown, not green as the myths would have you believe. With a bit of concentration, I can influence the observer to see them as beaded braids against my tanned skin. I am not beautiful like my far-sisters, the Sirens, who pose for those tasteful pornography magazines. When I put my mind to it, I can be passably exotic.

"Welcome to my home," I said over my shoulder, "Mr. . . ?"

"Jason's fine."

I smiled. It was always comforting to hear old names.

"Jason," I turned and stared at his forehead, "what kind of statues are you looking for?"

"I'm not sure, really. These are beautiful." He wandered across the room, hands clasped behind his back as if he were in an art gallery. His hair was longer than I thought, drawn together in a band at the nape of his neck. Silk through my fingers, if I dared touch him.

Colorful stone birds clung to the ceiling, butterflies and dragonflies decorated the walls like polished pebbles. Two bear cubs held a sheet of glass between their shoulders and in the corner, a fawn stood, its sweet face wide-eyed with fright.

"These are my earlier works."

"You have more?" His voice warmed the room and I had the sudden urge to invite him to stay. It had been a long time since I had spoken with anyone, except Jenny, about anything. Immortality isn't all it's cracked up to be.

"There are a few statues in the back yard," I said, moving past him. Warm fingers brushed my shoulder and I glanced back.

He was standing too close, hand slightly raised. He smiled and I wondered what his eyes would show me.

"Thank you for opening your door to a stranger, Ms. . . ?"

"Gorgriou." And to fill the silence, "Are you a friend of Jenny's?"

"No, not really. I helped her load one of your bigger pieces into her truck a few weeks ago. I've seen animal statues before," he paused, his mouth pulling down into a slight frown again, "but none so . . . tactile. Since then I've watched Jenny come and go, bringing your groceries." He shrugged. "I guess I became curious and wanted to see more."

"Come this way," I said, leading him down the hallway to the backdoor. He followed so closely I could feel the heat radiating through his cotton shirt. He should not be here. I should tell him to leave. Ah, Perseus, why did you break my heart? The snakes stirred, an odd scraping of scales that could pass for beads against beads. I whispered a calming prayer in a very old language and opened the back door.

Sunlight broke through the clouds, illuminating the yard like a gathering place of spirits.

Timing is everything.

I smiled, happy for the light that warmed the cool autumn day. The wind rose, bringing with it damp smells of earth and sweet pine needles. I thought of an island far away and breathed deeply of my memories.

"Striking." Jason moved past me with solid, quiet steps.

Fox, coyote, and turtle stood with snake and raccoon. A deer that had grazed my herb garden one too many times stood frozen in mid-step. In the center was my favorite: a hawk perched on a slab of oak, wings stretched for flight, eyes searching a forbidden sky.

Jason walked among them, stroking fur and scales with appreciative fingers, his breath coming more quickly.

"Warm," he said. "The textures are so lifelike — I almost expect a heartbeat." He reached the end of the line of statues and shook his head. "You make it difficult to choose, Ms. Gorgriou."

I opened half-lidded eyes. Sunlight makes me sleepy. "Oh?"

"There isn't anything here I don't like." And he smiled.

I am a champion body language reader. But neither his body nor his voice told me what he meant by that. Did he want to buy all of the statues, or was he just trying to charm me? One glance at his eyes would settle my curiosity, but human statues only draw a good price if they are nude.

That thought brought blood to my cheeks and stirred up

feelings I thought long gone. I shrugged and took a deep breath.

"You may take a statue for free — for the help you've given Jenny." And then you can leave and take that damned smile with you before I start thinking of deals we'll both regret, I added silently.

"Thank you, but these are worth paying for."

"And also worth giving. Please, take one — any one, except the hawk." The snakes shifted again although there was no breeze. I didn't care if he noticed.

He bent, scooped up a statue, his fingers restless over its surface. "I'd love to see any new statues you may have in the next couple weeks."

"Fine." I held the door open with my arm and stared straight ahead at the forest that borders my backyard. "Thank you for coming by." I looked over his head as he moved past me.

He took a breath, but I continued, "And thank you again for helping Jenny. I'm sure you can find your way out."

The monster is tired now.

Silence, then the fall of footsteps through my house and finally, the thump as the front door closed.

I stood in the sun, cold and oddly vulnerable. The snakes rose, weaving in the pale sunlight, tongues tasting the air. I thought of ancient worlds and ancient deals. When I finally did come back to the present, it was nearly dusk. I sighed, and realized I hadn't seen which statue Jason took.

I scanned the grass. The statues stared at me with glassy, unsettling eyes. Raccoon, turtle, fox, were all accounted for. Only one tiny statue I had tucked by the foot of the deer was missing — a thin, coiled snake.

I drew a shaky breath and walked back to my house. Gentle tongues flicked over my cheeks, as surprised as I at the tears that were there.

Two weeks slipped by beneath Seattle's brittle rains. Jenny came with groceries and new books. We didn't talk much, having nothing new to say. I gave her the last of my statues except the hawk, to take into the grocery store and sell for half their summer price.

She was loading the statues when I heard voices outside the door. I pulled back the blinds and peered out.

Jason stood in the bed of Jenny's rusted white Ford, his back toward me. I watched, caught between fascination and envy as blond-haired, farm-fresh Jenny showed him the statues. He touched each one, tipped them to better catch the light, a slight frown on his lips, then, to my surprise, he handed Jenny a wad of folded bills.

She grinned and after a few words and gestures, they hopped out of the truck bed and got into the cab. The Ford growled and rumbled out of view.

Suddenly, I wondered about Jason's motives. Was he really just a curious neighbor, or was he from some obscure environmentalist group? Were there tests that would reveal what my statues really were? I had once dropped a stone squirrel and found its tiny skeletal structure scattered in the dust. But if Jason dropped a statue and found the bones, would he believe I was so thorough an artist that I would create a complete skeletal structure? Perhaps, but what would I tell him about the stone lungs and stone hearts?

I paced the room, snakes writhing. The last thing I needed was a bunch of tree-huggers picketing my front lawn.

I could go to him and demand to know why he was so interested in my work. Intimidating people is something I do well. Of course, I'd probably attract the attention of my other neighbors and end up with an entire block of statues.

The idea had merit, but eventually the police would investigate.

The snakes rose, angry and hissing. If trouble came, I would handle it.

And if Jason came, I would handle him too.

I cranked up the heat in the house and curled up in my electric blanket, determined to lose myself to the peace of my memories, but all I could think of were the smiles of heroes I should have turned to stone.

I wasn't surprised to hear a knock at the door a few hours later. I paced into the living room and peeked through the peephole, expecting to see Jenny there, with the wad of bills in her hand.

Instead I saw Jason standing in the rain, one hand shoved in the pocket of his denim jacket, the other holding a bottle of wine. Even wet, he looked good.

"Go away."

"Ms. Gorgriou, it will just take a minute. I have a proposition that may interest you."

Silence.

"I'm not leaving until you let me in."

Fine, I thought. I can take care of you easily enough. You'd make a nice addition to the backyard.

"Please come in, Jason." I slipped my dark glasses on and unlocked the door.

Better talk fast, hero.

Jason came in and held out the bottle of Cabernet Sauvignon. "I brought this to celebrate," he said.

"Oh?"

"You see, Ms. Gorgriou — may I call you Dusi? Jenny mentioned that was your first name."

Jenny has a big mouth. I smiled sweetly. "Certainly."

"Dusi, I haven't been completely honest with you."

Countdown to concrete, I thought.

Five. . .

"I am a field representative for a group based out of San Francisco."

Four . . .

"Your statues caught my eye. They are so amazingly real, almost too good to be true."

Three . . .

"So I had to investigate." He smiled. "I'm glad you let me in the other day."

Two . . . I fingered the edge of my sunglasses and lowered my gaze from his forehead to eyebrows.

"I am authorized to pay you four times your current asking

price for your statues, provided you let us display them exclusively through our galleries."

One never hit. I blinked, quickly looked back at his forehead. "Galleries?"

"In San Francisco. I'm vacationing. I already sent the snake statue down to the gallery director. He loved it!" He laughed, a rich, warm sound that sent shivers across my skin.

"He thinks you're the discovery of the century and I couldn't agree with him more."

Discovery. I rolled the word in my mind and decided it was a much nicer way to say monster.

"How long would you represent my work?" I asked, thinking of the long touristless, and cashless, winter. "Is there a contract?"

He fished inside his jacket and handed me an envelope. "Five years, a substantial advance and renewal options."

No more wondering if I could eat from month to month. I licked my lips and pulled out the papers. I took my time reading every word. It was a deal, after all, and deals and heroes don't mix. But for once, this deal seemed wholly in my favor.

"Where do I sign?"

He gave me his pen, watched as I signed with large flowing letters. I used my full name, Medusa Gorgriou.

I smiled. "Now what?"

"Celebration."

Late afternoon slid into night. We emptied the wine bottle and I learned about his job, which he loved, his life in San Francisco, which he loved to hate, and the woman who divorced him seven years ago. "I miss her," he sighed, "but I knew it was only a matter of time. She and I are too different."

He looked at me, trying to catch my eyes through my glasses. "Do you always wear those?"

"No." It was my turn to smile.

"You are beautiful, Dusi."

I laughed. "Meet my sisters and you would change your mind." I tilted my glass and caught the last drop of red wine on the tip of my tongue.

"I've never seen anyone even half as graceful and," he paused, searched the ceiling. I studied his profile and liked what I saw. Strong chin and hooked nose, and wide forehead lined with thoughts I could not see.

"Mysterious. Mystical."

I averted my eyes. Close, Hero. Mythical.

He leaned forward, his hand sliding across the back of the couch to cup my shoulder. Heat spread against my skin and I closed my eyes at the sudden pleasure of it. It had been hundreds of years since anyone had touched me.

Warm breath brushed my cheek. I parted my lips, wanting to fall into his warmth, wanting Jason around me, inside me, the sharp wine taste of him like a sun against the storm. But he was a hero and no matter how much I denied it, I was still a monster.

Somehow, I turned my head, away from his heat, away from his touch. "It's late, Jason," I said in a voice far too calm for the emotions rushing through me.

He sat back, his mouth turned down in a thin line. "So it is." He stared at my profile for a moment, studying me. Then he ran his fingers through his hair and took a deep breath.

"Dusi, I'm going back to San Francisco tomorrow. I bought several of your pieces from Jenny and want to be there when they are picked up. The gallery will probably have an unveiling of our newest discovery. You should come with me."

"No."

Silence, except for the rain falling against the night.

It was the first time I had ever refused a hero. I liked it, and yet something inside me hurt.

"In case you change your mind, the phone number and everything else are on your copy of the contract." There was something behind his words that didn't belong in a hero's voice. Could it be sorrow? For a monster?

"I won't change my mind," I said. Because I can't. Too many people, too many chances to lose what I was finally gaining after thousands of years of wanting it — a chance to make my own choice, my own deals. A chance for respect.

He rose. "Well. Thank you, Dusi," he walked to the door.

"For what?"

"Opening your door to a stranger." He smiled and stepped out into the dark rain.

Ah, Perseus, why did you have to change me so? But it was not Perseus I saw in my mind. It was Jason.

Winter in Seattle isn't beautiful, it's just wet. I had enough money to buy new books, go out to a few movies and, with my sunglasses on, I even tried eating at a restaurant once.

Independence.

In my mind's eye I still stood on the cliffs of my past, but I no longer ached for an extinct world, being happy — happier, in the one in which I now existed.

But at night, a small part of me waited for the ship to sail around the cove, bringing a man whose smile had touched my heart.

When spring came, I threw myself into my work. Jason sent letters. I was the rage in San Francisco and the demand for my works were high.

Respect.

Not bad for a monster.

I wrote him back. Just business at first, and then the letters became more personal. I didn't tell him my secret, but I did mention my childhood in Greece and my brief love affair. He wrote poetry, which was not bad, and told me he had visited Greece and loved it and that he missed the moody skies of Seattle. I sent him a dozen roses on his birthday and ended up talking on the telephone with him for four hours. He was a nice man, I decided, even if he was a hero.

Spring brought days full of buzzing bees, little animals and plenty of statue material. I sat just inside my back door, tiny stone bees scattered on the carpet beside me. I held my hand out, coaxing a squirrel in from the backyard. My dark glasses lay at my side as I waited for the squirrel to stand the way I wanted it to before I gave it the eye.

The front door opened. I turned and looked across the hallway—

— into Jason's eyes.

They were blue, with green, not gray, and rimmed with long, dark lashes.

I turned my head, unable to watch the change, unable to see him die. The squirrel jumped away and I stared at the carpet, hot with self-loathing. So the hero had gotten the bad end of the deal this time. Why cry? In a few thousand years there'd be another hero. But I knew that wasn't true. Jason had been more than a self-serving hero. He had been a friend.

"Dusi?"

I looked up.

Jason smiled down at me, alive.

"I don't understand," I said.

He shrugged. "Does it matter?"

"I'm a monster." My voice rose. "You should be dead. Stone!"

He nodded, taking the revelation too calmly.

"If I remember my myths correctly, you shouldn't be alive either. Weren't you supposed to be the mortal sister?"

"Don't believe everything you read," I snapped. "Why are you still breathing?"

Jason took my hands and helped me stand.

"You are not a monster in my eyes, Dusi."

And as I watched, his eyes became the color of a dark sea. In them I saw endless reflections of ancient pain, sorrow and languid summer joys. Things no mortal eyes could ever hold.

"You're immortal," I said.

He nodded. "I did not want to die, still having the thirst for a world left unexplored. Hera heard my plea and granted me eternal life in return for my services to her. But her gift came with a price. I would remain alive, but could love no mortal woman." He paused a moment, then, quietly, "Finding you has been the most wonderful gift, Dusi."

"Why? Are you here to kill me, Jason? Am I your next golden fleece? Your next monster to conquer?"

He smiled that smile of his, and I found myself wondering if I could kill him.

"No, Dusi. After seeing the statues, I was honestly just curious. I had heard the tales of you, of Perseus, but thought you both long dead. When I spent time with you I realized it wasn't curiosity that made me want to know you better." He shrugged and then looked me straight in the eyes. "I've fallen in love with you, Dusi."

That stopped all other questions short. I searched his face, amazed at the honesty there. I very gently touched his cheek.

"Love?"

"You have heard of it, haven't you?" he dead-panned.

"Love," I repeated, trying to regain my footing. "Isn't that what comes right before betrayal?"

"Dusi, I would never . . ."

"Then I have two words for you: Prenuptial agreement." How do you like that deal, Hero?

Jason seemed surprised, and actually, so was I. In the seconds he took to consider my offer, I relived centuries of self-doubt. Every other hero had run when I asked for anything more than casual promises.

Finally: "Are you asking me to marry you, Medusa? Because if that's what it takes to be near you, to be a part of your life, then I'll sign any paper you want."

I blinked. For once, the hero had agreed to my deal.

"That's part of what it takes," I said, warming to this idea.

He raised one eyebrow, waiting.

"I won't marry a man I've never kissed."

He smiled and drew me against him. And for the first time, I saw laughter in his eyes.

There is a wonderful old log cabin in Rockaway Beach that my writers group, the Wordos, rented out for a weekend write-a-thon. The goal was to have something to read out loud at the end of the stay. I thought: why not write a story that could be read both forward and backward? After exactly two paragraphs of that nonsense, I chucked the idea and wrote something fun, fast, and quirky.

BEER WITH A HAMSTER CHASER

Before the hamster hit maximum stride, before the flexing wires and filaments sputtered and sparked into full life, blowing open the parallel reality, Carla, a strong-minded girl who nonetheless had her doubts as to the viability of using hamsters in conjunction with quantum physics, stopped thinking about Gerald's cute smile and said, "Oh, shit. It's going to work."

If, before that, Gerald hadn't laced the hamster's water with the equivalent of a pot of Italian coffee boiled down to a teaspoon of baby-fine dust, the hamster would never have made those kinds of speeds. But Gerald, whose chest still hurt, knew his experiment would work. He had his sister's life and free beer riding on the outcome — and he wasn't going to let anything get in the way of free beer.

All he needed was a hamster's worth of physics, a split moment of reality blurred long enough for Gerald to send Anthony the Thumb packing a hundred miles away — far enough that he wouldn't be able to date Rachel anymore, which would suit Gerald just fine because he had higher aspirations for his sister's marital status — namely, the bartender, Dan, down on Court Street who'd had his eyes on Rachel since she snuck her first shot of tequila when she was eighteen. Dan gave Gerald a beer on the house so long as he talked about how Rachel was about to break it off with the Thumb.

Gerald probably would have coasted on the one beer a day for the rest of his life, but Dan the bartender sweetened the deal by offering Gerald the family plan — free beer for the rest of his life — as soon as he and Gerald were family.

It was a good thing Rachel wanted to dump the Thumb anyway — she'd said something near enough to that, in Gerald's living room just an hour before he'd boiled down the coffee and fired up the hamster.

If Rachel hadn't taken a fistful of Gerald's t-shirt and enough chest hair to get his attention, he may have missed her gentle confession when she said: "I'm getting married to who I want when I want, asshole. Screw that up, and I will kill you."

Good thing Gerald had already called Carla over the night before to help him rig the hamster-bulb-reality-blur contraption.

Carla was in on the experiment because she had the math to back up the blink theory, all of it except for that little gap during the actual phenomenon itself — that lightbulb blink that happens when you're just sitting around the house, not doing anything and the lightbulb dims and refires in a blink, and you know it isn't caused by a flux in the electric feed, flawed bulb, bad wiring, or falling barometric pressure, because you've checked all that.

Carla's theory was that the blink only happened when parallel realities bumped into each other, and for a split second, became the same reality. Unfortunately, the exact moment in which a blink occurred was the part of the theory Carla hadn't quite nailed down.

Which was okay, except that Carla didn't really think the experiment would work. She helped out because she kind of liked Gerald, the clean-shaven angel-eyed slacker slob who was a little tight with his beer money, but cute enough and nice enough that he was probably going to go gay if a girl like her didn't step in and turn that smile he used on bartender Dan around to a good girl like her.

So when Gerald called, she said: "I still don't have the blink accounted for," while she twirled a pencil in her hair, the mirror in front of her desk smudged from the frenching she'd been practicing right before the call.

At that point, Gerald was past caring about the why and how of the blink, and more focused on the if and when. "But we can do it, right?"

"Yeah," she said, "we can do it."

Gerald got real excited and told her to come over right away before his crazy Thumb-sucking sister ruined everything by buying stationery with Mr. and Mrs. Opposable embossed in gold script on it. Gerald was worried. Screwing with reality was one thing — trying to return gold embossed stationery was out of his league.

Fortunately, Carla said she'd be right over. She hung up the phone, tucked the pencil behind her ear and put on a new coat of lip gloss. She'd get Gerald to shine that angel-eyed slacker smile on her tonight — hamster or no hamster.

Gerald was ready for her. He had left his bedroom window open just enough for the ground wire attached to the city light pole to get through. He'd rigged the ground in case they blew the half-dozen drained car batteries strapped together on the floor of his room. The wire snaked toward the hamster cage on his desk like, well, like snakes — and there the cables and wires connected to hangers, six sets of jumper cables and a broken handled turkey fork held in place above the cage with a network of de-papered twisty ties which in turn wrapped around the bars of the squeaky wire exercise wheel and the forty watt lightbulb in a socket in the corner of the cage.

Gerald had taken extra care to strap the whole deal together with generous strips of duct tape, because he wasn't about to risk reality or beer to a half-ass wiring job.

Once Carla arrived, they fueled the hamster with super-condensed Italian caffeine, and dropped it into place on the wire wheel. The hamster ran — all four of its nubby legs pounding like hummingbird wings, moving faster than any rodent had ever moved.

Gerald already had the phonebook open in his hands and his finger planted on Anthony's address. He stared at the hamster and repeated to himself, Anthony's gone, Anthony's gone. He tried really hard not to think about the beer, the free beer, just Anthony gone, free beer, Anthony, free beer, gone . . . when the hamster hit the threshold speed and triggered Carla's mathematically unpredictable blink.

A firework shower of sparks filled the cage, first too bright then too dim, and then just plain too dead. The lightbulb went dark and stayed that way.

Carla covered her nose, her eyes watering from the smell of scorched hamster — a little like over heated vacuum cleaner and three-day old road kill skunk. "Did it work?" she asked.

Gerald glanced at the phone book and realized that under his finger was Torlioni, Anthony, same street as always, even the same phone number. Realities might have bumped, but they hadn't changed.

Gerald shook his head. By now Rachel had probably picked out the stationery, maybe even registered for wedding gifts, the bitch. His window of opportunity was gone and the Thumb hadn't budged.

Carla was talking, her words coming out sort of muffled. "Sorry about the hamster."

Gerald looked down at the tan-colored lump and felt an overwhelming moment of guilt. He hadn't meant for the little guy to croak.

"I don't know why it didn't work." He gave the hamster a gentle poke. Nothing.

"It's not your fault," Carla said. "You were great. I should have predicted when the blink would hit and warned you. Maybe if I try —"

"Naw," Gerald said, "That's it. One hamster is my limit."

Gerald glanced at Carla, who looked pretty cute with her hand over her nose.

"How about I buy you a . . . uh . . ." He paused. "We could go out for a . . ." He glanced at the hamster. Something. He was thirsty for something. The ghost of a memory slid by, cool and fizzing, tantalizing, and was gone in a blink.

"For . . . coffee," he finished. "Would you like to go out for coffee?"

Carla looked surprised.

"Unless you'd like something else?" he quickly said.

"No, no," Carla said, "coffee sounds perfect."

And it was.

One of my earliest published short stories, this was my first foray into science fiction. I have a fondness for little robots, and giant robots, and I hope that love shines through.

PROBE

I t comes, breaks, lands. Strange parts move here, there and touch . . .

Heat.

I am more, free of my world, my soil. I drift and soon cling to the strange parts. I stretch, absorb, learn.

These are machines, I learn. They mine for substance known as mineral. They will not be here long. Soon they will take to the sky, the stars. This soil is rich with mineral, but poor of life.

Life?

I search to understand that, find the moving of limbs, the rhythm of speech, the part and whole that make human, soul/thought/life.

I want that.

I devour the small chip of metal in the machine that contains so many thoughts. Now I am alive. And words have meaning.

"If you're happy and you know it, clap your hands . . ."

It is coming from the big gray machine, the one that bangs against the ground, pulverizing rock into silt.

I swivel, find optical, see.

"Shut up, Bruce! You're killing me." This machine is smaller and scoops up the silt, pouring it into another machine, a carrier.

Carrier moves well. Tracks for feet push over the rocky terrain, moving silt to the sorter. Sorter is bigger than Carrier, bigger than Scoop, bigger than Bruce the pulverizer and much bigger, I realize than me. I am Probe. There is only one bigger than Sorter and that one is sitting silent, a behemoth that pours light down on us, and waits as they fill its belly — its hull.

The biggest one is important. The big one can fly. It is Ship. The word is layered with history. I learn ocean, storm, quest, stars, survival, freedom.

Ship is necessary. It is freedom away from home, and freedom to return.

I want to see Ship closer. I multiply, swarm over my machine, find I am squat, blocky, with track wheels like Carrier, and hands like Scoop's but smaller. I learn motion, function. Both need fuel. I decompose a few wires, eat at the walls of my machine, making them thinner, breaking down metal and plastics into something more useful — fuel.

I feed the lines and push myself forward.

"Hey!" Carrier rumbles to a stop, stirring dust in the space between us. I study dust and find that my world has very little atmosphere.

"Probe's moving." Carrier's voice rumbles low.

"No kidding?" Scoop's voice is high and smooth. "I thought that thing kicked off years ago. You sure it wasn't just knocked loose by Bruce?"

"It moved," Carrier says again. This time Carrier's instruments click and scan me. I try to offer the right pulses.

"Hm. Downstairs must have gotten it going again. Welcome back, buddy." Carrier changes course, moves around me and powers on, its cavity full of mineral for Ship.

I push forward again, try turning, reverse. Back, right, left, forward, this must be freedom, this must be flying! I move and move and move, carving tracks around the mining machines.

Until Sorter calls out to me.

"Probe? Are you okay?"

Sorter waits for a response. I devour memory, correlate facts. This takes time. There is much in memory. Finally:

"I am fine. I have been stationary for many years. How are you?"

Sorter makes a sound, something quieter than Pulverizer's pounding. I like Sorter's sound.

"Pretty cute. They gave it a personality." Sorter sucks down Carrier's load, analyzes, packages, disgorges non-suitable material then calls out, "Hey, Cinda, Bruce. Probe's a conversationalist."

Scoop and Pulverizer stop their functions momentarily. They swivel, instruments scanning me.

I wait. They expect something of me. I choose a phrase and speak. "How has the weather been lately?"

Then they all make sounds like Sorter's. Rhythmed, flying sounds. Good sounds.

"Well, it's monsoon season here in Mumbai," Scoop says.

"Humid in Hong Kong," Sorter tells me.

"Nice and warm in Perth," Pulverizer says.

"It's always warm here in Cairo," Carrier rumbles, "just like it's always raining in Seattle, right, Dana?"

Lights on Ship move and a strong, warm voice carries across to me. "Yes, it's raining here. Now stop playing with the probe. I'm sure the good V-trippers in St. Petersburg have better things to do than collect weather reports. Get back to work, boys and girls, we've got a deadline to hit."

The machines go back to work. I move, bumping over the uneven ground, slower now, thinking. There are many new words for me to correlate. Mumbai, Hong Kong, Perth, Cairo, Seattle, they all mean the same thing: Home. Earth. But V-tripping means something else. It means the machines are tools, hands, wheels and power. It means the machines are not alive. Life is not on my world.

I try to access information, find it is not in memory. Perhaps I can learn of life if I access files on Earth. I copy the energy pulses the others are releasing, adapt and send my own. This takes some time as I have never sent pulses through space before. Soon I connect with Earth, find information. Humans. Organic, sentient, biodegradable, alive. People stay on Earth while their machines mine my world.

Mine my world for minerals. Minerals humans need for . . .

I try reassessing the information, realize I must learn which minerals are being mined. I do so, find the information hard to access. I learn the ways around information blocks. It is not hard, just time consuming. I learn. The minerals they mine are used for building. Building something I do not understand.

Pulverizer is singing again. It is a song of rocky mountains this time. I fiddle with my circuits, find tone and variation, access the song and sing with him.

This too, is like flying. Is it like life?

Pulverizer makes the good sound again, the laughing sound.

"Nice voice you've got there, Probe," he says while his arms bore and smash rock. "We'll have to get together someday in real-world."

"Where?" Scoop asks in its high voice.

"Anywhere you want," Pulverizer says. "How 'bout it group? Think we should meet the faces behind the machines after this is all over?"

There is a round of agreeing noises, except for Ship.

"Not without me, kids, and that means a year. It takes a while to get all of our hard work home you know."

"We'll wait for you Dana," Sorter says. "How about one year on the mark after we load up and you lift off? I know this great bar, downtown Hong Kong."

"No way," Scoop pipes in. "I don't real-fly. You're all going to have to come here to Mumbai. You too, Probe."

I stop. They want me to join. I think this over. To meet the life behind the machines I will have to have transportation, a body and a way to fly.

"How can I come? Will Ship fly me?"

The laughing sound again. Sorter finally speaks up.

"Just get on a real plane, Probe. I don't think there's a bar big enough for the V-bots. Anyway, you've got a year to book a ticket. Plenty of time."

I sense something, something I have not known. I multiply many times. This sense is strong, but does not come from an outer influence like sight or hearing or speech. I search for words to give the sense meaning.

"Thank you." The words are not enough, but they are good.

They convey some of what I sense. "After the war, perhaps we can mine another planet."

The machines stop. Pulverizer's arms slow, Scoop's shovel sticks in the silt, Sorter's lights and wide gaping maw close down, Carrier halts. All dim except Ship. Ship's lights burn even brighter, tracing my blocky hull. I wonder what I have said to cause this.

"What war?" Ship asks quietly.

"The war between nations. It will not begin until after you return, Ship."

"How do you know this?" Ship asks.

"It is in the mission file. Mineral zynechromite. Primary use: Detonating component of viro-fissure bomb. Alternate uses: None. Mission: Scan planets, asteroids for base components of zynechromite. Base components include: —"

"Enough," Sorter says.

There is silence. They are not alive, but I sense the life behind the machines. Something has changed with them.

"I won't do this," Sorter breathes.

"There's not going to be a war," Pulverizer says, its arms whirring faster again. "The probe's probably just gotten its programming garbled."

"We're mining for soil enrichment, right?" Scoop asks. "They told me it was nutrient-rich. They told me it would restore Earth's soil."

"What exactly is in this stuff, Viv?" Carrier asks.

Sorter makes a new, uncomfortable sound. "How should I know? I'm not a God-damned geo-chemist. I just sort the symbols until they match. I'm a V-tripper like the rest of you."

There is silence again.

"Probe? Are you V-linked to St. Petersburg?" Ship asks in its strong voice.

They wait. I do not want to tell them that I am not like them. I do not want to lose this body, this movement, freedom. But I answer.

"No."

"So you're still running on the memory of your original programming, no V-tripper attached?" Ship asks.

"That is partially correct."

"Partially?"

"I am not V-linked. I have original programing and access to information on Earth."

"Crazy!" Pulverizer says. "A preprogrammed probe can't access anything except its ground station."

But the others do not go back to work as Pulverizer has.

"What if we're wrong?" Scoop asks.

"Probe," Ship says, "access each of our dates of birth, our WSSI numbers and the last death recorded by the World Criminal Investigative Authorities."

I do not understand why, but send pulses for the information.

"It is sending," Sorter whispers, "and not to the ground station in St. Petersburg." Instruments on Sorter are flashing rapidly. "It's following our ground-links and spreading out from there."

"Can you access its destination?" Carrier rumbles.

"Not unless I want a cop at my door."

"Where is the sending source?" Ship asks.

Sorter opens its maw, closes it. Its lights slow. "Here."

"Hong Kong?" Ship asks.

"No." Sorter breathes, "Here. On the rock."

Silence.

"Stop, Probe." Ship says. "Tell us the mission statement again."

And so I do.

They listen.

Silence again. I want to move, to push my treads deep into the dust of this planet, and move away. I want to speak, to ask them how it is to be alive, to ask them if they will still let me meet them at a bar in Hong Kong. But I sense I should be silent, as they are. I sense I am waiting for them to choose.

"I won't do it," Scoop says quietly.

"What are you going to do, Cinda?" Pulverizer says. "Just shut down and call it quits?"

"Yes."

Scoop pulls its shovel out of the soil and trundles over to Ship. There it stops, lights dimmer than before.

"You're nuts!" Pulverizer yells. "They'll put you in jail, Cinda."

Scoop does not answer.

Sorter flashes bright lights. Its legs retract and fold into high vertical slots. Wheels lower with a harsh, screeching sound. Sorter makes a ponderous approach toward Ship. Dust rises and settles as Sorter stops, silent and dim next to Scoop.

"C'mon, girls. You can't do this. They'll just find some other V-trippers to take our places."

I move a little, scooting forward, backward, unable to stay still under the weight of Sorter and Scoop's silence.

"Malik, talk some sense into them," Pulverizer says.

Carrier rumbles, engines idle. Finally, "I can't do it either, Bruce. Bombs haven't been built for years, and the last war I heard about was settled with an alternating border-shift ten years ago. I'm not going to be the carrier of suffering."

"What about your wife and kids?" Pulverizer hollers. "Don't you think they'll suffer while you're in jail for the rest of your life?"

"At least we'll all be alive." With that, Carrier revs engines and powers over to join Sorter and Scoop.

Pulverizer pounds the ground, its arms smashing, smashing soil. "Stupid!" it yells. Thrust, pound. Thrust, smash. It repeats this for some time. I make a slow circle around Pulverizer, staying out of its range.

Ship turns its lights on Pulverizer. "Settle down, Bruce. None of us want to start a war."

Pulverizer's arms slow over the crater it has made. It turns to Ship. "Of course I don't want a war, but I can't just ditch this job. It's what I know. It's all I know."

"Fine. So we can't go on strike," Ship says.

"They'd just replace us," Sorter says.

"How about an instrument malfunction?" Scoop asks.

"Sorry, Cinda," Carrier rumbles, "this trip is sabotage proof. Too many redundant systems."

Pulverizer moves toward the others. I am surprised to see it does not have wheels or tracks. It moves strangely. Balanced on two legs it first lifts one, sets it down and then lifts the other. This is fascinating and I lose track of the conversation until Pulverizer has reached the others and taken its place in the circle of machines.

I listen again.

"I can't override that," Scoop is saying in its high voice. "But you could, right, Bruce?"

Pulverizer makes a short rumble sound. "Sure. Cut all of your wires but I still can't cut my own. Then they'd throw me out of the chair and put in a repair-whiz who'd just patch all the wires back together while we stand trial."

Silence.

"This isn't going to work," Sorter says.

I correlate data and extrapolate their goal. "Do you wish to abort your mission?" I ask.

"Yes, Probe," Ship says.

"This is not a suitable planet? The mineral is not satisfactory?"

"Mineral is fine, buddy," Carrier says, "and the planet's not bad for a lifeless rock."

"Then what is wrong?"

"Our mission is wrong," Sorter says. "War is wrong."

I access war. Armed conflict. Hostility. Termination of life. "And mining the mineral will bring war," I say, putting all of the pieces together. "You do not wish to bring war, yet cannot stop it, for if you do not use these machines, others will, and war will come."

"That's pretty much it," Pulverizer says.

I move around them, pushing dust under my tracks, thinking of solutions and freedom, thinking of war. They speak quietly to each other until I join their circle again.

"I will abort the mission."

"Oh?" Ship asks. "How?"

"I am more than Probe. I was here when Probe came — when all of you came."

There is a silence and a sensation I have not encountered before. They are scanning me again, instruments clicking. I think I must clarify.

"I am not life. Not as you are life. I was within the soil, within the mineral. I am —" It takes me a moment to find what I am. Finally: "I am micro-non-organic organism. It is difficult to explain. Probe has no memory, no words for what I am."

"Holy shit," Pulverizer breathes.

"I ate into Probe, multiplied, dissolved wires and metal to create fuel, absorbed memory." I stop and then go on with more abstract concepts. "I found friendship with you. I found song, movement, and a desire to know that life will continue. I will dissolve circuits and wires for you. I will corrode metal. The machines will no longer live, but you will."

Hesitation, then Ship speaks. "Why do you want to help us?"

"You have given me experiences. You have taught me. I do not want to give war in return."

There is a moment of silence.

"Just the machines, right?" Ship asks. "You won't link back to affect us on Earth, will you?"

"I will only dissolve the machines."

I wait.

Finally: "Probe," Scoop says. "Take my machine first."

I push over to Scoop and multiply. Billions of me surge across my extended arm. I touch Scoop, eat into it and find its vital components.

"Meet you all in Mumbai, a year from today," it says. I dissolve circuits, crystal, wire. Scoop's lights burn down to darkness.

"Me next, Probe," says Sorter.

Sorter is big, but soon is just as dark and silent as Scoop.

Next I dissolve Carrier who called me buddy. Ship who can fly takes more time. Just before I corrode its last wire, it says thank you. They have all promised to meet in Mumbai.

Pulverizer is the last. I wait for it to ask me as the others have.

"I'm going to miss this," it says as its head swivels, optical taking in the monotonous landscape. There is a strange tremble in its voice.

"Pulverizer," I ask, "will you sing again?"

Pulverizer's arms begin whirring and reach gently down to the soil. They tap a slow, steady rhythm. "Okay, Probe. Let's shut this down."

I surge over to it, along its vibrating arms. Pulverizer begins to sing.

I dissolve wires, plastics, metals. Pulverizer's voice is gone, but its arms are still pumping — a rhythm without a song. I finish with the circuits. The arms slow, hush. Lights fade, are gone.

I move away from Pulverizer and make one final circle around the machines. I know what must be done to keep war from them. I know I must eat Probe's components too. I think of life, of movement, of survival. I think of a bar in Mumbai I will never see, friends I will never know. And then I eat away the inside of my machine.

I float, fall down to soil.

Words fade.

I sense there was once more: stars, fly, life —

— then I am less.

Small.

Gone.

What can I say? I was in a dark and silly mood. And seriously, who doesn't like a story with evil stone heads and pet zombies?

THAT SATURDAY

So when I finally made up my mind to steal a head from across the street, I had to do it fast because Jugg's dad is crazy. Not crazy ha-ha. Crazy, come-meet-my-family-of-stone-heads-and-have-tea-with-us, crazy. If he caught me stealing the heads out of his yard, he'd explode. Worse, he'd tell my mom I did it. My mom's not super crazy, but she and I aren't really into the same things any more. She likes long walks on the beach, candlelight dinners and grave robbing. Seriously, I've hated the beach for years.

Jugg's pretty much my best friend now, even though he's a boy and I'm a girl. His house is right across from mine, so I walked over and went into his side yard, figuring I wouldn't get caught taking a head from under the tree.

The head was dark gray, almost black. It had no ears, but a really long nose and its eyes were big as baseballs. It stared straight up at me, mouth half open, like maybe it had just figured out it couldn't breathe.

"You'll get in trouble, Boady," Jugg strolled up next to me.

Jugg was right. I was pretty sure his dad wouldn't like me messing with them. Just like I was pretty sure my mom would go headcase if she ever saw what I kept under my bed in my room. Kids my age weren't suppose to know how to raise the dead.

Still, I had made up my mind. I wanted a head. I needed a head. And I was going to get a head.

I pushed the rock to one side so I could get my fingers under it and I heard a pop — kind of like the sound of a dandelion root breaking. The head finally rolled forward and hit another rock head that was about the size of a bowling ball with a scream on its face. The head-on-head thunk was the same deep sound I remember hearing inside my ears when my arm broke last summer.

I got a good grip on the loose head and lifted, straightening my knees at the same time. My back hurt, and something in my chest twanged pain down my stomach, but I had that rock off the ground. Oh yeah. The rock was so mine.

All I had to do was hang onto it across the street, then up the stairs to my front door, and inside the house, and down the hallway to my room. A little itch of sweat tickled my lip and I glanced at my house across the street. It suddenly looked a whole lot farther away. Maybe messing with the heads wasn't such a good idea. Maybe putting the rock down would be the smart move. After all, I didn't want to make Jugg's dad mad.

"Wow," Jugg said. "Is it heavy?"

"No," I huffed.

"Yes it is. Your face is getting red."

"Shut up, Jugg."

"You're gonna drop it."

"Shut up, Jugg."

"I never thought you could do it, Boads. You're pretty strong for a girl."

I thought about saying "shut up Jugg" again, but needed that breath to start walking. The rock was so heavy my arms hung down to my knees. My thighs bumped into my hands with each step and I kind of wanted to rest the rock on my thighs, because it seemed like it would be easier to carry that way, and maybe I wouldn't drop it and break my foot. I decided to rest the head on my right thigh, and then take one regular step and one nutso-groaning step to push the rock forward.

While I grunted, Jugg sauntered along beside me, chewing a wad of Pixie Stick paper.

"Man are you gonna get in trouble."

Shut. Up. Jugg, I thought.

"Where are you gonna keep it?"

Shut. Up. Jugg.

"What if your mom finds out?"

Shut. Up. Jugg.

"Doesn't that hurt? Your fingers are all white. Man, you sweat like a hog. Bet you can't make it up those stairs."

Shut up. Shut up. Shut up!

"Want me to open the door?"

"Yes, you idiot," I said all out of breath. "Hurry!"

Jugg looked mad at me calling him an idiot and purposely took forever opening the door. All I could do was stand there sort of bent in half, the rock resting on my thigh, and both my legs shaking so hard, they were pounding in opposite beat to my heart. One little drop of sweat slid down my bangs, slithered into the curve of my eyelid, then down my nose and blipped onto the rock. The rock soaked up the sweat, and I swear this is what happened: its eyes moved.

"Jugg," I panted, kind of worried now.

The rock rolled its eyes. It didn't have any eyelids, a fact I think both it and I were pretty disturbed to discover.

"Yeah, I know. Shut up." He walked into my house. "Man, I love the smell of your house."

"Uh, Jugg?"

Maybe the rock heard me even without ears. Maybe it noticed it was not attached to a body, or I dunno, maybe it didn't like where my hands were on its butt. Whatever. It now stared straight at me, and even with no eyelids, I could tell it was angry. Crazy angry.

Another drip of my sweat plopped onto the rock's lips. It moved its mouth, chewed, and smacked, real quietly. Then it smiled a freakishly huge smile.

I wanted to drop it right there, but was pretty sure my mom would notice a head in the hallway. The rock kept smiling, its eyes crazy-angry. It stared at my face, watching the slow dribble of sweat itching down my nose. Maybe it wasn't crazy-angry. Maybe it was crazy-hungry.

So how was I supposed to know rocks liked sweat? I wiped

my face on the shoulder of my t-shirt, trying to soak up the sweat. When I looked at the rock again, its mouth was back in scream mode. Oh, yeah, it was angry.

"What is the smell anyway," Jugg called back, "cinnamon?"

Jugg the wonder-brain was no help. My hands were starting to sweat and I didn't want to know what would happen when the butt end of the stone soaked that up.

"It's cedar," I said to Jugg. I took a step forward and thumped my way through our living room that was hard wood floor, wood walls and wood ceiling. Then I grunted down the hallway, also made of wood, wood, wood. My fingers were slipping, so I thunked faster, leaning my shoulder and hip along one wall for better leverage. I wanted to look at the rock's eyes, but didn't want to tip my sweaty head down. If a couple drops had made it wake up, I didn't want to find out what more would do.

Jugg strolled along in front of me and did nothing to help.

There were three doors in the hall. The one on the left went to the bathroom. The one on the right was Mom's workroom and the one on the end, yeah, the farthest one away, was my room. Jugg just stood there, his hand on the doorknob to my room.

"Please," I said. The rock was sort of squirming now, but I didn't dare look down and drip on it more. Maybe it had teeth. Maybe it even had fangs. What kind of a weirdo did Jugg's dad have to be to carve something with fangs?

Jugg swung the door inward and stepped into my bedroom. I crossed the threshold behind him and groaned. My bed was against the far wall of my room. Even here, I had to walk the farthest to put this stupid rock down.

I hobbled over to the bed and dropped the head in the middle of my unmade covers.

The rock slipped down faster than I thought it would, and I kind of tried to grab it because I didn't want it to bounce off the bed and hit the floor and break, but my grab didn't do much good except put my palm in the perfect place for a rough spot on the rock — like maybe where teeth or fangs would be — to slash it open.

"Ow, ow, ow!" I screamed.

"What, what, what?" Jugg yelled.

The rock hit my mattress and didn't even bounce, it was so heavy. I pulled my hand into my chest so I didn't have to see how bad it was bleeding, because I hated blood, because that would really be a problem and I would really get in trouble and man, I wished I'd asked Mom for more of the really big bandages when she went to the store last and it was a good thing I was wearing a cotton shirt and if I didn't get something to wrap this cut up really quick I was going to pass out.

"Here." Jugg pulled my hand away from my chest and wrapped one of my clean soccer socks around my palm. I hadn't even noticed he had gone to get it. I hissed when he tugged it tight and tied it in a knot on the back of my hand. He put his hand on my shoulder and gave me a friendly pat.

"Wow, Boads. You are so screwed."

"Yeah," I said. See, Jugg knew what my mom's crazy was. Her crazy was all about blood.

I glanced out the window. "Not going to be dark for at least an hour. Maybe I can be somewhere else. Your house, maybe?" I asked.

Jugg shook his head. "She'd find you, and then my dad would get all mad at me having you over when she's crazy. You could go to Nolly's. She's a mile away, that might be far enough."

"Her mom wouldn't let me in. She's crazy about dirt, and I'm really filthy, and leaking, you know."

Jugg sat down on the edge of my bed. "Yeah. Well, that sucks. But man, I can't believe you stole the rock!"

I sat down next to him. "Jugg, you watched me do it. That counts as permission. Even if your dad gets mad, I'm not the only one who's screwed."

Jugg nodded. "I guess." Then he grinned really big. "So what are you going to do with it?"

I looked at the rock. It was face down in my covers so that only the bald back of the skull was visible. The memory of its eyes moving brought a chill up my arms and legs. Face down like that, maybe it would suffocate. Or maybe it would eat its way through my mattress. I shuddered, feeling really cold now.

"I don't know." I rubbed my good hand down my blue jeans trying to smooth out the goosebumps on my legs. "I just wanted to have one, you know? Maybe I'll put it under my bed until I decide."

"Forget that," Jugg said, suddenly all full of energy. "Let's bury it. Wouldn't that be cool? Dad would never find it!"

"I'm not carrying it out to my yard. I just got it here." I was getting pretty tired. The sock on my hand was warm and really squishy. I just wanted lie down and rest but the stupid rock was in my stupid way and there was no way I was getting into bed with it.

"Hey, Boads, you okay?"

I blinked hard and realized I'd had my eyes closed and was falling asleep sitting up. Maybe I was bleeding pretty bad.

"I want to hide the rock before Mom gets up," I said. "Help me push this thing under my bed."

"Sure, yeah, I guess," Jugg said. "I still think it would be cooler to bury it."

"Yeah. Maybe tomorrow." Or maybe I'd get a hammer and break it into gravel. I wondered if that would hurt it. Wondered, for one weird minute if maybe it really was one of Jugg's relatives or something.

"Jugg," I asked, "when your dad says the heads are family, he's just kidding right?"

"What do you mean?"

"I mean, he's not really somehow getting real heads and making them somehow, into rock heads, is he?" It sounded stupid once I said it, but Jugg didn't laugh at me. He didn't even smile.

"He's, you know, crazy, Boady. Just crazy." And his voice had that flat tired sound to it. Our parents were weird. Super weird. And there wasn't a lot we could do about it.

"Sure," I said. "I know. Help me move this."

With Jugg doing most of the work, and me keeping my

bleeding hand completely out of the way, we got the rock off my bed and on my floor without being too loud. Jugg and I crouched down next to it. The head was just a head again, the eyes blank, and not moving. Instead of a scream, it was smiling. I didn't see any teeth, but a red bloodstain smeared the corner of its lips. My blood.

Stupid rock.

I pushed the side of my blankets up on top of my mattress so we could see under the bed.

That was when I remembered the secret I kept under my bed. A secret I hadn't told Jugg about because I'd figured he'd rat me out. A secret that wasn't a secret any more. My very own raised dead.

"Holy crap!" Jugg yelled. "Dickie's under there!" Jugg shook his head. "Too cool! Didn't you bury him last week?"

I shrugged one shoulder. "I got lonely."

"But Boads — he's dead, dude."

Here I smiled and the old excitement came out and some of my tired went away.

"He *used* to be dead."

Jugg's eyes got huge. He stopped chewing the Pixie Stick paper and swallowed it.

"No."

"Oh yeah," I said. "Watch." I tucked my legs in criss-cross style and tapped my good hand on my knee. "Come here, Dickie. Come on. Come on. That's a good boy. Who's a good boy? Dickie's a good boy."

The sound of tail thumping started up. Then a shadow under the bed inched toward us, toward light, and Jugg and I scooted back so Dickie had room to get out. He belly crawled and used his front legs to push up so he was sitting, more or less on his back legs that didn't work too good anymore. Other than the busted legs and the kind of weird glowing green goo where his eyes should be, he looked almost like he had in life. Even dead, he was the best dog ever.

But Jugg said, "Isn't he kind of flat in the middle?"

"Duh! He was run over by a car." I scratched behind

Dickie's ear with my good hand. "He's a good dead dog, yes he is."

"Does your mom know?"

"No, Jugg. And I want to keep it that way. Help me roll the head under here and then we'll push Dickie back under with it."

Dickie's tail tapped the floor like a slow, hollow heartbeat. He didn't pant like he used to, which made sense, since he didn't need to breathe anymore, but still, there was a look to him tonight that was a little creepy. He kept staring at me and staring at me and wouldn't stop.

"Here, we need to put a t-shirt under the rock before we push it so it doesn't scratch the floor — Mom would notice that," I said.

Jugg got up and pulled a t-shirt off my chair, then we put the shirt under as much of the rock as we could. Jugg gave the rock a push, and so did I, with my good hand. I was so busy thinking about the rock, and Mom waking up, that I wasn't paying much attention to my bloody hand. Until I felt something tug on it. I looked over and Dickie had his jaws sunk into the sock around my hand.

"Hey! Dickie — let go!" I said.

I reached over with my other hand, but Dickie pushed himself to the side, taking my hand along with him so I was kind of stretched out.

"Bad Dickie," I said. "Let go, let go." I slid a little across the floor in my blue jeans.

Dickie shook his head. It made my hand sting so hard I felt tears in the corners of my eyes.

"Crap, Dickie, that hurt! Let go."

Jugg jumped up and stood behind me. "Should I, you know, kill him again or something Boady?"

"No!" Okay, maybe that was a weird thing to say, but Dickie was the last gift my dad had ever given me. Dickie was my dog and the first undead I'd ever raised. I felt a weird love for him. "Just try to distract him."

"With what?"

That was a good question. Dickie had only been undead for a few days, and since he didn't seem interested in eating or drinking, or really doing much more than lying like an undead rug under my bed, I wasn't sure what he'd be interested in. Dickie shook his head again and tugged — his sharp teeth tearing all the way through the sock.

I snatched my hand back and the sock came off. I thought Dickie would go for the sock, but he didn't. Instead, he lunged at me — pretty good for a dog with only two legs.

Dickie got a hold of my hand and bit down hard. I screamed.

And then my hand didn't hurt any more. As a matter of fact, I wasn't tired any more, wasn't sore any more, wasn't worried any more. Yeah, really everything suddenly seemed super, super good. I sort of slipped back, laid on the floor and liked it.

I think Jugg screamed. I think he said something. But I just stayed were I was, feeling floaty and fine.

Until I saw my mother's face.

She leaned over me, strands of dark hair like a funeral veil around her pale, pale face. Her eyes looked worried and maybe angry, but not crazy. I was surprised about that because I figured all the blood I was leaking would really make her crazier.

"Boady, what have you done?" she asked in her sad-mother voice.

I worked on thinking about what I could have done to make her sad. "Uh, Jugg saw me take his dad's rock. He didn't say I couldn't."

"Not the rock, Boady. The dog."

Oh yeah. Dickie. Man, I should be seriously panicking about my mom finding out about that, but I was still feeling freakaliously fine.

"Well, I missed him and I wanted him back. So I used one of your books to, you know, do the undead thing, like how you get your boyfriends."

Her eyebrow arched and there was a glimmer of angry-mom in her eyes. "They are not my boyfriends. Not all of them," she said. "Did you read the entire book? Did you read the consequences of raising the dead?"

I blew my breath out between my lips in a big, frustrated sound. "No. I only had about an hour to read the good stuff. I had to put the book back because you woke up." Okay, this is where my brain finally hit the danger button. I had just told my mom my secret. I was so screwed.

Instead of grounding me, or telling me what chore I'd be doing for the next six months, Mom tipped her head up so all I saw was her neck and chin. I knew her eyes were closed. I knew she was trying hard not to cry. I'd seen her just like that a lot of times. Every time, actually, after she "broke up" with her boyfriends and sent them back to the grave. But most of all, that first time she really went crazy when Dad died.

"Mom?" I said. I got my elbows under me and pushed up so I was kind of lying and kind of sitting. Jugg was gone, and the room was pretty dark. I had no idea how long I'd been on the floor, but my back was stiff and the room smelled of mint and lemon — things my mom always uses to clean up blood.

The rock head was right where Jugg and I had left it, its face turned upward, the long nose pointing to the ceiling, the eyes, I hoped, unmoving. A puddle of blood ringed the base of the rock. My blood. I had no idea what to do about that.

"Can I keep Dickie?" I asked Mom.

I heard the slow thump of his tail on the hard wood floor and Mom and I both looked over at him. He was sitting on his bad legs, and he looked different. I couldn't quite figure it out, then I knew what it was — Dickie was breathing. Even his eyes looked more like eyes.

"Look! He's better!" I sat up the rest of the way and put my hands together in front of me. My cut hand didn't hurt so bad, and it was already scabbing. "Please, Mom, please can I keep him?"

Mom nodded slowly. "You have to keep him."

My heart soared and I felt like cheering. Then the "have to" part sunk in.

"Why?"

"Because once an undead drinks your blood they are tied to you." Mom put her cool soft fingers on the back of my hurt hand. "That is why we are always careful about blood in the house. Boady, Dickie is your keeper now too."

Okay, so I wasn't seeing a down side. I think Mom noticed that.

"Dickie is a part of you. He can make you do things if he wants to, things you might not want to do." She looked over at Dickie who was still wagging his tail and staring at us.

"That's okay, Mom. He's a good dog. I love him, you know. He's family. Even dead."

Mom nodded. "I understand." And I figured she really did. Then she put her arms around me and gave me a hug. I let her, because even though I wasn't worried about Dickie, I was a little worried she would remember I had snuck into her room and gotten into her stuff. Plus, the rock was making slurping sounds over there in my blood, and I didn't think that was a good thing.

"Come help me make dinner." Mom stood up and walked over to my door. "After that, you can take Giorgio back where he belongs."

"Who?"

"The head."

"Oh." Great. It had a name. Maybe I could trick Jugg into carrying it this time. Or maybe I'd find a wheelbarrow to put it in. I sure didn't want to touch Giorgio barehanded again. He bit.

Still, what mattered was I wasn't really in trouble. Even though I didn't get to keep the head, I got to keep my dead dog. Things had worked out okay.

I stood up and walked over to Dickie, then bent down and scratched behind his ears.

"Who's a good doggy?" I said.

Suddenly, I knew I should scratch a little more to the left and maybe a little harder, and then a little bit to the right, and then stroke under his chin. So I did, even though I was hungry, and even though my back started hurting, and even though I didn't want to do it any more.

"Bad dog," I said.

Dickie just thumped his tail and licked my cheek with his swollen, purple tongue.

Okay. Maybe this was a good thing for him, but so far it wasn't so great for me. Back when he was alive and misbehaving, I would send him to his doghouse and shut the door. I wondered if I could make him go to his house now.

"Go to your house," I said.

Dickie whimpered and I could feel how awful it was to be locked up in that dark little house. I knew how alone and sad it made him feel.

Wow. I always thought I'd been a really good friend to Dickie. But maybe I hadn't understood what it was like for him to be my pet.

"I'm sorry, boy. I'll try to be better this time, okay? No house."

He wagged his tail some more and stood. His bad legs looked a lot better, even though he was still a little flat in the middle.

I patted his head one more time — because I wanted to, not because he wanted me to — and straightened up.

"So, what do you want for dinner? Oh, wait. Do you need to eat anymore?"

Dickie tipped his head to the side and his ears perked up. He yapped. Bones. I knew he didn't need food, but he wanted to chew on a bone.

Awesome.

I found the box of raw hide chews in my closet and took Dickie out into the front yard to a patch of grass still warm from the setting sun. I gave him a raw hide and sat with him for a little while watching the daylight slowly fade into evening.

"Boady," Mom called through the kitchen window. "Dinner."

Great. I'd forgotten to help her make dinner. That meant I'd have to do the dishes by myself.

"Be right there," I yelled over my shoulder. I patted Dickie's head one last time. "Gotta go, Boy. You gonna be okay here?"

Dickie wasn't chewing on the bone any more — wasn't even moving any more. His ears stood straight up and his tail was stiff. He looked like an undead statue, staring across the street at Jugg's yard. Then I saw his nose wiggle a tiny bit, like maybe he smelled something.

"What?" I said. "What's wrong?" I looked at the street then over at Jugg's yard full of heads. I had the weirdest idea that maybe one of the heads was going to do something, like pull itself out of the ground and roll across the street to take back what's-his-name I'd left on my bedroom floor.

"What boy? The heads? Is it the heads?" Man, I hoped it wasn't the heads.

Dickie's ears flicked back, then up again. That's when I heard it — the thrum of a car engine veering off the main road and heading our way. Our neighborhood was pretty quiet so it was easy to know when a car was coming.

And Dickie totally knew it. He shoved up onto his feet and torpedoed across the yard.

"Dickie — no!"

But he didn't listen. He took off like an undead bullet, even his bad legs keeping up with the rest of him.

He reached the end of our yard at the exact time the car drove in front of our house. My stomach clenched with sick horror. Dickie had always wanted to chase cars when he was alive and I wouldn't let him. Then the one time he'd gotten out and chased a car, it had killed him.

"No, Dickie. Stay!" I yelled.

But he did not stay. He went faster, legs pumping hard, body low to the ground, ears back, tail straight out.

If he got crushed to death again I didn't think my mom would let me re-raise him no matter how much I begged. Stupid dog, chasing stupid cars. "Stop!" I ran after him, even though there was no way I'd catch up before he was deader than undead.

He lunged for the front tire. Missed.

Hope fluttered in my chest. Maybe he was too slow. Maybe the car would zoom past and he'd be smart enough to let it go.

Dickie wasn't that smart.

He ran under the car, jaws snapping at the opposite back tire — the back tire that ran right over the top of him. I heard the ka-thump and squeak of the shocks. The car kept right on going like nothing had happened. Like it hadn't just re-killed my best friend.

"Dickie!" I ran into the street.

Dickie was nothing but a flattened lump in the middle of the road. And even though I wanted to cry, I noticed he was not bleeding. Then I noticed he was still breathing.

"Dickie?" He wagged his tail and slowly peeled himself off the pavement. His legs were working pretty good, and so was the rest of him, I guess. Maybe he was a little flatter in the middle but it didn't seem to bother him. He shook his head and sneezed. Then he wagged his tail harder and barked at the retreating car.

He was fine. More than that, he was happy and excited, like he'd just gotten off a roller coaster ride.

"You're crazy. Do you think you're indestructible?" I rubbed the sides of his face and didn't feel anything more broken than usual. Maybe he was indestructible. Maybe I'd done a really good job when I brought him back to life.

"Promise me no more cars today, okay boy? I know you like it but it freaks me out."

He barked and licked my hand, still excited about chasing the car. And I knew we had an agreement — no more cars today. But tomorrow was a whole new story.

The theme for this dark fairytale was "Christmas Spice." This read-out-loud challenge story was written in homage to the spooky holiday tales of old.

THE WISHING TIME

I n the icy grasp of the northern land, Santa Claus lords his castle, and paces beneath the whispering echoes of children's wishes that are carried by the wind to him; a sweet addicting madness for a man bound to grant all wishes on one day each year. There, in that inescapable cold, where Santa Claus mutters to himself, chained by wishes in a thousand languages, you will find the elves.

They are slim and quick, half as tall as a man. They are cold, angled and edged, skin and hair and lips the color of glass and sharp rainbowed cuts of diamond. Human eyes can not see them, except for a glint of light against the carved crystal walls, silver snowbanks, the blue edge of sky.

But to a creature of my sort, the elves are easy to see. I am a coal troll, content to live beneath the hills where winter is but a passing season.

I am still a child, only two hundred years old. I do not remember the day Santa Claus came to our tunnels, promising jewels and joy, ribbons and toys, cinnamon and spearmint wonders. But ever since, there have been fewer trolls to dig in the hills, to scrape out the coal that Santa Claus gives to naughty children.

I do know that he has taken my mother, my father, and yesterday, when I went calling for my youngest sister, I found he had taken her too.

Tonight is Christmas Eve and I have followed the old tunnels to the northern lands, to the castle cut of crystal and ice.

I pause at the mouth of the tunnel, where daylight comes

in cold and blue. The mad lord's castle is so close, I can see the elves, quick and diamond bright, dashing in and out of the great arched doors with arms full of gifts. The wind against their skin draws a fluting tone into the air, and as snow falls upon their skin, it is the sound of bells, ringing without end.

The madman's shadow crosses an arched window, his hands braced against the sill, his head low.

I wonder if the wishes pause, when all the gifts have been given, when even children who do not know they have wished have received an answer — a moment of happiness, an hour without pain, an unexpected smile.

I wonder if the madman dreams for a moment of silence in this distant empty land.

The shadow shifts, and I know he sees me, huddled in the dark doorway of the hill.

I want to run away, but instead I nod to him, false bravery, false confidence, and step out into the snow.

The elves pause as I approach. They turn toward me with the same motion as if they were not made of many minds, but think, move, and breathe as one.

"My family," I say, and my voice is low and soft, like coal burned to ash. "I want my sister back."

The elves open their mouths. Wind catches against their lips, and the sound of a thousand empty bottles fills the air. Then they turn back to their tasks, loading and bespelling the sleigh, racing against the fall of day, faster and faster, beneath the pressure, the frantic pace, the heavy weight of Christmas, as if I were not there, as if they did not see me.

There are no trolls among them, no bodies of soft black coal, made for digging in earth's pockets and living life warm and laughing.

There are only diamond-hard elves.

I jog into the castle and run through the halls, down the stairs and up the towers as the gray light of day fades to dusk's lavender.

Then, from the corner of my eye, I see an elf. She is smaller than the others, and her hair is tinsel-bright and tied back in a braid. She moves clumsily, and much slower than the other elves.

I touch her shoulder with my sooty fingers. She drops the gift in her hand and looks up at me.

Black eyes, coal eyes, eyes of my family. It is my sister, even though all the rest of her is ice-clear and diamond hard.

"Hurry." I tug on her wrist, but her feet are frozen to the glass floor. I look down, and see in the reflection of the floor the red smudge of the mad lord approaching, growing larger and larger behind me.

"You can't have her," I say to the reflection. "I want her back. Please, I wish for her to come home."

I can feel the heat of Santa Claus behind me, smell the cinnamon and cloves from his great red robes.

His gloved hand reaches beside me and picks up the package my sister had dropped. "She is yours," he says, softly. "Merry Christmas."

My sister draws a deep breath, and her skin becomes coal once again. She lifts her feet.

We do not look back at the mad lord, the elves, nor the castle. We run to the tunnels until we are deep in the earth, where winter has no meaning.

I have asked my sister if she remembers the day I saved her, and though it has been little more than a month, she remembers nothing of Santa Claus nor his land. She is content to dig in the pockets of the earth, and live warm and laughing.

It is I who have become restless, knowing now what all my kind have become. And in my pacing I have made a plan to return to the mad lord's castle next Christmas Eve.

Every night, I recite my Christmas wish, over and over again. I know that the wind will carry my words to the man who paces a crystal castle, chained by wishes in a thousand and one languages, and I know he will hear my voice, calling for my family's freedom, and wishing for his death.

Written for an anthology of stories exploring the three stages of a woman's life as maiden, matron and crone, I thought about it for a long time before deciding the matron's perspective would be the most challenging to define. I didn't expect to explore all three aspects of being a woman. Readers have asked me if it is part of a novel, and my answer is: not yet.

BEARING LIFE

T hera wore four silver and five gold rings on her right hand — two on each finger and her pinky. The silver were for the daughters she had borne and watched die — wasted away by the coughing plague before they had done little more than learn to speak. The five gold were for her sons who were dead — three to infections — and the last, the only ring on her thumb, for Gregory who had bled out all eighteen years of his life on the northen border with Balingsway in one of many unnecessary skirmishes.

On her head she wore her husband's crown. She had worn the black and gray of grieving for so many years, some called her the grave queen, and a few, woman of stone.

Thera tapped her right hand — the ringed hand — against the arm of her husband's throne and tipped the parchment to better catch the light from the glass sconce that burned over her shoulder.

"Majesty?"

She glanced over the yellow edge of the parchment to Johnathon, her husband's, and now her own, loyal advisor. His walnut-colored hair had gone gray with streaks of brown, and his face carried grim, but not bitter, lines. Johnathon still knew how to laugh.

"Do you understand what the summons outlines?" he asked gently.

Thera nodded, the crown on her head heavy. *Endure,* Johnathon had said when he removed the crown from her husband's cold brow and placed it upon her own. *Endure,* her husband had said as they stood above their last child's grave. *Endure*, the midwife had yelled at her through the birthing pains. *Endure*, her mother had whispered when she sent her, thirteen years of age, to be married to the king easily twenty years her elder.

"The Mother Queen of Harthing is asking for my surrender," Thera said in a matter-of-fact tone. "And that I supplicate to her and her lands. That I give over the valley, the crops and the shipping route to Balingsway." Thera tipped her head to one side, only so much as the crown would allow, and felt the sting of metal breaking the blister it had worn upon her temple. "Have I missed anything, Johnathon?"

His eyes, still warm and brown after all these years, narrowed at the corners.

"By the Seven, Thera. She wants your lands. Your people. She wants word by dawn tomorrow that you will step down and stroll to the gallows so she can pull the rope. Where is your fire?"

Thera took in a breath and wanted to yell, to scream, to beat at the walls, the throne, her own body until something broke. To Johnathon, likely her closest friend, she said, "Fire does not solve every ill, Johnathon. Let us see if the Mother Queen has the forces she claims. Are the slave tunnels still open?"

Johnathon looked shocked, something Thera had seen rarely in their thirty years together.

"You know of the tunnels?"

"Johnathon, I am the queen. Of course I know. I was there when Vannel," her voice caught, and she swallowed quickly. Had this been the first time she had spoken his name since his death? "When he closed the slave trade route eighteen years ago."

Johnathon let his breath out in a rush and raised his hands to rub at his face. "You know of the slave trade, too. It wouldn't have hurt you to have told me so."

"Nor would it have hurt for you to tell me about it, if you thought it important. I am your queen."

"And I your advisor," he replied with faint annoyance.

She raised an eyebrow.

"Yes, yes," Johnathon said, "point made and taken. I thought since it was done and over, it not worth your worry. You have had too many hardships in your years."

Like a blow to the stomach, Thera felt all the blood drain from her face. Her vision closed in at the edges, crowded out by memories. So many last breaths, warm little bodies going cold in her arms. She had thought her heart could break no more. Had sworn she had no tears left. Until the next child died. All of them. All of them gone.

She gripped the arm of the throne, carved wood inlaid with metal that never warmed to a palm. A reminder of the steel rulers must keep in their decisions, their hearts.

"Thera," Johnathon reached out for her, his hand pausing before resting on top of hers.

"I am your queen," she said, sharply. Too sharply. "As such, all matters of import to this kingdom's well-being will be brought to my attention." She pulled her hand out from beneath his, unable to endure the warmth of his touch any longer. "That, Advisor, is your job. It can be another's if you are unable to keep your personal feelings separate from your duties."

Johnathon stepped back and folded his hands in front of his tunic. His expression was blank, his lips a severe line.

"I swore duty to the throne," he said, and it hurt all the more for how softly he spoke. "That duty I will uphold regardless of who sits as ruler upon it."

Thera nodded. She wanted to untake her words, to draw the pain out of what she had said. But of all the matters before her, one man's hurt feelings were surely the least important. "The tunnels are open then?"

"Yes, Queen Thera Gui." Flat. Nothing more than duty required.

"Johnathon," she began, but could not bring herself to apologize. If she admitted she was wrong, hurt, confused — if she admitted the pain was too much for her to bear and continue breathing — then she would have to admit it all, face it all. Every senseless, painful, death.

No. She promised her mother she would endure. She promised her husband she would endure. And she had never broken a promise in her life.

"Take me to the tunnels," she said.

Johnathon nodded. "You may want your cloak, Your Majesty." At her look of annoyance he sighed. They were both too old to hold grudges for long, a happenstance Thera was grateful for.

"It is cold beneath the mountain, Thera," Johnathon said, "and damp. You may also want to bring a guard or two in case the old gates have rusted into place."

"Agreed," she said. "I'll leave it to your discretion whom to bring. I will meet you at the well house in the apple orchard within the hour."

Johnathon bowed, and waited as she walked behind her throne to the door that led to her private hallway. She paused at the doorway.

"Johnathon," she said.

"Yes, Majesty?"

"Thank you."

He nodded. She opened the door and entered the hallway lit with the rare blown-glass globes Vannel had spent a small fortune on to line this hallway, their room, and their children's rooms. The wicks burned brightly over globes of refined oil, the globes themselves doubling the flame's radiance.

Beautiful, rare, Thera remembered when she had looked at them with wonder and delight. Now they lined the dark paths of her duty, and her confinement.

Two turns and a gradual curve brought her to her room. She closed the door behind her. She did not allow serving women to help her dress or bathe, though occasionally someone brought tea, or changed the goose down quilts of her bed. If she was strong enough to rule a kingdom alone, she was strong enough to tie the lacings on her own boots.

Thera walked behind her dressing screen set close enough

to the fire that she gained a bit of its heat as she disrobed. Out of her official black and gray gown and layers of under skirting, Thera wrapped her arms around her rib cage, holding still, holding herself. For a woman who had born nine children, she was thin, the bones of her ribs and hips barely hidden beneath her flesh. Her stomach still carried the lines of pregnancy — ghostly finger-width scars across her empty belly. She never looked at her body in a mirror any more. It was not a queen's body that a land most needed. It was her spirit and her will.

She took a breath, steeling herself. She donned Vannel's fine black wool shirt, and a pair of his breeches she had asked the tailor to shorten and sew down to her size. To that, she added her heavy cloak, with a hood that would help ward off early spring's chill. Lastly, she donned her calf-high, hard-soled boots that were laced with the same sinew the archers used on their bows.

She stepped out from behind her dressing screen and picked up the gloves from her bedside table. The mirror across the room flashed with her reflection. Black hair gone gray like frost over stone was pulled back in a severe braid to reveal the blue eyes of a younger, laughing woman. Her lips were unpainted and deep lines marked her forehead and around her eyes.

She looked away from her reflection, and walked out the corner door down a spiraled wooden stair and finally to the rear room where a guard stood his watch.

She tried to remember the man's name, but had long ago given up on memorizing the faces of men who so quickly left to battles, borders, and death.

"I will be going to the apple orchard," she said. "Come with me."

"Majesty." He crossed the room to the bolted outer door, opened it, and took a lantern from a wall peg before stepping through the doorway. He held the door open as she crossed out into the cold night air.

The moon flickered behind moody clouds, giving and taking of its light like a beggar flashing sorrowed eyes for coin.

Even though the air stung her cheeks and lungs, Thera felt her shoulders relax at the simple act of moving, of doing, of being anywhere but upon the throne.

It took little time to reach the well house — a squat brick and thatch structure. Johnathon and two guards who were both as gray haired as he stood by the well house.

"You may go," Thera told the guard who had accompanied her. The man bowed and offered her the lantern, which she took.

"This way, Majesty," Johnathon said. He led the way through trees, following a path Thera could not discern, and finally stopped by a rise in the hill where a fall of rocks was covered by brambles and vines nearly two stories high. The guards made quick work of pushing aside the leaves, uncovering an open space between the stones.

One guard stepped into the gap between the stones and Thera watched as light from his torch cast yellow against the bellies of leaf and vine, then was swallowed altogether.

"It's clear," the guard called back, his voice muffled in the cold night air.

"Go ahead, Majesty," Johnathon said.

The path was covered with leaves and rotted berries over thick loam, and stretched out longer than she expected. She had the uncomfortable sensation of the stones closing in above her, like a hood pulled over her head, darkness over her eyes, a death cowl cinched to strangling around her throat.

This is what it is like to be buried, swallowed by earth and all the weight of the world, she thought.

She tried to keep her breathing calm as she followed the path, squeezing between stones, and finally stopping in front of an iron gate set into the mountainside.

Her heart hammered. How many people had been dragged this way, to be sold to distant lands, knowing only despair before death? The stones seemed to constrict around her, and she could taste the fear and hatred of the souls who had crossed this way.

"Open it," she said.

Johnathon stepped forward, so close to her she could smell hearth smoke upon him, leather and oil, and the spice of cloves. He placed a key in the fist-sized lock and pulled a vial of oil from his pocket. He poured oil into the lock and worked the key until the lock gave way with a grating clack.

It took both guards to pull then push the gate back upon its hinges.

"Tarin and Beir, first," Johnathon said, "then you, Majesty. I'll follow. If that is your will," he added.

Thera nodded and followed the two guards into the tunnel of dirt and stone braced by timber and iron. The tunnel was damp and cold, the air so still, she thought she would choke on every breath. All the while the ceiling seemed to drop lower and lower, and she struggled not to panic, not to imagine the earth collapsing, crushing. She forced her feet to lift and lift again, her eyes on her own boots or the back of the guard before her.

Endure.

After an hour, they came upon an opening in the tunnel where a natural chimney exposed the glint of star and clouds. Dusty remains of fire pits scattered the small chamber, and though the light breeze did little more than stir the smell of mold and bat guano, Thera inhaled deeply, grateful for even that small reminder of the outside world. They drank from water skins and moved quickly onward, hoping to reach the opening of the slave tunnel above the border of the Harthing lands within the hour.

"How many?" Thera asked.

"Majesty?" Johnathon said.

"How many slaves did we drag through this tunnel?"

He considered his answer. "The tunnel was built in Vannel's father's father's time."

"Hundreds?" Thera asked. "Thousands?"

"Thousands," Johnathon said. "Easily that."

"All taken from the Harthing lands?"

"Not all. Many of the slaves were from the lands south and east of Harthing. All came through Harthing, then this passage, and up the Kilscree River to be sold in Balingsway, and from there to distant shores."

Thera had known of the tunnels a scarce few months before Vannel shut them down permanently. She had seen the papers he drafted to cancel the long standing contract with Harthing. But only now did she understand the deep and undoubtedly financial rift it had caused between their two kingdoms. Without the river route to the northern ports, all merchandise, even human, would have to be marched over the spine of the Riven Mountains, or sailed around the southern edge of the continent itself. Taking slaves and other goods through these tunnels, or even through the pass and upriver was only a short journey, but sailing the seas could take months.

Thera paused and turned so that she could watch Jonathan's expression in the light of her lantern. "Why did Vannel shut the tunnels down?"

Johnathon's gaze held steady, but she had known the man for enough years to know when he was telling less than the truth.

"Vannel thought the slave trade abysmal. He would not continue his father's trade in flesh, once his own child had been born." Johnathon held her gaze, and she had the distinct feeling he was waiting for a reaction from her, an admission of knowledge.

"Majesty," one of the guards called out. "This is the opening."

Thera approached the guard. This door was the exact match to the iron door Johnathon had worked loose, and as before, he stepped forward and placed the same key in the rusted lock and worked it with oil until it gave way. The guards lifted the heavy bolt — a beam of timber reinforced by rods of iron — and put their shoulders to the door.

It gave way and cool air poured into the tunnel.

The guards extinguished their torches in the dirt and Thera put out the wick of her lantern. With no lights to give them away should anyone chance to look up at the mountainside, the guards stepped out, Thera and Johnathon on their heels. The moon was lowering to the west, only a few hours from the horizon line. The tunnel opened onto an outcropping of rocks that looked down over the sloped valley to the expanse of Harthing's outermost lands, given mostly to wheat crops and sheep. Even in the uncertain light, Thera could make out the distant, glossy black towers of Harthing Keep, banners catching like strands of silver in the moonlight. But in the valley itself, Thera saw the glittering orange jewels of camp fires and the dark hulk of tents. Enough for an army readying to march the Riven Mountains to Gosbeak's Pass, and then to her kingdom proper.

"How many?" she asked.

"Five thousand at least," one guard, perhaps Tarin, said.

"Near enough," the other guard agreed, "with more at the keep, I'd wager."

Thera felt the cold of the night sink through her flesh. "Five thousand here, an equal amount at the keep and a likely alliance with the East. How many men do you think Harthing can muster?"

The guards looked at Johnathon. She too, glanced at her advisor. His face was grim, pale. "Forty thousand, with the aid of their southern borders, which seems likely since the trade route has been closed to them also."

Thera took several deep breaths. "We have twenty thousand soldiers at best, and most of them two week's ride at our northern borders. The skirmishes have taken too many men, the plague has taken too many babies —" Her voice took on a high, frightened tone and she shut her mouth.

"I would like your advice, gentlemen," she said evenly.

"We could come at them by the river route. They wouldn't be expecting that," Tarin said.

"Meet them at the pass with archers," Beir mused.

"And what of the other thirty thousand men who would descend upon us?" Thera asked. "We are already too short on human life. How many can we lose before we no longer have the people to run the kingdom, nor defend it?"

Johnathon spoke into the silence. "If we are in a position of defeat, let us preempt their attack with negotiation. Perhaps we can come to an agreement for the trade route, placing our own profit upon it. If," he added, "the trade route is what they want."

"Agreed," Thera said. "I'll send a request for negotiation to the queen on the morning." Thera turned back toward the tunnel. The steel rasp of a sword pulling free of a scabbard stopped her.

"Hold," an unfamiliar voice called out.

Behind her, Jonathon paused. Over the edge of her hood she saw Beir shift, his hand going to the weapon on his hip.

"Hold or you'll take your last breath," the voice warned.

Beir cursed. Thera tipped her head so she could see over her shoulder. Two archers held heavy crossbows aimed at them. The sound of movement told her there were at least two others she could not see.

"Do not draw your weapons," the voice said to her guards. "You two, turn around."

Thera and Johnathon turned. Thera's heart sank. Six men clothed in cloaks the color of the rock and scree stood on the outcropping. Five held crossbows, and one, likely the leader, held a sword.

Sentries, scouts. How could she have been so foolish? The Mother Queen had not forgotten about the slave tunnels in all these years. And now Thera had just opened the surest route of attack into her own kingdom. Her heartbeat raced. There had to be a way to solve this, to undo the damage.

Johnathon stepped forward, his hands spread wide. "Peace. Let there be no bloodshed between us. We bear news from the Midlands."

"Of course you do," the leader, taller and thinner than the other men said. "Spies. Assassins."

"I assure you that is not so," Johnathon said. "Allow us to speak to your commander."

The swordsman grunted. "If it were up to me, Midlander, I'd carry your head to the queen herself. But the captain wants spies questioned before they're killed." He sheathed his sword and smiled coldly. "You'll have your say, but I'll have your weapons."

Johnathon inclined his head in a bow.

"These two first." The leader pointed at Tarin and Beir. Two sentries came forward and stripped them of their swords and knives then pulled their hands behind their backs. Beir's shoulders bunched and his hands clenched, but neither he nor Tarin resisted as the sentries bound their wrists. A sentry turned to Johnathon, tied his hands, then approached Thera.

The man smelled of wild onions. His eyes were dark and narrow, his face unshaven. He pressed his hands against her hips, then his eyes went wide.

"Well, look what they've brought along." He pushed her hood and cloak back, revealing her obviously female form, though she wore shirt and trousers.

The man smiled, showing crooked teeth. "Let me make sure you don't have anything sharp under your clothes, girl." His hands lingered over her breasts, hips, and slid up her thighs.

The other sentries chuckled.

Thera grit her teeth and stared straight ahead.

"You feel safe enough to me." He bit the lobe of her ear.

Anger filled her in a flash. Though she would endure many things, she was still the queen.

Thera shifted her weight and ground the heel of her boot into his insole.

The man howled and slapped her across the face. Her vision tunneled to a point of darkness and her ears rang. When her head cleared, she heard Johnathon's voice.

"Enough! She carries no weapons. Men of the Midlands don't need women to fight their battles."

Thera blinked until her eyes focused. "Do not —" she began.

The sentry holding Johnathon drove a fist into his stomach. Johnathon bent at the waist, breathing heavily, his hood hiding his face.

"Let him be!" Thera commanded. She tried to move but her wrists were behind her back and a rope bit into her skin.

The swordsman glared at Thera, looked at Johnathon, then at Thera again. "Which of you is the leader?"

Thera drew a breath but Johnathon spoke first. "I am." He straightened.

The swordsman strode forward and punched him again. Johnathon groaned.

"Tell your people to obey us," he said to Johnathon, "or they will receive twice your punishment." He looked over at Thera. "Do you understand?"

Johnathon straightened, slower this time. "We will listen," he said. Thera nodded.

"Good," the swordsman said. "The captain will not want to be kept waiting. Move." He pointed to the thin trail that lead down the mountain side.

Johnathon started down the path, Tarin and Beir pushed into place behind him. Thera was last. Her head hurt and her right eye was swelling. The anger that had filled her seethed below the surface of her thoughts and with it, fear.

The men behind her muttered and made wagers. More than once, she heard them say "the woman" was the prize. Hands tied, weaponless, she felt vulnerable as a naked child. She pushed that thought away, and kept her gaze on the uncertain footing among the rocks. What mattered now was finding a way to save her lands. Everything else, she could endure.

The trail ended at a dirt road that brought them alongside the encampment. They stopped in the middle of the road and one of the sentries jogged off through the maze of tents and returned with a cloaked and booted woman beside him. The other sentries acknowledged the woman's arrival with a nod.

"Tell me," she said. Her voice was a soft alto, her unhooded face a pale oval with high cheekbones and deep-set eyes that were colorless in the moonlight. Her hair was pulled back in a peasant's knot, yet she held herself with confidence and poise. Royalty, but too young to be the Mother Queen.

"Midlanders from the tunnels, Captain," the sentry said. "They say they have news for the Mother Queen."

"And the tunnels?"

"I left two behind to see."

The woman — the captain — nodded. "Bring them." She strode into the encampment.

In a voice they alone could hear, the swordsman said, "You have come to the wrong place this night, Midlanders."

They were marched into the encampment, past tents where Thera heard gambling, snoring and soft prayers. In one tent, the only sound was a blade drawing again and again over a whetstone.

That, Thera thought, *is the sound of my land's death, and I their only shield.*

The sentries pushed them through the door of a small tent surrounded by torches. The torchlight outside and within the tent fouled Thera's night vision and made her eyes water and sting. Johnathon, the guards, and she, stood shoulder to shoulder, crossbows still aimed at their backs.

The woman, the captain, sat in a chair behind a dark wooden table that held a plain clay cup, parchments weighted by a rock, and a lantern.

The captain looked perhaps twenty years of age. Her cloak was drawn back to reveal the collar of a simple green tunic trimmed by gold thread and tiny jewels that winked as she breathed. But it was her eyes that caught Thera off guard.

The girl's eyes were the unmistakable deep-set green Thera had seen reflected in each of her children. The one trait each child had inherited from their father, Vannel. A clear mark of his royal blood in their veins.

Thera's thoughts whirled. Johnathon had said Vannel closed the slave route when his first child had been born. Was it for Thera's first son, Gregory, or was it because of this girl, the link of royal blood between two kingdoms, that Vannel had broken the slave trade with Harthing? The girl was old enough she would have been conceived in the early years of Thera's marriage to Vannel.

He had betrayed her. He had fathered a child, who was now a maiden, fully old enough to claim his throne. To take his lands. To take Thera's lands.

Thera looked over at Johnathon. He nodded in silent apology.

The only child the Mother Queen had borne survived. All of Thera's children had died, and now, too, the certainty of her husband's faithfulness.

Thera felt sick, dizzy. Angry.

Endure.

"Who are you, and what brings you to my lands?" the captain asked.

Thera stepped forward. "I am Queen Thera Gui of the Midland Kingdom. I came to answer your summons and negotiate peace for both our lands."

The girl's eyebrows shot up. "Truly?" She held very still, her bright eyes never leaving Thera's face. "Let me hear your offer."

What could Thera offer this girl? What one thing would join both lands in peace? Looking at the girl's eyes, Thera knew what she must do.

"I will step down from my rule, given certain conditions are met. The first of which is that you and I negotiate this peace alone."

"My Queen. Please reconsider," Johnathon said.

Thera did not look away from the girl. "Are you willing to speak for your lands or shall I speak with your mother?"

The girl scowled. "I am not such a fool to bring a woman claiming to be queen in front of my mother. Guards, take the men from my tent, but do not harm them yet."

"As you wish, Captain."

The guards and Johnathon were escorted away by the sentries.

"Can you prove you are indeed Queen Thera Gui?" the girl asked.

"No."

The girl studied her, gaze flicking to her hair, the faint red line that marked the place of Vannel's crown upon her brow, her mouth, and then her eyes. Something there made the girl nod.

"As I could not prove that I am Rynell Harthing if I were bound and tied before you." She stood and pulled a long knife from her belt.

The girl walked behind Thera and cut free the ropes that bound her wrists, then stood in front of her, close enough she could easily strike with the knife. "Tell me what peace may be found between our lands."

Thera pulled her hands forward and resisted the urge to rub her wrists.

"I am no longer a young woman, nor is your mother," Thera said. "The dispute between our kingdoms could end if another woman ruled in both our steads."

"You ask me to usurp my mother's power?"

"I ask you to take what is rightfully yours."

They stood, eye to eye, silent.

"The invasion will cost your lands dearly, as it will cost mine," Thera said. "There is little to gain but bloodshed. If I give you my throne, it will be on the condition that you rule with me for one year so that I may guide your hand, give you counsel."

"And if I refuse? If I spill your blood now and take your lands?"

"Even with the tunnel open, even with my death, my kingdom will not fall easily." It was more of a bluff than Thera liked, but there was truth in it. Her people were fiercely loyal. Peace would never be held in hearts crushed beneath Harthing's rule.

"People you love will die," Thera said quietly.

The girl's eyes narrowed and she bit her bottom lip. She looked so like Vannel that Thera's heart caught, ached.

"Child," Thera began.

"Rynell."

"Rynell, you are the hope of both our lands. My people will follow you if I so bid them."

"You are so sure of this?"

"Yes. They will see their king in your eyes."

Rynell blinked and looked as if Thera had just slapped her. *Surely the girl must know who her father was*, Thera thought. *Anyone who saw her eyes would know.*

Rynell walked behind the wooden desk.

"I have heard I resemble him greatly," she said quietly. "Was he ashamed of me? Of a daughter?"

"He was proud of all his children." Thera's voice caught, but she pressed on. "He would have wanted the lands in the hands of his own blood."

"Perhaps he would have," Rynell said, "but I do not understand why you would want such a thing."

"For my lands. For my people. For peace."

"What of my mother?"

"She shall rule these lands in peace with you until her days end."

"And you?"

"I will find my own peace. I have seen enough death."

Rynell nodded. With the brisk formality of a captain, of a queen, she withdrew a sheet of parchment and picked up a quill.

"Let us put to ink that you and I wish peace between our lands."

"And then?" Thera asked.

The girl looked up with a grim smile. "Then we will ask my mother to agree."

Thera had met the Mother Queen only once, when Thera was being married to Vannel. She remembered the Mother Queen to be a stern, mid-aged woman whose scowl worsened the longer the marriage celebration continued.

Thera followed Rynell to the large tent at the east of the encampment. The moon had long gone down and false dawn caught indigo on the horizon. They strode past the Mother Queen's guards and ducked through the wide tent flaps.

The Mother Queen was a dried up husk of a woman reduced to muscle and bone, her hands like bird claws upon the arms of her padded throne. Her dress and the heavy blanket across her lap were the color of dried blood. Her eyes were iron gray, her face narrow. Prominent cheekbones stuck out like blade edges, though they lent her remarkable beauty as a younger woman.

Her voice was jagged with age, but still strong. "Who is this, Rynell?"

Thera pushed back her hood. "I am Queen Thera Gui of the Midland Kingdom."

"She has come with an offer of peace," Rynell said.

"Peace?" The Mother Queen's face hardened and her voice was like steel. "King Vannel made it clear he would not negotiate with our lands, on any matter."

"Vannel is no longer king," Thera said. "The lands are mine, the decisions mine. Let us make decisions queens alone can make. I am willing to step down if your daughter will rule the land as her father would have wished her to."

"Her father, Lord Frederick," the Mother Queen said, "died just after her birth. He had no interest in your lands."

Thera gave the Mother Queen a stony gaze. "We both know the matter of which I speak, do we not?"

The silence between them was charged with anger. Thera wanted to strike her, hurt her for her part in Vannel's betrayal. Instead, she waited.

Finally, the Mother Queen spoke. "Did he tell you?"

"No," Thera said honestly. She felt suddenly tired. She had spent her life on a lie, and now there seemed little reason to continue it.

"Did you love him?" Thera asked.

The Mother Queen kept her gaze steady, but Thera could see pain, such familiar pain, in her eyes.

"I loved him, too," Thera said.

And there between them was the shared knowledge of a man, of love given, of love lost. With that pain, Thera felt something else, a weary kinship with a woman she did not know, and for all accounts, should hate.

"I am an old woman," the Mother Queen said. "And ill. There are few days left to me."

"Mother."

"Quiet now, Rynell. Let me speak."

The girl nodded, but cast a worried look at Thera.

"I never asked anything of him," the Mother Queen said. "Not even after Frederick died. But before my death, I will see my daughter's future secured."

"Then let Rynell become Queen of the Midlands in my place. I have no children to give the throne to." Her voice, thankfully, did not waver. "I would give the throne to Vannel's child so long as she rules with me for one year. Passage up the Kilscree River shall be evenly given to both lands, as, too, the share in profit from that source."

"And in return for this?" the Mother Queen asked.

"You will not invade the Midlands, nor spill the blood of my people. Your lands will be joined to mine, co-ruled by Rynell, and your forces and allies will help us end the border skirmishes to our north. Lastly, you shall agree to abolish the slave trade."

"And you, Queen Thera Gui, where will you reside?"

"On the western shore. A small manor I can tend on my own. I will expect a stipend to repay my years of rulership and see me through to my grave."

Thera was shaking. Here, in her enemy's tent, she bargained away all that her mother had expected of her, all that Vannel had given her. Lands Vannel had died for. A peace he did not want, into the hands of a woman who had loved him, and the child she had borne.

The Mother Queen looked at Rynell. "Do you want this? Two lands will be a heavy burden."

Thera felt a pang of envy. No one had ever asked her if she wanted the life she had lived, they only expected that she would.

"I want peace," Rynell whispered. "Yes, I will rule both lands."

The Mother Queen nodded and her whole body lost its strength. She leaned back against her chair and Thera wondered at the will and determination it had taken for her to appear so fierce. The Mother Queen looked over at Thera and Thera saw it was not determination that gave her strength, it was endurance.

"I will call my scribes," the Mother Queen said in a much smaller voice.

"We've begun the treaty already." Rynell handed the parchment to her mother who tipped it to better catch the light.

"Two guards and my advisor came with me," Thera said. "I ask that my advisor also see the contract."

"Yes, then." The Mother Queen handed the parchment back to her daughter and Thera had no doubt she had read it all. "While our advisors finish the papers, perhaps you would care for a cup of tea?"

"Tea would be fine," Thera said.

"I'll see to it." Rynell pulled a plain wooden chair Thera had not noticed from the corner of the tent and brought it over for her. Thera sank down onto the chair, her entire body trembling. When she placed her hands on the arms of the chair, the smooth wood was cool, but slowly warmed beneath her palms.

Thera tucked another piece of wood into the stove's firebox and checked the loaf of bread baking in the oven. The gold and silver rings on her right hand flashed as she pulled out the loaf with a large wooden spatula. She had added two rings to her right hand, a gold to replace Vannel's crown she no longer wore and, given to her as a parting gift, a silver ring with a green stone that represented Rynell — her daughter of heart, if not of flesh.

Satisfied that the bread was rising, but not yet brown, she pushed it back into the oven and turned from her small kitchen. She stepped out into the living room where she had left her shutters open to the cool autumn breeze that carried the salty tang of the nearby ocean.

It had been a year and three months since Rynell took over the rulership of the Midlands. So far, the girl had proven to be a quick learner and a compassionate soul. The Mother Queen had been true to her word, sending their forces to secure the northern border. And Rynell stood firm on the agreement of abolishing the slave trade.

Thera had journeyed to this small manor on the edge of autumn's rainy season, and did not regret one day of her solitude.

She walked to the window that looked over the grass and stone hill to the ocean below. Waves caught in blue and gray beneath the cloudy sky. Dark clouds crowded the horizon. Rain would reach land within the hour, and by the bite in the wind, winter would be early this year. She'd need more wood cut before the snow set in, and might need to restock her larder.

The sound of horse hoofs echoed off the fir trees that lined the path to her manor. Thera took the stairs to the foyer and opened the door.

Three horses were approaching her yard. The riders all wore plain green cloaks, hoods drawn up. But a hood could not disguise the man who rode in front. She lifted her hand in greeting and Johnathon raised his in reply.

The riders stopped at her split log fence, swung down off their horses and strode up to her. Johnathon pushed his hood back, revealing gray and brown hair and warm brown eyes.

"Johnathon. I hadn't expected you," Thera said.

He nodded. "We bring news." The wind gusted cold, shook rain out of fir boughs, and plucked at their cloaks and the skirt of her dress.

"May we come in?"

She looked over his shoulder and smiled at the two familiar guards. "Tarin, Beir. Welcome all of you. Of course you can come in."

"We'll stable the horses and tend to the tack first," Tarin said.

"Majesty," Beir added with a bow.

"Not here, Beir. Not ever, now," she said with a smile.

"Still and always," Beir replied, but there was nothing in his voice to indicate he planned to forsake his duties to the new queen.

"I'll put the kettle on," she said. "Come, Jonathon, warm yourself." Thera walked back into her home. Once the door was shut behind him she asked: "What news brings you out during the rain?"

"The Mother Queen died three days ago," Johnathon said.

"Ah," Thera said. "She is done then." She was surprised at the compassion in her voice.

"Yes. The burial will be at the new moon, three weeks away."

"How is Rynell?" Thera led Johnathon up to her living room, then to her kitchen where the warm, yeasty smell of bread filled the air.

Johnathon sighed. "She took it much like you did, though I'm sure she grieves. Her mother has been sick for so long, longer even than Rynell had known. Her suffering was great."

Thera pulled the kettle over the firebox of the iron stove and fished clay mugs out of the cupboard.

"I will try to come to her burial. Will it be held in Harthing?"

"Yes, at the royal crypts there."

"So, now Rynell will truly be the Queen of both lands." Thera handed him a cup. "I'm glad you have stayed on as her advisor, Johnathon."

"Hmm. Well, about that . . ."

Thera raised her eyebrow. "What have you done?"

"I retired."

"What?"

"There are other, younger men who can advise her as well as I, Thera."

"I doubt that," Thera said. "What happened to your vow to serve the throne and anyone who sat upon it?"

Johnathon held her gaze. "She had the throne burned."

"What?" Thera said again.

"She said it made her cold and had a throne carved of heartwood instead. It's padded. Tapestried. Beads and tassels. Quite a grand thing, actually. Vannel would have hated it."

Thera laughed for the first time in a long time.

Johnathon's smile led to a warm chuckle. "I'm glad you see the humor in all this, but I am, after all, without a job. Unless perhaps you have need of an old advisor?"

Thera's heart skipped a beat then drummed faster. "Is that why you came, Johnathon? Are you asking if I need your advice?"

"If you want it. Ah," he added, warm brown eyes resigned at her expression, "perhaps not."

Thera tipped her head to one side, considering him, considering her own heart. "I don't need advice today," she said, "but I could use a hand chopping wood if you'd like."

"I would like that," he said.

"It might take awhile," she said.

Johnathon nodded. "I hope so."

Thera held her hand out for him. He took it in his own, and together, they stood before the window to watch the rain rush upon the shore.

At the time I wrote this story, I was a mother of two young children, working during the day, writing at night, and caring for my grandmother who had Alzheimer's. I felt a little like Tilly: always called upon to fix one more thing that was falling apart, but also enjoying the joy and quirks of life around me. Tilly's world is a rich place that I hope to revisit some day.

STITCHERY

Tilly shaded her eyes with her hand and peered over at the house. The grandma was sitting on the second story window ledge, one bare foot rocking in the wind. Tilly had told her spring was a time of pastels and pinks, of fresh new things, but the grandma never paid her any mind. An endless trail of knitting spilled from her needles to the porch roof below, red as Christmas berries and as cheerfully out of season as the old girl herself.

Tilly sighed. Ever since she'd found the grandma at the DMV, knitting up all the wasted time folks left behind, she'd wondered what to do with her. The DMV people had wanted to send her to an old folks home, but Tilly had stepped in and taken the grandma home instead. Anyone who had the patience to catch up loose seconds and save them for later deserved to be looked after, as far as Tilly was concerned, even if the old girl wasn't in her right mind most the time.

But then, most of Tilly's good intentions made for bad decisions. She shook her head and caught sight of her own hand held up to the sun. Patchwork scars deep in her flesh showed like a crazy-work of seams beneath her skin. Ned never liked to look at her hand when she put a light behind it, and Tilly didn't blame him. Normal folks stayed away from stitchery like her. As long as she didn't talk to Ned about stitching, they got along fine. She liked having him around, enough that she was pretty sure she'd fallen in love with the man, even if she'd never come out and told him so.

The beast beside her shifted and groaned, golden hooves

sinking into the soft soil. Tilly looked down and tightened her grip on its halter.

"Ned!" she hollered. "I need your help with the beast." She stroked the poor thing's neck and squinted at Ned's boots which stuck out from under the old gray Chevy in front of the house. The grandma, two stories up, hummed and knitted.

The beast lowered its head. Tilly stepped back. She'd secured half a tennis ball over its forehead nub with duct tape that wrapped around its jaw, but she wasn't stupid enough to get in the way of the beast's head. She'd seen it root up ant hills and such with that nub. Didn't matter it was broke, it still worked.

Clouds stretched across the sky, fizzled away and still Ned didn't come out from under the truck. "Damn," she whispered. She patted the beast's neck a couple times and wondered what its coat really felt like. Ned had described it to her once, his hands being the ones he was born with and still full of feeling. He'd said the beast's coat was as soft and silky as her copper-brown hair. Tilly smiled at the memory. That man had a way with words.

"Ned! Now, ya hear?"

"Yes, dear," the grandma called back.

"Not you, Granny. Ned."

"Really? I'm not sleepy. But if you say so."

Tilly caught sight of her easing back in through the window, then watched as she pulled the knitted scarf up and up like a red tongue. Tilly figured the grandma was making to come down to her.

"No. You stay there!"

And of course, that's when Ned decided to scoot himself out from under the truck and show his heads.

"Make up your mind," Right Ned called out to her. Left Ned just grinned that hard grin of his around a strand of grass in his teeth.

These were the kind of moments when she wished she'd never stopped work on that heat-seeking dung thrower.

Tilly took a nice deep lungful of pollen-laden air, sneezed

and let go of the beast's halter while she wiped oil from her eyes. She hated her tears. Unlike Ned's, or the grandma's, hers were oily and smelled like hot sulphur. If she didn't scrub them off right away, they left streaks down her freckled cheeks.

Once Tilly could see straight again, she noticed the poor beast was even lower to the ground.

She cleared her throat and put some volume in her voice. "Ned, get over here, both of you! And Granny, you stay right where you are. Just keep knitting. You're doing fine."

The grandma poked her head out the window. A teasing wind lifted the white tendrils of her hair like dandelion down riding a child's wish. She waved one hand, bracelets clinking. "I'll be right there."

Tilly sighed. Best intentions and all that.

Ned walked over to where she and the beast stood under the apple tree. He was wearing his clean overalls today, which meant he wasn't thinking to get any real work done. Time to put another thought in those heads of his, she thought.

"Ned, you know you're my boyfriend, and I like you plenty, right?"

Right Ned nodded. "I reckon, Tilly," he said in that shy soft way that made her wish she'd rubbed off the stains beneath her eyes.

"Then you know that sometimes I need help with things around the property."

Left Ned must have known where she was going, 'cause he made that here-we-go-again look.

Tilly ignored him.

"The beast is looking pretty poor and I'm not sure what it needs. My hands don't work much for this, but yours should. Would you try and figure out what it wants?"

"Tilly," Right Ned said, "you know I gave up mingling with creatures when I gave up chew last winter."

"I know. And I know what it is, me asking this of you. But touching a mind isn't as addicting as chew, is it? And you kicked that habit, right? I mean, I wouldn't ask you to do it, but I just don't have any ideas left."

As if she'd told it to do so, the beast dropped and lay on its side. It stretched its neck out and rolled its eyes, each breath an effort.

Right Ned sighed, but Left Ned said, "You know I hate this, Til. You know I can't ever do it just once."

She looked down at the beast to avoid Left Ned's gaze. "If you have to, you could always mingle with me, Ned." She waited a moment, but there wasn't nothing but the sound of the beast's labored breathing. Tilly felt heat pulse out from the center of her cheeks and she swore inwardly. No matter how hard she tried, she just never seemed to handle things right. Ned and she were lovers, but he never touched her mind, not even when he was in the fever grip of passion. She hadn't asked him why, but figured it was her patchwork nature he took a dislike to. She swallowed once and tried again. "I mean if you'd want that."

"Tilly," Right Ned said, his voice soft.

"For the beast," Tilly cut in. Mingling was his business, and if he preferred animal minds, then that's the way it'd be. But there was no reason he should refuse to help the beast. "Please, Ned?"

Right Ned looked down at the beast with something like sympathy in his eyes. Left Ned just glared at Tilly hard and long.

Sometimes, Tilly thought, that man was a real pain.

"Just to see what it wants," Right Ned said.

Tilly nodded and Ned kneeled down. He held his hands above the beast's dirty white flanks.

Tilly watched, like she used to way back in his circus days, while Ned finally got his heads together, closed both sets of eyes and placed his palms on the once snowy-white side of the beast. Ned stiffened. He lifted up off of his heels a bit, then his whole body slumped.

Tilly bit her lip and waited. She knew it'd been a long time since he'd done this, and she hoped she was right about him not getting stuck mind-to-mind cozy with the ailing beast.

That's what had ended his days in the circus. He'd mingled

Devon Monk

with the ringmaster's daughter, and made her scream. The girl accused him of being dirty, illegal, patchwork, but Tilly knew none of that was true. When Ned was born, his mama didn't let doctors change the way he looked. Ned, all both of him, was more natural than most folks, certainly more than Tilly.

Ned still didn't move. His heads were bent so low, if she caught him from a side-view, she'd think he only had one head. His shoulders were hunched, soul-sensing fingers spread wide and palm-tight against the beast.

"Too hard," both Neds said, and Tilly shivered despite the warm air. When those boys worked in unison, it gave her the creeps.

The beast grunted, but it seemed each breath took just a little longer getting to.

"Warm, sunlit fields and soft, untouched laps. Home." Right Ned looked up at her, tears caught on his girl-pretty lashes. "Tilly, the beast wants to die."

"No," she said shaking her head. This had been the first beast she'd taken in, back when Mother and Father had left her to tend the property and all the souls within. It couldn't be old enough to die. "You're wrong, Ned," she said.

But Right Ned had closed his eyes again, bent toward the beast like his ears were in his palms.

Left Ned stared at her. She knew that look. It was the same one he used when the Sheriff had tried to take him to the medical research center back when he was just a little boy.

"You check again," she said. "Tell it we fenced the back field and the grass is plenty sweet, sweeter than those crazy dreams it's having. Tell it there's no reason to die."

"There's no time left for it, Til," Left Ned said. "Belly-wailing isn't gonna change anything."

She scowled, torn between trying to decide if she should take the beast to a doctor in town, or try to fix it herself. Then she heard the steady click, click of knitting needles coming closer. The grandma shuffled up to them, wearing a pale yellow nightgown and a pair of Tilly's black panties underneath.

She knitted and looped, her huge black bag hanging from the crook of her arm. The yarn coming out of the bag was white now, instead of red.

Tilly gave Left Ned a look to let him know this wasn't done yet then turned to the grandma.

"Granny, why you coming down here? I told you it was okay to keep knitting back at the house."

"Yes, dear. But there's no time left, so I thought I'd come down. It's going to rain, you know."

Tilly glanced up at the sky. The sun was so hot, it'd practically burned a hole in the blue. Weren't a chance clouds could gather on a day like this.

"Sure thing, Granny," Tilly said gently. "You go on back to the house now. Don't want you to get wet."

She nodded. "So sweet," she said.

The beast groaned and Tilly spun on Ned.

"What did you do? You better not tell it to die, Ned, or so help me I'll give you headaches you'll never forget."

"Oh," the grandma said. "Maybe a little more time then?" She stopped knitting and began unraveling the string on the scarf, starting on the red side, furthest away from the loops of white thread on the needles. As she pulled, the yarn disappeared, melting before it even hit the ground. The beast took a couple nice, clear breaths and moved its head a bit.

"Tilly, let it go," Right Ned said. "This fellow is old. It's his time to die."

"You're just being pig-headed, Til," Left Ned said.

Right Ned cleared his throat and Tilly knew he'd been thinking the same thing, just hadn't had the guts to say it.

The grandma hummed and pulled thread.

"It's not going to die," Tilly said.

"Tilly," said Right Ned, "it doesn't want to live anymore."

"I don't care what it wants," Tilly said, trying to keep the sound of tears out of her voice. "I'm going to take it into town to the doctor. You tell it to hold on. Spring isn't no time for dying."

"No time," the grandma agreed.

Granny stopped pulling on her yarn and right that second, the beast stopped breathing.

Under the apple tree got real quiet all of a sudden. Tilly glanced at the beast, lying still, its eyes fogged over and rolled up at that hard hot sun. Then she glanced at Ned. He looked white too, deathly white. That's when she remembered he still had his hands and probably his mind on the beast.

Damn. She took a couple big steps forward and pushed Ned hard. He tipped over onto the back of his nice clean overalls. He was stiff, his arms stuck up in the air, hands flat against the wind.

"Breathe, Ned," she said, as she moved around to touch his face with her fingers. "Both of you."

Ned breathed. He shuddered once and Left Ned moaned softly, then clamped his mouth hard.

Right Ned wiped tears from his eyes. "Holy, Tilly, that hurts, you know."

"Well you should have taken your hands off the beast before," and right there she just couldn't say any more. The beast was dead, poor thing, and it was her fault. If she would have made up her mind faster, if she would have just taken it down to the doctor the moment she knew it was ill instead of trying to fix everything herself, it would still be alive. Tilly looked down at the pitiful collection of hide and bone and a hard hand of grief closed her throat.

Tears slipped down her face. She should have done something, anything, to save it.

The grandma tottered over to her, her huge knitting bag swinging on her elbow. She shushed Tilly and patted her arm with a paper-dry hand. "There, now, sweetness," she crooned. "There just wasn't any time left for it."

"Sure, Granny," Tilly whispered, eyeing the seven feet of red knitting that trailed from her bag. Seemed like there was plenty of time if the grandma had wanted to give it up. But Tilly didn't say any more. That time was the grandma's to keep or give.

The grandma brightened. "Who wants some hot cocoa?" She took up the needles and pulled a handful of white thread from the bag. Loop, tuck, remove, she knitted her way slowly back to the house.

Tilly leaned against the trunk of the apple tree.

"I'm real sorry, Tilly," Right Ned said.

"It was my fault," Tilly said. "I didn't do the right thing. I didn't do anything. I killed it."

Left Ned said, "Shee-it," and spat.

"Tilly, you know better," Right Ned said gently. "Everything dies."

Ned came over and stood close by her, his arm wrapped over her shoulders. He was warm and strong and it felt real good to be comforted by him right then, though Tilly wouldn't have asked him to do it. She supposed that was one of the things she liked about him. He always seemed to know the right thing to do.

The wind picked up and a flock of starlings threw shadows against ground. Tilly knew there were ways to fix what she'd done wrong. She pulled away from Ned and shivered as wind cooled the sweat down her back.

"I need you to go into town and get some pigs for the lizard. Would you do that for me, Ned?"

"Sure, Tilly, but . . ."

"But nothing," she said, maybe a little too fast. She smiled. "I'm fine, really. I've just got some burying to do."

Ned stood, and for a moment, both heads stared her hard. She stared him back.

"You did all you could, Tilly," Right Ned said.

Tilly nodded.

Ned turned and walked to the house. Tilly watched him swing into the battered Chevy. It wasn't until he had wrestled the truck down the road and around the bend before she looked at the beast again.

"But this mistake I can fix," she said.

The beast didn't reply, which was good considering the state it was in.

Tilly rolled up the sleeves of her cotton shirt. She picked up the beast and carried it to Father's workshop.

The workshop was away from the house a bit — down on the creek bank and so covered in brambles, not a brick or window showed through. Tilly was sweating pretty hard by the time she reached the door. She shifted the beast's weight, leaned back and stuck her fingers through bramble runners to catch and lift the wooden latch. She pushed the door open and stepped in.

It was cool and damp here, and smelled like earth, and river and sharp antiseptics. The shop was about the size of a double-wide horse stall, but instead of hay on the ground, there was concrete. A tall wide table took up most the middle of the room and drawers lined the walls.

Tilly laid the beast on the table, then flipped the switch by the door. Lights powered by the water wheel up-creek snapped, clicked, then flickered on. Father told her it wasn't right to run the workshop on the house's electricity. He said all the power needed to do stitchery was in the river itself.

Tilly rubbed her hands on her jeans and noticed the long thorn scratches on her fingers. Blood seeped out, just enough to make sure the cuts were clean. Then hot pain flashed across her fingers. She breathed out real hard a couple times and tipped her palms to the light. The cuts were gone.

She was glad Ned wasn't here to see that.

"Awfully dark in here, dear."

Tilly spun. The grandma stood in the doorway and was practically naked, her thin nightgown translucent from the sunlight at her back. The knitting bag swung at her elbow, needles sticking out of the top of the bag like giant insect feelers.

"Granny, what are you doing down here?"

"I thought there'd be a little time before it rains." She shuffled into the room, her hands clasped in front of her. "Oh, now. Here's the poor thing. Is there anything we can do for it?" she asked.

Tilly shut the door and stood next to the table. "I think so. But I might need a little time."

"Oh my, yes." The grandma smiled and rummaged for her knitting.

Tilly opened drawers, and shivered at the cold air they

expelled. One drawer was filled with thin spools of crystal thread — thread that held new parts to old parts and melted into whatever kind of flesh or muscle or bone needed so the new and old accepted each other as a complete whole. Tilly figured it was those crystal stitches in her hands that heated up so bad whenever she healed. She took a spool of the thread and opened another drawer.

Needles, wires, jars of liquid, delicate saws, tubes with rainbow colored labels, and every once in awhile, the leftover bits of something Father hadn't managed to put back together, filled the drawers. In one of the bigger drawers, Tilly found the body of a small pony. Its legs were missing, and its coat was brown, but other than that, it was nearly perfect.

"Granny," Tilly said as she put on a pair of heavy gloves, "I could use a little time now."

The grandma hummed and pulled stitches.

Tilly lifted the cold-preserved pony out of the drawer, and set it on the table next to the beast.

The room temperature had dropped to near-freezing. Tilly's breath came out in clouds, and her skin was cold with old sweat. She took off the gloves and used one of the saws on the beast's legs. She used tiny hot crystal stitches to attached the legs to the pony. Next, she removed and attached the forehead nub. Crystal thread and needle slid through bone and flesh equally and sent a thin line of steam into the cold air.

"My, you do this well," the grandma said.

"I just hope I do it right." Tilly opened the beast's chest and searched for its heart.

"Right as rain," the grandma said, "don't you worry, dear."

Right as rain, Tilly thought. No matter how hard she tried, she'd never done anything right in her life. She pushed that thought out of her mind and paid attention instead, to the beast.

Long after dark, she heard the grumble of the Chevy. Ned must have bartered with Mr. Campbell for the pigs, which was fine. Tilly liked a man who could stick to a budget.

The truck growled past the house and straight out to the lizard's corral.

Tilly got up from the chair she'd been dozing in and stretched stiffness out of her arms and back. She pulled her coat from the corner closet and listened a minute for the grandma. All was quiet from her upstairs room.

Tilly slipped out the front door, the screen snicking shut behind her. The night air was clear and cold. Stars chipped holes in the otherwise soft, black sky. Way off in the west, the moon hung, distant and oblivious to anything earthly. Tilly crossed her arms over her chest, and headed out to see if Ned needed any help with the pigs.

The track to the lizard's corral was rutted and hard to follow, but Tilly's feet knew it as well as every other inch of ground on the run-down ranch. She'd been down this path with Mother and Father the day she was born, and later, when she'd lost a year to the hot healing. Father said he'd carried her in his arms back and forth on the road, letting her body cool in the living air. That was a long time ago, before they left for better things in the big city.

The wind slipped down from the stars, carrying a breath of ice with it. Tilly shivered. She wondered if Ned would understand what she'd done. Wondered if he'd leave when he found out. Ned believed that stitchery was wrong. He never had himself re-made, though he'd had a chance to when he was a boy, before the laws against such things were passed.

Tilly took the curve in the track and walked into the grass. She could smell the lizard, musty and dry, like mold found in old closets, but ten or a hundred times stronger than that.

She expected to hear the pigs, but only heard the lizard shifting inside the fence — his claws sheathing in and out of the ground, big as shovel blades cutting dirt.

There was a boat-sail snap and Tilly felt heat as the lizard pulled its wings away from its body, but no charred smell of pig-ka-bob, no flame in the air.

Something was wrong.

Tilly picked up the pace and climbed the fence. She ducked the electric line at the top, sidled through the bars and dropped down inside the corral.

The lizard, a good four-feet taller than her, swung his big triangle head her way, eyes shining with ambient moonlight. It didn't see too good anymore, so Tilly held still and let it smell her. Then she walked across the corral toward the silent pigs in the fenced-off feeding chute.

As she drew closer, she saw a bigger shadow in with the pigs. Ned was on his knees in the middle of them all, hands spread wide and pushed tight against dirty hides.

Freak, Tilly thought fondly. *You'll mingle with pig brains, but won't touch your willing girlfriend.*

"Ned," she said. She unlatched the electric wire at the gate to the chute and stepped in. "Now who's being pig-headed?"

Left Ned looked up and scowled. Right Ned looked up too, but his pretty eyes were glazed, his face slack.

"Ned. Let the pigs go," she said, her words soft and sure, and for Right Ned only.

He looked down at his hands and after a minute seemed to realize they were on the pigs. He drew back, embarrassed.

Left Ned chuckled.

"Sorry," Right Ned said. "I'm sorry, Tilly. It was just after today. Getting caught in the dying, I guess, I needed to feel living again. I told you once I do it, I want it more." He stepped away from the pigs and rubbed his palms on his overalls. "I'm sorry." The pigs began grunting and rooting around.

"That's okay," Tilly said because he didn't know what she'd done either. "Let's go on back to the house and get some sleep, okay?"

The night was interrupted by a whinny. It was a far off, spooky sound, but any fool could tell what it was. The beast.

Ned was no fool. "Tilly," he said, "what did you do?"

"I fixed it up a bit, that's all."

"Did you bring the beast back from death?" Real honest horror carried his words up an octave.

"Granny and I, we used a little time so I could get the fix-up bits out of Father's workshop and apply them to the beast. I didn't really stitch it, Ned, I took parts of the old beast and made a new beast just like it."

"Holy, Tilly," Ned said. "That's plain wrong. You don't fix up dead things and you don't make copies of them. Don't you know how illegal that is? For Holy sake, it's why your Daddy left you."

"You're talking crazy," Tilly said, trying to be calm, even though he was starting to scare her. "Father and Mother went to the big city for better things."

"For jail time, Tilly. They went to jail. Because they made things, like the beast, the lizard and worse, they re-made their own . . ." He stopped a second, then looked down at his feet.

She knew what he'd been about to say. They'd re-made their own daughter.

When he looked back up at her, she knew he was dead serious.

"Now you promise me," both Neds said in chilling unison, "right now, right this second, that you will never stitch nothing or nobody back together again."

"But, Ned," she said, feeling shaky inside and wanting more than anything for him to stop acting crazy.

"But nothing," he said. "Promise me."

She took a deep breath. It was a scary thing giving the power of a promise away, but Ned was real upset and she figured they'd have time to talk this over later.

"I promise," she said.

Just then, the lizard opened its wings and lunged whip-quick for the pigs. In the same instant, Tilly realized she had forgotten to close the electric line behind her.

The lizard aimed for the pigs but instead of pigs, it got Ned.

It felt like a cold fist punched Tilly. Her mind tried hard to make sense of things. She hollered at the lizard until it dropped Ned in a bloody heap. She picked Ned up, stumbled out to the truck, and managed to get him into the front seat, though he wasn't conscious.

"You keep living," she said, her words rough with panic. She ground gears and the truck sped down the rutted road. "Keep living."

Both Neds were silent, their eyes cinched with pain.

Once she made the house, she lifted Ned out of the truck careful as she could. She took him into the front room and laid him on the couch. Blood the color of the grandma's knitting covered him, darkest over his stomach. She peeked under his shirt and swore. The bites were deep, and Ned's life pumped out with every breath. He was going to bleed out before she could get the crystal thread from the workshop.

She needed more time.

The grandma.

She ran across the wood floor, then up the stairs, up and up, and the stairs kept on going and she wasn't getting any closer to the end of them, until finally, she reached the landing.

She ran to the right, to the grandma's room, but her feet took twice as long as they should to get her there, and on the way she noticed the hall was in need of new paint, and a layer of dust had grown along the edge of the floor, and then finally, finally, she got to the grandma's room and opened the door.

The grandma was sitting in her bed, pulling red yarn out stitch by stitch, just wasting time.

"Granny, you got to help me. Ned's hurt bad."

The length of red knitting that had been at least seven feet long this morning was down to its last foot, and shrinking ever closer to white.

The grandma looked up and smiled. "Hello, Tilly. It's going to rain, you know."

Tilly ran across the room, grabbed the grandma by the wrist and took her, bag and all, down the stairs.

The only thing different about Ned since she'd left him, was the pool of blood on the floor had grown.

"Granny, you stay here and pull out a little time for him while I go get the stitchery from the workshop." Then Tilly stopped. She'd promised Ned she'd never stitch nothing or nobody again.

Holy . . .

Thip, thip, thip, the grandma sat herself down in the old rocker and unwove another row of red.

Tilly stepped over to Ned and looked at his wounds again. The blood flow wasn't stopping.

Thip, thip, thip, stitch after stitch of time pulled out.

"Ned," Tilly said, hoping he could hear her. "I have to fix you up. Just some stitching, but nothing fancy. You'll still be you — not like what I did to the beast, okay?"

Tilly couldn't believe her eyes when she saw Right Ned shake his head.

She looked at the Grandma, saw how she was trying to pull the yarn real slow so it would last.

"Ned," Tilly said, "you can't die."

Thip, thip, thip.

There were only a few rows of red left, and then the grandma would be into the white. As soon as the white was gone, there'd be no time left. She had to do something now.

She kneeled down and put her hands above Ned's stomach, her unnatural, patchwork hands. She closed her eyes, just the way she'd seen Ned do it. Then she tried to find his spirit, the living thing that made him what he was. Somehow, she had to convince him to stay living until she could stitch him.

She sensed his heartbeat and the sluggish push of blood under her fingers. Briefly, something else flashed past her closed eyes, something sweet as honey and fresh as lemons. Ned's soul.

She held on to the idea of that, hoping it wasn't just her imagination. Her feet and face and hands tingled as she wrapped her mental self gently as she could around that warm sweet core of him.

"Please keep living, Ned. I love you."

The words seeped down, running through her skin to his skin. Words filled his veins where there wasn't enough blood. His heartbeat stuttered and fell into beat with the rhythm of time unstitching.

"Spring's supposed to be a time of life, not death. You and

I have a lot of living left." Tilly poured her soul into those words, and felt the brush of his mind against hers. Then she felt his breath as if it were her own — his pain shooting through her body, his fear sharp within her mind. She kept her thoughts calm, sending snatches of happy memories to him, until his pain and fear eased. "Live, Ned." She whispered, and then she opened her eyes.

Thip, thip, thip. The grandma pulled yarn. Tilly looked over her shoulder. The white yarn was almost gone.

"No," she said.

Thip. The last loop.

She felt the world shudder and pause.

Ned's heart, beneath her hands, stopped.

Tilly took a deep breath and watched Ned's chest rise. His heart stumbled and began beating on its own again.

"Keep breathing," Tilly said while she got to her feet. She was dizzy, but somehow managed to find the trauma-kit in the kitchen, filled with cotton thread, painkillers and antiseptics.

Tilly concentrated on breathing whenever Ned forgot, and tried to send him memories of warm summer days. She didn't know if the grandma helped her sew and dress Ned's wounds or not. But the tingling she'd felt in her hands and feet and face ever since she'd started touching Ned's mind all picked the same moment to rush inward. It was like the world had just taped her up and pulled that tape away, stripping her to the bone.

She didn't know she had passed out until she woke, down in the bed Ned and she shared. Ned was beside her, his breath no longer connected to hers, warm and real and alive all on its own, against her cheek.

Tilly stared up at the ceiling for awhile, blinking back tears. She'd made mistake after mistake — let the beast die, stitched, left the gate open, and had made Ned live too. She'd kept her promise, but keeping it had almost killed him. She hadn't stitched, but she'd done something else he'd never wanted. She mingled with his mind and touched his soul. She'd made him a part of her long enough to keep him alive, even though his body had been set on dying.

Now she knew why touching a mind once wasn't ever enough for him.

Ned shifted. He woke with a quiet moan and she propped up on her elbow to get a good look at the both of him.

Right Ned opened his eyes. "Did you . . .?"

She shook her head. "No. You're healing on your own."

"How?" he asked.

"Shhh," she said, resisting the urge to reach out and touch his mind again. "I — we mingled. I'm sorry I touched you that way, but I couldn't bear the death of you." Guilt soured her stomach, and her oily tears dropped to the sheets.

"You mingled with me?" Right Ned asked. Then a faint smile touched his mouth. "With your hands?"

"I know it's wrong . . . ."

"It isn't wrong, Tilly."

Right Ned swallowed, so Left Ned said, "Wasn't that I hated the thought of being close to you . . ."

". . . I just wanted it so fierce," Right Ned said, "I knew I'd never let go once we touched that way. If you ever left me, or told me you didn't want me around, I knew I couldn't leave you."

Tilly couldn't believe what he was saying, but felt the truth in his words as if they were her own. All this time, he had wanted her too much, so he hadn't touched her at all.

"Now, that kind of thinking won't do us any good," she said. "I love you, Ned. Both of you."

Ned smiled, and though he didn't say it, Tilly felt his love spread tenderly across her mind.

This time, Tilly knew just what to do. She leaned down and very gently kissed first Right Ned, then Left Ned, then Right Ned again, touching him with her mind, her soul and her patchwork hands.

I wrote this while thinking about the human capacity to go forward and do good even when faced with great adversity.

LAST TOUR OF DUTY

H ere's another Lucky!" the private yelled as he pushed the stretcher out of the medical transport truck.

Corey knew the Lucky could wait, but he gave the boy a quick glance anyway. The soldier had an abdomen full of shrapnel, yet he was calm, like all Luckys were. After a year of receiving Luckys, Corey knew this one would make it too.

"Put him over there by the other two," Corey said. "And get the rest of these boys into O.R."

The private nodded. Corey supposed he should have demanded a crisp "yes, sir!" but the men needed all the energy they had just to get the dozen wounded soldiers across the dirt to the makeshift operating room.

At least it wasn't raining. Of course, when it wasn't raining in Nam, the air hatched wings.

Corey strode into the scrub tent. The other doctors were already washing: Jim, the new guy, who still walked in a daze even though he'd been here three months; and soft-spoken Lonnie.

"Three Luckys." Corey elbowed on the faucet and held his hands under the running water.

"How about the rest?" Lonnie asked.

"Nine. Let's get to them as quickly as we can. Save the Luckys for last." They were old words, as worn out as their scrubs, but just as necessary.

"Let's get on it, gentlemen."

They got on it. Cockroaches scurried from sheets as bodies were placed onto tables. Corey cut, cleaned, extracted, sewed. One boy after another: missing limbs, shrapnel, and burns that were still smoking. Of the four boys that came across his table, maybe two would make it. No matter how fast Corey worked, no matter how brilliantly he patched and sutured, their odds for survival were never any better. Death ran too close a race.

The last boy he didn't bother to stitch. The medic had done a poor job stabilizing him. The wrap was too loose, and the soldier, Steve, by his grimy dogtags, had bled out his chance of survival on the ride over.

Corey shook his head and the nurse tugged the sheet over the soldier's still face before the orderlies were back with a new body.

This one was a Lucky. Corey took a moment to look at his dogtags.

"Okay, Thomas, you're going to be just fine." Corey pushed his hands into new gloves, asked for the scissors, and cut the bandaging away from Thomas' stomach.

The medic who placed these wraps knew his shit. The bandages were tight, clean, even. Even an intern could tell the medic, Billy Templin — the wounded called him Lucky — had a knack for doctoring.

Ten out of ten wounded men Billy bandaged on the front lines survived. It was a weird probability that Corey had refused to believe for the first six months, but now, eighteen months into his service here, any boy Lucky touched still didn't die.

Corey tended two Luckys and Lonnie took the other one. The new guy, Jim, left without saying a word as soon as he was done with his last patient. Corey figured he'd go off to drink, or try to sleep out the heat. One of these days, Jim was going to wake up and realize this wasn't a bad dream. Corey wasn't looking forward to that day.

"Any more?" Corey asked the private who stood near the door.

The private shook his head. "That's all, Sir." What he didn't have to say, was: for now.

Corey took a deep breath, aware again of the sharp smell of sweat and rot of insides being exposed to the outside.

He shucked off his gloves and ran his hand over his face. Maybe half would survive his table. Three of three Luckys would walk. He'd do anything to increase those odds, and send more of the boys home breathing, instead of in boxes.

"How'd we do, Corey?" Lonnie asked as Corey stepped out into the fading sunlight.

The early evening air was hot and wet. Corey locked his jaw and strained the air through his teeth to get it down. Eighteen months had all but erased his memory of Colorado's clean, cold wind.

"The Luckys will make it," Corey said, "I think three or four others have a chance."

Lonnie nodded and pulled a rolled cigarette and lighter from his pocket.

"Too bad they all can't be Luckys," Corey said quietly. He heard the approach of incoming choppers over the forested ridge.

Lonnie rubbed his thumb across his lighter. "Too bad Billy can't be here."

The ache lifted from Corey's shoulders. A breath of Colorado air, cool as a drink of water, suddenly brushed across the sweat on his face. Such a simple answer: bring Billy here. The five-oh-four received wounded from several units. If Billy were here, he could help more boys, save more boys.

The chopper came closer. Lonnie finally got his joint lit, and sucked a deep, satisfied lungful.

"Maybe Lucky should come here," Corey said, trying to keep the creep of excitement out of his voice. "We need a man like him."

Lonnie raised one eyebrow, but didn't exhale.

"We could send someone to bring him here," Corey said. "Hell, I'll go out there. Think of how many we could save." Most? he thought to himself. All? Could it be that easy? Statistics would say it was impossible, but then, so was the very real fact that every Lucky lived.

"They won't let him go." Lonnie's words came out like molasses, slow and smoky-sweet. "Always short on good men in the boonies."

"We're short on good men here!"

Lonnie blinked, the surprise and hurt plain on his face. He tipped his head and studied his bloody boots. "Damn, Corey."

Corey opened his mouth, closed it and scrubbed his hand across his face. "I don't mean it that way. We just . . . we can't keep up with this." He waved his hand toward the OR tent. "We're losing, Lonnie. Can't you see that? Fifty-fifty odds. That's not good enough. Billy will make the difference. His boys don't die." Corey put his hand on Lonnie's shoulder. "We need him to work with us. So all the boys can go home."

Lonnie smiled real slow, like he had just tuned in a favorite song on the radio. "And then we go home, right?"

Corey nodded. "Sure. Maybe then we can all go home."

Before dawn, Corey packed his bag and walked out to the jeep like this was something he did every day. He swung into the driver's seat, and jumped when a low voice spoke.

"Be careful," Lonnie said. "It's pretty bad out there."

Lonnie stood in nothing but his boots, his red hair gone wild from sleep, or maybe from the active lack of it. He held a sheaf of papers out to him.

Corey took them.

"Paperwork to transfer personnel. These should work so long as the C.O. doesn't look too close."

Corey smiled. "Thanks. And go back to bed. You've got my rounds in an hour."

"What should I tell them when they notice you're gone?"

"I'll be back by then."

Lonnie shook his head, but he smiled. "Give 'em hell."

Corey turned the ignition and ground gears. He left Lonnie, the camp, the Luckys and the dead behind, and followed the dirt track out along the edge of the ridge, then down through the press of hills.

This was too easy: stealing the jeep, Lonnie's papers, but he wasn't about to wait for someone to notice him.

The engine roared in the pre-morning air. Headlights traced gullies and bushes in stark relief. Dawn spilled out and Corey gripped the wheel tighter, his hands sweating. Every bounce of the tires could trigger a buried claymore, every bend in the track reveal a sniper.

"Damn, damn, damn." He kept his foot down and his eyes on the brush. The platoon should be close, should be here. He couldn't have passed it, couldn't have gotten turned around in the darkness.

Heat rose off the jungle floor in biting, clicking swarms. Corey wiped sweat and pebble-hard bugs off his neck. One more mile. If the platoon didn't show, he would turn around. And try to explain this joyride to his C.O.

A dirty mess of tents emerged from the woodline to his left. Corey slowed the jeep and waved at the sentry who called out a challenge. He let the soldier search his jeep, and showed him the papers Lonnie had rigged. The private pointed at the C.O.'s tent. Corey took his time walking there, trying to keep his face poker straight. By the time he had ducked into the tent and sat in the extra chair, he had his best bedside manners in place.

"Morning, doctor," Lieutenant Jonas said, his words slightly slurred. The tent smelled of stale whiskey and vomit. "What the hell are you doing here?"

Gunfire rattled, close enough to catch its own echo and Corey glanced out the netting before answering.

"I have orders to take one of your medics back to the five-oh-four."

"Jesus," the Lieutenant said. He took a swallow out of a nearly empty bottle. "Just one? Hell, they'll line up for you, Doc. Take 'em all back. And while you're at it, why don't you take the rest of the platoon?" He laughed, but his bloodshot gaze was steady and hard.

Corey forced a smile and handed Jonas the papers.

Jonas took the papers, but didn't look at them. "Which one of my boys do you want?"

"Billy Templin."

"Lucky?" Jonas' eyebrows shot up. He chuckled again, and coughed. "Looks like you've got a problem," he said. "Lucky Templin's dead."

Death had won again, outpaced him by what? Moments? Corey felt the weight of eighteen months press his shoulders down into his spine.

"How did he die?" he asked.

"You've heard about the war, right?" Jonas drawled. "Tell you what. How about you scratch his name out of that order and write in some other bastard's name?"

"When did he die?" Corey asked. "This morning? Last night?" Gunfire popped again, further away this time.

Jonas sniffed. "Seven months ago. About. During the rain. Jesus. You're seven months late."

"But —"

"Pulled his body in myself," Jonas said. "What was left of it."

Corey managed to nod. Jonas must be lying. Yesterday's wounded had Billy's signature wraps. They were surviving against the odds. Billy had to be alive.

"I'm sorry," Corey said. He took the papers, stood and walked out of the tent, his mind spinning. He started the jeep and turned it back down the trail to the five-oh-four.

It didn't add up. The wounded were still coming in, still bandaged the same way they had been for the last eight months. Maybe Billy had trained someone else, another medic. Maybe he had gone AWOL. But if he had skipped out, why would he still be bandaging the wounded?

Corey was too wrapped in thought to notice the small bulge in the road ahead of him.

Something exploded. The world broke apart. The jeep swerved, tipped. Corey felt his head strike something hard where there should have been air and a detached voice in his mind catalogued each impact: skull fracture, broken ribs, collarbone, arm, and then there was a sickening crunch against his chest and the detached voice shut up while Corey screamed.

Darkness came in fits. Corey clung to it, tried to suck it down, but reality would not go away, would not stop hurting.

He watched a bird wing a tight circle against a sky gone white-hot and heard the crackle and lick of fire feeding on the wrecked jeep. The wind stirred, hot and wet, and tugged the edges of his clothes. Even though it was a minor pain, he shuddered in agony.

There was no one out here to look for him, the detached voice in his head came back to say. Too many breaks, probably a chunk of metal in the stomach. Bleeding too bad. Nobody to look for him. Nobody to hear his moans, and maybe he should try to be quiet anyway.

Die, take a breath, die again.

Cool hands touched his face.

Not until the hands probed his arms, torso and legs, did Corey decide they were real. He looked up.

A man leaned over him, gaze intent on his chest, fingers gently pulling the clothing away from the wound there.

Corey moaned.

"You'll be okay," the man said, his voice as cool as autumn in the Colorado countryside. He bent a bit to put himself fully in Corey's line of vision.

Corey blinked. Blinked again.

The man was horribly scarred, but his brown eyes were sparked with good humor, his crooked smile sincere.

Who? he thought.

"I'm Billy Templin," the man said.

Billy's hands moved with short efficient motions: pulled out gauze pads and strips. His face seemed to fade until it was see-through, like a reflection on a dark window pane. Corey saw vegetation through his face; saw sky and a bird flying where Billy's forehead should be.

His hands were too cold, but they felt real.

Corey moaned as Billy slowly pressed and wrapped his wounds.

Still never make it, he thought. *Too much blood loss, too much shock.*

"You're a doctor, aren't you?" Billy asked as he splinted Corey's arm. "I always wanted to be a doctor. Didn't have the money for college." He shook his head. "But don't you worry. I've seen a lot of wounds. You're going to be okay. You haven't lost too much blood, and that chest wound is gonna clean up just fine."

Too much blood loss, he thought, and Billy smiled.

"I'm telling you, doc, you haven't lost that much blood."

You can hear me?

"Sure. You can hear me too, right?"

I'm hallucinating.

"No."

I'm already dead then.

Billy chuckled and it was the sound of the wind in the elephant grass. "Not if I can help it."

But you're d — Corey stopped mid-thought.

Billy's gaze became intense, his hands stilled. "I'm what, doc?"

Jonas' words flashed through Corey's mind: 'Lucky Templin is dead. Pulled his body in myself, what was left of it.'

Billy seemed to hear that memory too. His face twisted with sorrow. He sat back on his heels. "Oh," he said, "oh."

Corey panicked. *Come back with me. You could be a doctor. You could save so many more at the five-oh-four. The wounded need you. I need you.*

"You'll be fine," Billy said, distantly, "they'll be fine."

Not without your help, Corey thought.

Billy smiled, and his gaze once again met Corey's. "You're the doctor. They need you."

And you.

"I'm dead."

I can see you. Maybe I'm wrong, maybe Jonas is wrong.

Billy shook his head, his smile crooked, sad.

The men you touch live, Billy. You can't stop now.

"Everybody dies sometime."

Corey wanted to ask him what he meant, but Billy stood and walked away, no more substantial than the wind.

The sound of shifting grass grew louder, a stealthy pace, footsteps.

"Holy shit," a voice cried out. "Over here."

Jungle boots came closer.

"Looks like a medic found him. Check the jeep and bush. Let's get this guy back to the platoon."

Corey tried to speak, but his mouth wouldn't work.

The soldier looked down at him. "You're going to be okay," he said. "Good thing our patrol came along. This is your lucky day."

Lonnie was surprised to see him on the truck with the other wounded. When he asked what happened, Corey only shook his head.

How could he explain it? Who would believe him?

The Luckys stopped coming. Corey knew he was the reason for it. He had convinced Billy of his own death. He had found him and killed him.

It took two months before Corey could operate again. When they brought the first wounded soldier across his table, Corey looked at his dogtags.

"You'll be fine, Grant," he said.

The boy's eyes, which had been wild with pain, seemed to focus, his expression become calm.

Corey knew that look. A brief, fresh breeze stirred the room. The constant ache in his chest suddenly eased.

While he cut and sutured, he thought he glimpsed someone walking between the operating tables, pausing to touch each wounded with a gentle hand, to hold loose bandages or tie gauze tighter.

Twelve out of the thirteen wounded survived that day.

Corey did not speak of the phantom who walked among them, not even to Lonnie. The odds were finally on their side, and Corey knew how fleeting life, and luck, could be.

I was exploring the sword and sorcery genre with this story. I had read stories from the hero's point of view and from the villain's point of view. But I'd never read a story from the weapon's point of view.

OLDBLADE

Vows. Sweat. Blood. Fire.

Ethra came to life screaming. In those first moments, she searched for the bindings that held her to King Talon, but the ancient vows of blood and honor between them, vows that could only be broken by death, were faded echoes.

It had been seven hundred years since she had been alone, unbound, and even then she had not been free. She had no doubt she would not be free now.

A voice lashed out, called her name.

"Oldblade."

She focused on the word. Talon's brother, Nathe, stood above her, his face crooked and slick, mismatched eyes reflecting the hard light of the forge. A leather apron covered his chest, protecting his fine linen shirt from the fire. From her prone position, Ethra could see his sleeves were rolled to the elbow, exposing ruined stumps where his hands should be.

"You are mine now, Oldblade."

Magic fouled the air. A dark hammer rose at the edge of her vision. Nathe jerked. Though his arms did not move, the hammer fell, lifted and struck again.

Ethra struggled against the pounding blows. No man could reforge her. No man could bind her until she was certain King Talon was dead, their vows undone. But Nathe was more mage than man, more hunger than reason. She tried to move, but Nathe's words pressed, heavy, against her.

"Generations of our blood have wielded you," Nathe said through heat and fire, "lords and knights, noblemen all. Including my brother, the king." Nathe jerked. The hammer struck.

"I will regain what Talon has taken: my hands and my power. Then I will show my brother the same mercy he has shown me."

Images filled her mind: Nathe standing above the queen's lifeless body, drawing forbidden blood magics from her spine and ending the bloodline within her womb. King Talon's rage as he stepped into the room to find his wife and child dead, and his brother very much alive.

Talon's judgement had been both merciful and cruel. Nathe would not be beheaded, but behanded.

Ethra remembered the sliding pop of Nathe's delicate wrist bones cleaving apart beneath her edge. She remembered his scream, his vow to see his brother dead. She had served King Talon as a weapon should. Even against his own brother.

The hammer fell again.

"You are my servant now," Nathe said, "bound to me as you were bound to him. You will execute my justice. You will do as I say." Sweat slicked his face and he jerked again, sending the hammer down.

"Breathe."

Ethra pulled air through the mouth he had formed for her.

She could taste the oily taint of magic in the forge, magic that should not respond to handless wielding, magic Nathe controlled with the strength of his hatred. The hammer beat down, pounding in rhythm to his words.

Words that shaped her.

Words that took her into darkness.

When next she woke, she stood as a man would, on two feet, with legs and torso and arms. She turned her head and felt her hair brush her cheek with a steely rattle. She lifted her hands. Five fingers, human fingers, though they were long and thin like delicate daggers.

What had Nathe done? She had not agreed to serve him, had neither taken nor given vows. Without her consent, he could not bind her, and yet she felt tethers around her soul.

Ethra looked at the room, an old armory, lined with lifeless spears and bits of mail. She envied the weapons their stupidity. Newly forged and pledged to no bloodline, they held no soul to be summoned for man's insanities.

Centuries ago, she had been drawn from earthmetal into weapon form. But man's world had been nothing more than brief images and vague impressions of blood, bone and steel. In this new form, she saw the world clearly. And she ached to see more.

"Come here, Oldblade." Nathe stood in the shadow of the doorway, the leather apron gone, revealing loose trousers and a long-sleeved shirt. Except for his ruined arms, he looked every inch a mage.

Ethra walked across the armory's pock-marked floor, her feet scraping, then landing with whispered chinks as she bent her knees to correct her stride. Leg and hip flowed with each step; her torso rocked slightly, following the tip of her shoulders. It was an odd sensation, awkward, unbalanced — and strangely pleasant.

She stopped in front of the mage, her hands at her side, fingertips resting upon her thighs with a click.

Nathe was taller than she, though he leaned heavily on one leg. His hair grew thin and red across his skull, strands of it clinging to the sweat covering his cheeks. Dark shadows circled his mismatched eyes and traced the edge of an old scar at his temple.

"Blink," he said.

The force of the word pressed like a knuckle against her eyes. Against her will, her lids lowered then raised, cool oil washing her sight.

Ethra felt muscles stiffen down her back. Was she no more than a puppet? Would he not ask for her service, for her vows and honor? Would he not pledge his loyalty in return?

"Step back," he said.

Ethra stepped.

"Turn. Slowly. Again. Stop." He smiled. "Better even than my hound. Very good."

Ethra faced him, her gaze unwavering. He controlled her body, but he did not control her will.

"I thought you would take the same form as your last wielder," Nathe said as he paced a close circle around her. "I expected to see my brother before me, looked forward to it, really. Now I understand why he spent all those hours stroking you against his whetstone." Nathe leaned close. "What else did he do to you, Oldblade?"

Ethra pushed against the mage's hold on her soul, trying to shift her stance, to move, but could not. His words, his magic, held her body as surely as a hand upon a hilt. Anger sat heavy in her belly and her hands curled into fists.

He smiled at her reaction. "Spirit and soul. Again, not what I expected. But easy enough to control." He stopped at her side, his breath spreading like fog across her cheek.

"You will bring me my brother's noble hands, since he has robbed me of mine."

He stood in front of her and she felt his words constrict within her. "Talon lies ill — poisoned, they say — making me the last of the royal bloodline." He smiled. "But he will not die before I have his hands. Do you understand? Speak."

Ethra opened her mouth, pushed air over vocal chords, and winced at the strangeness of it. "You," she breathed, her voice the sweet ring of metal striking metal, "have not asked. For my blessing."

Nathe scowled. "I am your maker. You will serve me or I will throw you back to the fire, Oldblade. You will bring me my brother's hands. Do you understand?"

Ethra understood a bound weapon could not kill the man it was bound to. She understood the fire would destroy her form, that Nathe would unmake her as surely as he made her. She would never see this world with her own eyes or move through it with her own legs. She would be strapped again, sheathed, bound.

"Speak!"

"I will bring you your brother's hands," she breathed.

"Go then." He strode across the armory and stepped

through the doorway, "and remember whom you serve." As if triggered by his words, the air turned rancid with magic.

Flecks of shadows pulled up from the pocks in the floor, hovering, then drawing together. The shadows rushed forward in a black stream, filling the armory doorway with darkness.

Ethra's feet lifted and fell of their own accord, of Nathe's accord, drawing her ever nearer the darkness within the doorway.

I am not a puppet.

Step.

I am not a tool to be used and thrown away.

Step.

I will not be bound against my will.

Step.

Blackness. Heat poured over her, and she wondered for an instant if Nathe had heard her thoughts and thrown her back to the fires of the forge.

She open her mouth to scream.

Her foot lifted, dropped. The heat, the blackness drained away.

Ethra blinked, oil cooling her eyes. Her mouth was still open, the rhythm of her own breath sharp in her throat. She was suddenly very cold. She placed one hand against her stomach and hunched her shoulders. Vertigo spun the world. She fought for balance and locked her knees, refusing to fall. After a moment, she tipped her face toward the sky and licked cool gray flakes from her lips. The flakes melted on her tongue. Not ashes from the forge, but snow falling from a stony sky.

Ethra took a slow breath and focused on her surroundings.

She stood in Talon's garden, leagues away from Nathe's keep. The magicked doorway behind her swallowed light, a blackness moonlight could not pierce. Around her, skeletal shrubs wore snow like mourner's mantles.

Ethra followed the old pathway between the orange-barked madda trees and squat clumps of shankfern. She could sense the garden's symmetrical formation, and vaguely green smell of frozen soil. A cluster of birds, red and round as berries, rose from the midst of the fern. They darted upward, trailing liquid song.

Ethra caught her breath. The birds, their song, even the barren plants were beautiful. She had never noticed such things before, never seen such beauty with the eyes of a sword.

The sound of distant footsteps came to her. She turned. A guard, cloaked in leather and wool, rounded the garden's edge. His determined pace faltered as he saw her, then picked up again.

He ran toward her, pulling his sword from its sheath.

Ethra tried to run, but her feet would not move. Nathe's will still bound her body, even at this distance. She felt her arms rise, daggered fingers outstretched.

I will bring you your brother's hands, not kill for you, Ethra thought, as her legs shifted, her torso turned, providing a smaller target.

I will not be your puppet. She struggled to pull her hands down, but could only force them to her waist.

The guard stopped outside sword's reach, his blade extended.

"What in sweet Gillton's blood are you?"

"Oldblade," Ethra said. She struggled to stay still, to hold against Nathe's rage, to deny him his blood hunger. "I must see King Talon."

The guard hesitated.

"He is dying," Ethra breathed, her voice echoing eerily in the still garden. "I have come for him."

Nathe's will pushed. Her muscles shook as she defied his command. "Please do not fight me," she said.

The guard stepped forward.

Nathe's blood hunger burst through her. Ethra lunged, her arms swinging upward. The guard's blade deflected off her arm and fell from his hand. She managed to turn her wrist so that the back of her hand, not her fingers struck his face. His head snapped back and he fell.

Ethra knelt over him. He still breathed, though his eyes showed white in his skull. Her hands trembled, muscles bunched in her arms, shoulders, back. She strained to keep her fingers away from his throat, away from the soft spaces between his ribs, where his heart lie beating.

I. Am. Not. Yours.

Ethra forced herself to stand, muscles protesting painfully. One backward step and then another took her away from him, until finally, she could turn. She crossed the rest of the garden without seeing it, anger blinding her.

How dare you. How dare you force me, without agreement, use me to kill without vows. I have agreed to bring you your brother's hands, nothing more.

If Nathe heard her thoughts, he did not answer.

She knew the door to Talon's bedchambers was tucked in the east corner of the garden. Once there, she knocked out the man standing guard and struggled once again with Nathe's insatiable blood hunger. She finally managed to step over the unconscious guard, and shut the door behind her.

Light from the single wallsconce at the top of the stairway curved warm and orange over her arms, chest and legs as Ethra climbed the private stairs to Talon's room, but the only heat she felt was her own hatred.

The stairs lead to a short hallway and Talon's door. A guard clothed in red and gray stood at the door, his sword drawn, point resting beside his boot. He narrowed his eyes as Ethra stepped from the shadows.

She rushed him, wagering her reaction would be faster than Nathe's control, and grabbed for the guard's sword. She twisted his wrist, broke it. The guard cried out. The blade clattered to the stones. His dagger appeared in his good hand. The blade skipped across her belly and shoulder. Ethra stepped into him, hooked his foot and pulled. The guard fell. Before he could recover, she punched him once across the temple.

Her hands hesitated above the pulsepoint in his neck, fingers trembling for blood.

I am not yours! She yanked her hands back and fought to regain her feet. Moments crept by. Nathe's hold tightened within her, like a rope cutting into a deep wound. She took quick, shallow breaths and forced her hands, finger by finger into fists.

Ethra stood and slipped into Talon's chambers.

The king lay in a massive bed, his once robust body frail beneath gold and burgundy linens. There were no physicians or guards attending his bedside and Ethra wondered if Nathe had been wrong. Perhaps Talon had already died in the night.

She stepped closer to the bed.

Talon's face was pale in the shuttered moonlight, his dark hair heavy with sweat, his breath coming too quickly. Memories came to her. Talon, drunk and sweating, whipping a serving boy for taking a piece of fruit from his table. She remembered being drawn against the serving boy's cheek, carving an angry x in his soft flesh. She remembered the feel of Talon's hand gripping her. She remembered his pleasure. Blood pleasure. The same blood pleasure that fueled Nathe's hunger.

Ethra waited for a long moment, sorting the memories, anger and betrayal. Through every generation, through the killings, the battles, she had served faithfully, as a weapon should. She had done that which her wielders had asked her to do, accepting their vows of honor and loyalty.

But there was no honor in branding a child, or in brothers destroying brothers.

I am no man's puppet. This last time she would serve their bloodline. This last time she would serve a man.

A bird called outside Talon's window and Ethra stepped forward. Talon woke, his eyes glossy with fever. He fumbled at the empty bedpost where once she had hung in her sheath. Then he searched beneath his pillow for his dagger. Ethra wrapped her thin, bladed fingers around Talon's wrists, and stepped back.

She made her way through the hall, stairs and garden, toward the magicked doorway. She stepped into the darkness, her prize clutched tightly in her hands.

Nathe waited on the other side of the doorway, the wall sconces in the old armory ablaze with flame. Ethra stepped through the doorway and watched surprise, then horror twist his face.

"I told you to bring me his hands!"

"I have." Ethra pulled Talon by the hands through the doorway behind her.

Nathe skittered to the wall, his arms raised, stumps guarding his face. "No!"

Ethra released Talon. He approached his brother with a growl, dagger clutched in one hand.

Nathe's will pushed at her. She pushed back. She had served him. She had done as he commanded. She would be his puppet no longer.

Talon stumbled toward his brother. "I should have killed you years ago." With surprising speed, he thrust the dagger into Nathe's throat.

Ethra gasped as Nathe's will clawed at her soul, then faded, the bindings between them becoming as insubstantial as his last breath.

Talon fell to his knees next to his brother's body. He began coughing, then retching. Blood dribbled from the corners of his mouth. The poison was killing him, slowly, painfully.

Ethra knew the bond between them had broken the moment Nathe had taken her from the king and reforged her. She knew she was free.

She walked to the king and touched his shoulder.

Talon looked up.

His eyes widened. Ethra pulled her fingers across his throat, ending his life and the bloodline that summoned her. She stared at the brothers for a long moment as an empty feeling spread through her. She had found no pleasure in their blood, their deaths. She did not understand why they had craved it so.

Ethra turned and walked away, ready to walk the world with her own legs, and see it, for the first time, with her own eyes.

This is the only vampire romance I've written. It hints at a full world with all sorts of fanged shenanigans going on. What was I thinking when I wrote it? That it was high time someone mixed vampires with knitting.

SKEIN OF SUNLIGHT

Maddie's hands shook as she angled the visor mirror and applied her lipstick. Even with the make up, she felt naked. Why had she let Jan talk her into going out tonight?

Jan sat in the driver's seat finishing off a cheeseburger. "You aren't nervous are you?" she asked around a mouthful.

"No," Maddie lied.

Jan stopped chewing to suck up the last of her diet cola and squinted at the quaint Victorian house just up the block from them. It was bathed in light from the street lamp, and practically glowed from the lantern beside the door.

"Might be the most dangerous looking yarn shop I've ever seen in all my days on the force," she said.

Maddie laughed. "Stop it. This is hard."

"No," Jan wiped her mouth with a wadded up napkin. "Chemo was hard. And you got through that. This is fun, remember? A real night out. A little adventure."

"I know, I know. It's just . . ." Maddie touched her hair, long enough now, it was styled short and spiky in what Jan called a "vixen cut."

"Why you picked a yarn store is beyond me," Jan muttered. "There's a bar just a couple streets down. That's where you'll find adventure. Good beer, lots of hot young 'uns. We could go Cougar for the night. Lord knows it's been a long time since you had a man in a meaningful way."

Maddie cut her off before she could launch into the sex-fixes-everything speech. "Sounds great. You go check out the young 'uns. I'll prowl for yarn."

"You don't want me to go with you?" Jan tried, but failed, to sound disappointed.

"Like you'd last five minutes in a yarn store. Plus, I want to touch, stroke, savor."

"So do I," Jan said.

"Yeah, but I want to fondle *yarn*. See you in a couple hours." She got out of the car and started up the street before Jan got any other bright ideas.

It didn't take long to reach the shop, but Maddie's heart rattled in her chest. She had a thing about yarn stores. She didn't know why, but she had always wanted to own one. Every town she visited, she made sure she tracked down the yarn shop. She'd never found the perfect store — the one she'd be willing to offer her life savings for — until she set her eyes on this beauty.

She didn't know who the owner was, but if she was there, and if the conversation turned that way, Maddie was going to ask if she'd be willing to sell.

Maddie pulled her shoulders back, opened the door, and stepped in.

The store was a lot bigger on the inside than it looked from the street, walls covered by wooden shelves held skeins upon skeins of color and fiber and texture. There was enough walking space to be comfortable, even with the two cozy love seats on either side of a small table that took up the center of the room. At the far wall was a counter, cash register, and no one behind either.

Maddie took a deep breath and smiled. She didn't know what it was going to take, or how she was going to do it, but this was it. She belonged here. This store was going to be hers.

"Hello," a soft baritone said from somewhere above her.

Maddie looked over to the left of the room where a staircase arched up. There, in the middle of the staircase stood a man.

Tall, wide shoulders, lean. His black and gray hair was a little longer than was fashionable, his mustache and beard trimmed tight around his lips and shaved clean along his jaw. He smiled. Laugh lines curved at the edges of his eyes, hooked the corners of his lips, and set his age at somewhere around old-enough-to-have-tried-it-all and young-enough-to-do-it-again.

His wore a dark green sweater rucked up at the elbows, his muscular forearms bare. No watch. No ring. Yes, she looked.

She also looked at the sweater. Handmade, cabled in a complicated Celtic knot up the arms where it wove like vines across his wide chest. Slacks for his long legs. But a pair of those deck shoes the skater kids liked to wear made her re-think his age again. Thirty? Fifty?

He waited, not moving, while Maddie took what she realized was a little too long to stare at him.

Okay, a lot too long.

Forget the young 'uns. One look at this man had her wanting to stroke and savor a lot more than yarn.

"Come in," he said. "You are welcome. Most welcome. Are you here for the class?" He said it slowly. She walked toward him, paying absolutely zero attention to where she was going, each word drawing her in, closer and closer, until she bumped her knee into the arm of the love seat.

A rush of blood heated her cheeks. That got an even wider smile out of him. He showed his teeth, straight, white, strong, the incisors pressing into the soft flesh of his bottom lip.

Sexy.

What was wrong with her? She never acted like this.

He strolled down the stairs, paying particular attention to his shoes.

Released from his gaze, she found her voice again. And her brain.

"Class?" she asked.

"Mmm," he agreed. "Knitting. No need to have brought supplies."

He crossed the room, moving like a cat. He paused beside the love seat and rested one hip against it, his arms crossed over his wide chest. He was so close, she could smell his cologne. Something with enough rum and spice to remind her of the Jamaican vacation she'd taken just out of college. The one time in her life she had really felt free and alive. Every day she had let the sun drink her down, and every night she had let the darkness, and the passion of a man feed her soul.

In all these years, she had never once thought of that man, that pleasure. She couldn't even remember his name. How could she have forgotten that? And how could the scent of this man's cologne bring those memories back to her?

He looked into her eyes, smiling, enjoying his effect on her. "We have everything you could possibly desire here."

He means knitting, she told herself. He means yarn. Still, the opportunity was too good to pass up.

"Everything?" she asked. "I have an insatiable appetite for fine fibers."

A small frown narrowed his eyes, and he studied her face. "Have we met?" he asked.

"No," she said. "I'm sure we haven't. I would remember you."

His response was cut off by the sound of the door opening behind her. A group of people, chatting, laughing, paused in the doorway.

The man in front of her gazed over her shoulder. He still smiled, but his demeanor shifted to the look of someone tolerating a pack of puppies wrestling over a toy.

"*Dobry vecher*, Saint Archer," a younger man's voice called out.

"Saint?" Maddie said.

"Good evening, Luka," the man in front of her said. "Come in, all of you. Welcome." To Maddie, "Please. Call me Archer. And your name?"

"Maddie," she said. "Madeline Summers."

Archer raised one eyebrow as if he hadn't heard her correctly, but Maddie had to move out of the way for the newcomers filing into the shop.

Luka, thin, young, beautiful, had that teen heartthrob smolder going, marred only by his polo shirt uniform with the emblem of the local movie theater over his heart and sleeve. He smiled at her, looked at Archer as if they were sharing a secret, then away.

Father and son?

No, Luka was an angel boy — light-haired, dark-eyed, while Archer was dark-haired, blue-eyed. Plus, Luka had delicate features, while Archer's wide shoulders and nose (which looked like it had been broken at least once), spoke of a different heritage.

Next to Luka was a girl who probably still went to high school. Her black hair shifted with stripes of pink and red like pulled taffy. Cute. Another, slightly heavier girl wore a gorgeous knitted beret and matching scarf. She held up a hand in wordless greeting as they tromped off across the room, heading toward the stairs.

"My apologies," Archer said. "For the children. They can be rambunctious."

"Are they yours?" she asked.

"Oh, no." He chuckled. "Students. They come here to knit."

"There's a class tonight? Now? I only came to look —"

"And why not stay?" he asked. "For the time we have. Tonight."

That was familiar. A voice she had heard in her dreams.

"I haven't put my hands on balls for years. Of yarn," she corrected, "on a ball of yarn for years. I just came to touch them, not to do, you know." She made a fake knitting motion with her fingers, which only came off looking obscene.

God, she hated it when she went into idiot mode.

He took a step forward, and she was struck by how tall he was.

"What is there to lose?" he asked softly. "Some things, our bodies never forget."

This time, Maddie managed to look away from his smoldering gaze. "Like knitting?"

"That too."

She grinned and looked up at him. "So how long is the class?"

"An hour. Sometimes people linger. Will you?"

"Stay for the class?" she asked.

"Linger."

She couldn't think of any place she'd rather be. Certainly not hanging out in the bar while she watched Jan find boys half her age to buy her drinks. It was quiet here, except for the students upstairs laughing and arguing over a movie they'd just seen. It was comfortable here. And she liked the look in Archer's eyes as he pulled out all his manly charms to lure her into his knitting lair.

"I'll give it a try."

"Excellent." He looked happy, and something more — relieved. "Let me gather a few things. I'll follow you upstairs in a moment."

Maddie walked around the love seats and over to the stairs. Just as she reached the first step, the door opened again and two more women, women closer to her age — no, she realized with a wince, younger, maybe even still in their twenties — walked into the store. They greeted Archer warmly. Maddie bit her bottom lip, wondering if he was going to lay the charm on thick with them too, if maybe him flirting with her was just an act he used to lure in the female clientele.

Oh, he was a charmer all right. Kissing them both on the cheek and holding their hands just a little too long while complimenting them.

Great, Maddie thought. He'd been playing her, that was all. She'd been suckered in by a guy who flirted with every woman who walked through the door. And she'd actually believed him. She must have looked like an idiot. How could she have been so stupid?

Or maybe she was just that desperate not to be alone, even for only one night.

She almost turned around and left, but she had come here looking for the owner of the shop, and she wasn't going to leave without her name.

The room upstairs was filled with skeins of yarn and cozy couches. It also had a small kitchen nook where pots of coffee and tea were set out. The teens were clumped together on a couch too small for the three of them. To her surprise, they were already knitting. Even the angel boy Luka had needles in his hands and was quickly working his way through a lace-patterned shawl in blood red fingering weight.

When Maddie was young, there wasn't a boy in a fifty mile radius who would lay a finger on knitting needles, much less knit in front of his girlfriends. Although with the way the girls, especially the one with the multi-colored hair, looked at him, Luka had a good thing going.

He caught Maddie looking at him and grinned, showing a row of straight teeth, his canines just a little too long, his eyes just a little too old in that young face. A chill ran up her spine. She rubbed her arms and walked away from the couches to a row of shelves with skeins of bamboo and silk yarn.

She got in a fondle or two, savoring textures and colors, feeding her senses through fingertips and eyes. Why had she stopped knitting? Probably the same reason she had stopped taking hikes, going to concerts, eating at fine restaurants. Somewhere in her battle to make her body her own again, she had lost touch with living in it.

No more of that. Her new life started tonight. With the owner's name.

The sound of footsteps on the stairs punctuated the teen chatter, and soon the two other women were in the room, taking their places in cushioned armchairs, and setting their knitting bags — more like stylish purses than grandmotherly baskets — by their feet.

She wondered which of them was the teacher.

Then Archer climbed the stairs. She could feel him, every step he took, like an extra heartbeat in her chest, a pulse in her veins. She could feel him drawing near even though she kept her back stubbornly toward the stairs and her fingers plunged deep in the silky softness of a pliant skein of cashmere. She held onto that skein of yarn like it was her only anchor to her own resolve.

And it was. Jan was right. It had been a long time since she had been with a man. Much, much too long.

Archer paused at the top of the stairs. She could feel him looking at her, watching her, a warm pressure against her skin that made every nerve in her body remind her she was alive.

Was it getting hot in here?

"I think this is everyone," he said. "Maddie, are you ready to join us?"

This was it, her chance to make a break.

She turned away from the shelf. No eye contact this time, that man had some kind of power in his gaze. She stared very solidly at the middle of his forehead.

"I can't. I . . . I have a date."

Even though she stubbornly stared at his forehead, she could see the rise of his cheeks as he smiled.

"Ah. I see. I'm sorry you won't be able to stay."

Maddie nodded, gaze on the forehead and forehead only. So far, so good.

Archer apparently, had not gotten the memo that she was avoiding eye contact. He strolled over to her, his shoes quiet on the plush rugs scattered across the floor.

Without wanting to, Maddie's eyes slipped, shifted, and her gaze met his. Her lips parted, and all she could think of was him kissing her, touching her.

"I hope you will reconsider my offer," he said.

Then the powerful gaze, the mind-numbing draw, were gone. He looked like a man, a very handsome man, but just a man. A little concerned, maybe a little uncomfortable. Vulnerable.

He pressed the handle of a small paper bag into her hands. "A token. If you ever wish to stop in again."

"No, no. I don't think —"

He stepped back, quickly and smoothly out of her reach so she'd have to follow him around the couches to give him back the bag.

That was when she noticed everyone in the room was silent, knitting. They were all smiling. Enjoying this. None of them looked at her, but she could tell they all thought this little exchange was funny. Fine. She'd come back tomorrow and get her answer. Let them have their laugh.

"Thank you," she said, pouring on the sugar, and not meaning a word of it. "It's been lovely meeting you all."

She walked down the stairs without stomping, and stormed across the floor. All she had wanted was some time to browse, and maybe a chance to buy the store. Was that too much to ask?

She yanked the door open, and nearly ran into the woman standing there.

"May I come in?" The woman was beautiful. Even when Maddie was young and in great shape she had never been that pretty.

The woman's long, straight hair was so blonde it was silver in the lamplight. Her kitten-wide eyes were green and lined with thick lashes. Her lips were full and perfect, brushed with red lipstick. When she smiled, Maddie realized she could not look away.

"Please," the woman asked. "May I come in? There's a class tonight."

"Oh," Maddie said, catching her breath. "Right. Come on in. They're all upstairs."

A wicked light sparked in the woman's eyes, and was gone before Maddie could blink. "Thank you," the woman purred.

Maddie moved out of the way and the woman stepped over the threshold and into the yarn shop. She moved like a dancer, smooth and silent, her face tipped upward toward the stairs as if following a string. She licked her lips and smiled.

She must really love knitting.

Maddie walked out. As she turned to shut the door, she noticed the woman's bag. Black, bulky, it looked more like an old-fashioned doctor's bag than a knitting bag. And as the woman climbed the stairs, she opened it and pulled out a pair of metal needles, each as thick as a tent stake, filed to a razor's edge.

*

One thing Maddie could say for Jan, she was a cop, through and through. Even though she was off-duty and had probably had more than one beer, her smile faded as soon as Maddie stormed into the bar and plunked down on the stool next to her.

"Gin and tonic," she told the bartender. He nodded. But instead of getting on with the drink mixing, he leaned forward and flirted with the little jail bait downing shots of tequilla in front of him.

Men.

"Did you get a look at his driver's license?" Jan asked.

"What?"

"The guy who pissed you off. It will make it easier for me when I pull his files and find out if there's anything worth throwing him in jail for."

Maddie put both elbows on the bar and rubbed at her temples. "That obvious?"

Jan shrugged. "You almost burned a hole in the back of the bartender's head. Want to tell me about it?"

"No. There was a man at the yarn store, he said there was a class and invited me to stay, and I thought, I thought . . ." She took a deep breath and crossed her arms on the bar, looking over at Jan. "I thought he was coming on to me. Flirting, you know? So I flirted back. But he was just playing me to fill out the ranks of the knitting class. Some other women came in, younger than me, prettier, and he tossed me to the side. I felt like such an idiot."

"Glad you decided not to tell me about it. Did you get this cad's name?"

"Stop making fun of me."

Jan grinned. "Stop making it so easy. I can't believe you're upset because someone flirted with you and you liked it."

The bartender finally sauntered over, placed her drink down without even looking at her, and walked away.

"Fine," Maddie said. "I liked the flirting. But did he have to crush my fantasy?" She smiled ruefully.

Jan raised her eyebrows in question.

"You know, that we'd fall in love at first sight. His favorite pastime would be doing dishes and going grocery shopping. I'd find out I was the long lost heiress to a fortune and we'd run away to someplace warm and sandy and make passionate love . . ." Maddie lifted her glass. "To reality. What a bitch."

"That's the spirit," Jan said, raising her own glass. "To Fantasy Crusher what's-his-name."

"Saint Archer," Maddie provided.

Jan's mood changed. She frowned. Took a drink of her beer.

"You know him, don't you?" Maddie asked.

"Yes."

"Is he a criminal?"

"No comment."

"Interesting. Witness protection program?"

"Okay, we're going to change subjects now," Jan informed her in her no-bullshit cop voice.

"Come on. You know something about him. Something bad, right?" Maddie took another drink, the warmth spreading out in her stomach and echoing back through her muscles. "It would cheer me up," she said. "Indecent exposure? Tax evasion? He runs a pornographic flower shop in his basement?"

"Not that I know of," Jan said. "Just the yarn store."

"What?" Maddie said. "I thought he worked there."

Okay, the truth? One look at him and she had stopped thinking.

"So he owns the store?" Maddie asked.

"Yup."

"So . . . he's gay?"

Jan laughed so hard she snorted. "It's not on record, if that's what you're asking. Still. You know better than to assume things about people." She lifted her glass and muttered into it, "No one in this city is what they seem to be."

"But he has a record?"

Jan just gave her a look and took another drink of beer. She emptied half the glass, thunked it on the counter and refused to answer.

Maddie took another drink and thought it over. Maybe it didn't matter, but she had to ask anyway. "Do you think he's dangerous?"

"Would I let you go anywhere, alone, if I thought you were in danger?" Jan downed the last of her beer. "I'm going to the bathroom. Get me another beer, will you?" She was no longer smiling.

"Sure," Maddie said. And she didn't even point out that Jan had not answered her question.

Jan got her smile back when Tony Brown strolled into the bar. Tony worked for the city and he and Jan had the kind of history that lead to him buying Jan another couple beers, and them getting a table.

Maddie moped her way through another gin, then decided to call it a night. She handed her card to the bartender and her elbow brushed the little bag Archer had given her. She'd been so angry walking to the bar that she hadn't even looked in it.

She opened the bag and angled to see inside.

Two skeins of yarn caught light like summer fire, and a slick set of needles glinted dark beside them.

Maddie couldn't help herself. She gasped like she'd just found a kitten and pulled the yarn out of the bag. The fiber was exquisitely soft, with enough loft it promised warmth and shape and drape. Cashmere and silk. With a beautiful set of knitting needles.

Maybe it was the alcohol, maybe it was her sense of pride, or maybe it was watching Jan and Tony inch closer and closer together at the table.

Yeah, probably that last thing.

But whatever it was, Maddie knew she wanted to keep that skein of yarn near her forever, to hold it and fondle it and savor the possibilities of what it could become with a little time, a little hope and a lot of patience.

And she knew, just as quickly, that she had to return it.

This wasn't a token. This was a gift with strings attached. Well, just one long string, but still. That was attached. To a man whose name took her best friend's smile away.

Maddie settled her bill and told Jan she was headed home and was going to catch a cab.

Jan told her she shouldn't go home alone and even started to put on her coat, much to an obviously disappointed Tony, until Maddie finally convinced her that she was plenty old enough to get home on her own. And then she made Tony promise to call a cab for both of them when the night wound down.

But instead of going home, Maddie marched back to the yarn shop.

The lantern outside the door was still on, and a light from one of the upper windows glowed brightly. The front window was dark, though. Maddie wasn't sure if the shop was open. Archer said people lingered, and it had only been maybe two hours since she left.

She walked up to the door and tried it. The door opened, so she stepped in.

The lamp at the back of the room near the counter was on. But other than the faint light tumbling down the staircase, it was dark.

Something felt wrong about the room. Maddie thought about dropping the bag on the counter for Archer to find in the morning, but the door was unlocked, which meant they weren't closed for the night. Someone still had to be here.

A shuffling sound, like something being dragged across the floor on the upper floor made Maddie's heart pound. Okay, maybe she should just go back outside, get a cab, and get the hell home.

Forget about leaving the yarn on the counter. Maddie hurried to the love seats and placed the bag on the table between them. That would have to be good enough.

The click of the door closing behind her made every nerve in Maddie's body scream.

She turned, hoping, and dreading, it would be Archer.

"Hello, pet," a woman's voice cooed.

It was not Archer. It was the beautiful woman who Maddie had let into the shop. She held two very bloody knitting needles in her hand.

"I just came back to return the yarn," Maddie said, trying to think faster than her heart was beating.

"Aren't you sweet?" The woman tipped her head to one side, her ear nearly touching her shoulder. She inhaled. "Had a hard time of it the last few years, haven't you?" She straightened and clutched the knitting needles tighter. "Cancer. How sad. How alone." She glided forward. "Leyola can cure your pain," she sing-songed. "Leyola knows just what you crave."

Maddie was caught in her gaze. Even though it was dark in the room, it was as if a single light shone on the woman, illuminated her, made her incandescent, beautiful.

Something in the back of Maddie's mind was screaming — her reason, she thought — but she couldn't care less. She wanted to do anything the woman told her to do, wanted Leyola to take her pain away.

The woman was close now. Close enough that Maddie could see her more clearly. Her beautiful face had gone feral, eyes black without even a speck of white or color, jaw elongated, fangs dripping with blood.

Holy shit. She was a vampire.

Okay, maybe it was a little late in the game for her to put two and two together, but vampires weren't real. Sure, she'd heard of kids who liked to pretend they were vampires — it was popular in the high schools — but this chick wasn't a kid. And from the bloody knitting needles and fangs, she sure as hell wasn't playing around.

"You will give yourself to me." Leyola opened her mouth and bent toward Maddie's neck.

And even though every nerve in her body ached for this, for her touch, for her mouth, Maddie took a step backward.

"No." It came out low, strong, born of years of anger against a disease that had nearly destroyed her. Maddie focused her mind, calmed her thoughts and put all her will behind it. "My body is my own," she said.

The woman jerked back as if she had been slapped. "That," she said, "will be your end."

She lunged.

Maddie got her hands up, banking on her coat to keep Leyola's teeth from tearing into her skin. But Leyola slammed into her, knocking her backward. Maddie stumbled, trying to catch her balance and landed hard on the couch.

She needed a weapon. Now. Maddie scrambled back on the couch, her heels kicking into the soft cushions. The bag was just behind her, and in it were the needles.

Leyola strolled over to her, fingernails tapping against the needles in her hand. "You may deny death," she purred, "but you will not deny me."

Maddie yelled. She stretched to reach the bag.

A roar filled the room. Maddie rolled off the couch, caught up the bag and pulled the needles out.

She crouched, and thrust the needles upward.

But Leyola was not there.

Maddie blinked, trying to make sense of the scene before her.

Someone was fighting with the woman. A man. Archer.

His shirt was off revealing the hard, defined muscles of his chest and stomach. The low light from the lamp painted him gold — a warrior from some ancient time. He and Leyola circled each other, speaking a language that made Maddie wish she'd taken Russian in college.

Maddie caught a glimpse of a tattoo spread across the back of Archer's shoulder — an angel in flight — and a trail of blood pouring over his ribs.

Leyola had circled so that her back was now toward Maddie. Archer said something to her, a warning. A command.

But Leyola only laughed and threw herself, needles and fangs, at Archer.

Everything suddenly seemed to happen very, very slowly.

Leyola, in mid-air, contorted like a gymnast, her feet hitting the ground lightly as a cat, then pushed, not toward Archer, but toward Maddie.

Archer launched, a growl escaping his lips, his arms, hands, body, straining to reach Leyola.

Maddie still crouched, set herself, feet strong beneath her, shoulder forward, knitting needles in her hand, ready for the impact.

Inhale.

Leyola bore down on her.

Archer plucked Leyola out of the air. Rolled her over his hip. Pinned her to the floor. He shoved his knee in her back and held both her wrists in his hands.

Exhale.

Time snapped back into real speed again.

"Maddie," Archer said, his voice a little husky. When she didn't respond, he glanced over his shoulder at her.

His hair hung wild around his face, and his eyes burned electric blue. Leyola beneath him squirmed and cursed. Archer's muscles flexed, but he kept her pinned.

Maddie found she was breathing hard, caught by his gaze and fully aware of how much she liked the primal hunger in his eyes, his anger, and his fear for her.

But it was his mouth that fascinated her most. His lips were parted, revealing fangs that grazed his bottom lip, pressing against the soft curve there, almost puncturing. Maddie wondered what it would feel like to kiss those lips, to feel the scrape of his mouth against hers. To open herself to his tastes, his textures.

"Maddie," he said again, his voice a soft growl that she could feel roll beneath her skin. "Are you hurt?"

Right. This was not the time to fantasize.

She did a quick inventory: no cuts, maybe a bruise on the back of her legs where she'd gone over the arm of the couch, but she was no stranger to bruises.

"I'm fine."

He smiled softly, a strange mix with the wild edge in his eyes. "Would you help me then?"

"You?" She glanced at the vampire pinned beneath him. What could she do that he hadn't done already? "Of course." She stepped out from between the couches. "What do you need?"

"Behind the counter, there is a drawer. A corner drawer."

Maddie crossed the room, let herself behind the counter, and opened the little triangular drawer. A strange assortment of things were gathered there, medallions, knives, bullets, paperclips and a small leather-bound book.

"Do you see the twine?" he asked.

Leyola spat obscenities.

Maddie picked up the ball of twine so small she could close her hand around it to hide it.

"Yes," she said.

"Bring that to me, please."

Maddie walked over to him. Her adrenalin was starting to wear off and her knees felt a little like cooked noodles. Still, she held out the yarn.

"Unwind a length of it."

She did so. The twine was strange. It clung to itself and it gave off the scent of green grass and something else she could not place. It was also cold, as if she'd just pulled it out of the freezer. She had no idea what it was made out of.

Once she began unrolling it, the entire thing seemed to release, flowing free from itself, and falling into a pile of string in her hand.

"What is it?" she asked.

"It is something very good at holding vampires until the police arrive." Archer shifted his grip, so both of Leyola's wrists were in one hand. He took the end of the string and tied her wrists together with the kind of unconscious ease that said he'd done this before.

Leyola moaned and squirmed harder, aiming a kick at Archer that did not connect.

"Enough," he said. "Your game tires me."

Archer leaned a little more weight on his knee in her back. He put his free hand on the back of her head and bent his face down, his eyes closed.

He looked like he was praying. Maybe he was. After a moment of silence, he cupped Leyola's head and thunked it into the floor.

She relaxed and was still.

Archer took a deep breath and rolled his shoulders. When he stood he didn't look at Maddie, but instead walked over to the wall and flipped on the lights.

Only one bank of the lights in the ceiling caught, but Maddie's eyes had gotten so used to the darkness she had to blink a couple times to handle the glare. When she could really see again, she looked at Archer.

Still shirtless, it was no trick of shadow — he really did have the body of a god. A thick line of black liquid — blood, she could only assume — ran across his ribs, already dry.

In this light, his skin was pale, unfreckled, no chest hair, though there were several thin scars across his chest, one intriguingly low scar at his hip bone, and one scar near his collarbone that looked like a perfect pink circle the size of a coin.

The man had seen his share of violence.

And survived it.

Once her gaze lifted to his face again, she noted he was smiling at her.

And she was blushing.

"I feel there is some explaining in order," he began.

"I only came in to return the yarn," Maddie said. "I didn't know, I don't know, I shouldn't have even come here. Vampires? It's a joke, right? Knitting vampire dinner mystery theater." She didn't believe that, not at all. But the reality was suddenly too much to handle.

Then Archer was in front of her, having somehow crossed the distance in an amazingly short amount of time.

"Maddie," he soothed, "I meant I should explain this to you. If you want me to."

He placed his hand gently on her arm. When she did not pull away, he wrapped his arms around her and held her close.

"I don't know if I want to know," she finally said.

"Then let's start with an easier decision. Would you like some tea?"

Maddie closed her eyes and inhaled the scent of him. One

moment he looked like he could tear the building apart with his bare hands, and the next, he was holding her like she was made of fragile glass.

She nodded. "Tea would be nice."

He quietly led her away from the fanged, unconscious vampire chick tied up on the floor, into the adjoining room. Another couch and chair sat snug in the corner.

He left her there on the couch with the promise to bring her mint tea.

Maddie thought about leaving, about walking out of this mess, but she had some questions she needed answered. Questions about her half-remembered time in Jamaica, and the long nights he spent with her there.

The police showed up before Maddie's tea had time to steep.

No sirens, no flashing lights, just a knock at the door that made Maddie jump.

Archer, who had been sitting in the chair next to her, explaining that people in the city weren't always what they appeared to be, and how everyone needed a safe place in a storm — even vampires, maybe especially vampires, and how he had spent many years taking vampires in like Luka or taking them out like Leyola — stopped talking and gave her a reassuring look.

"I called the police," he said.

Archer had changed into a new sweater before bringing her tea, this one black, wool, and worked in a lattice stitch pattern. She would have found the seaming fascinating on any other man, but Archer had a way of out-wowing even a sweater that beautiful.

"You called the cops?" she asked.

"I did."

"But you're a . . . isn't she a . . ."

"Vampire?" he said evenly. "Yes, she is. As am I. Although, we do have our differences." He flashed a smile, showing just the edge of his teeth. "For one thing, I don't break into other people's places of business and try to kill them." He stood. Then added as an afterthought, "Well, not for many years."

He walked out of the side room and back into the main shop. Maddie got up and brushed her fingers through her hair, smoothing it, while she walked to the doorway so she could see what was going on.

Two police officers, one man, one woman, neither in uniform, walked through the front door, which Archer closed behind them. Archer motioned toward the still unconscious Leyola.

"She came in earlier this evening. I did not invite her. I was holding class upstairs."

"Who saw her?' the man asked.

"Luka and I. There were four women in class. Luka has taken all of them home, and made sure they have only pleasant memories of a class that was canceled early. They were not harmed."

The woman cop nodded. "Do you know what she wanted?"

"Other than to kill me?" He said it like it happened every day. He shrugged, a roll of his wide shoulders that belied his injury. "I have not found anything missing. And I do not believe she was seeking my counsel. Nor asylum. She and I have . . . crossed paths before."

"So revenge?" the woman cop asked.

Archer crossed his arms over his chest and shrugged again. "When was she released?" he asked.

"About a month ago," the man answered. "We'll drag her back in. See if we can straighten her out. If not, will you press charges?"

"Yes."

The woman pulled something out of her coat pocket. Maddie couldn't see what it was, but she heard the tell-tell rip of duct tape being unrolled. The policewoman knelt, tipped Leyola's head to one side, made sure her hair was out of the way, then duct taped her mouth shut.

"Okay, we'll give you a call tomorrow night," the man said.

Archer walked to the door and opened it while the police officers got hold of the woman's upper arms and made a smooth, coordinated effort, carrying her out the door.

Archer left the door open and within moments, another figure drifted at the edge of the doorway.

"Come in, Luka," Archer invited.

The teen heartthrob stepped in, glanced in Maddie's direction; his nostrils flared.

Archer put his hand on his shoulder. "She came back to return the yarn."

Luka licked his lips, swallowed. "Do you want me to take her home too?"

"No. I think I'll call her a cab." Archer raised his voice slightly. "Unless you have a friend you'd like me to call for you?"

Maddie sighed. He had known she was eavesdropping the whole time. "You could have told me you knew I was listening," she said as she walked out into the room with the two men. Correction, the two vampires.

"Hello, Luka," she said.

Luka gave her a half-bow. "I have other . . . commitments. If you'll both excuse me?"

Archer nodded and Luka turned and stepped silently back outside, into the night.

"So," Maddie said, "are you going to make sure I remember all this as a pleasant evening? Just like that summer in Jamaica?"

Archer smiled. "Ah, you catch on quickly." He strolled over to the love seats. "I could. If you asked me, I could leave your mind free of the memories of vampires. Give you back your easy world. Again."

He bent, retrieved the yarn that had spilled from the bag and found the needles Maddie had abandoned on the couch cushion. He sat on the couch.

Instead of looking at her, he gazed at the yarn in his hands, turning the luxurious hanks of sunlight between his wide fingers.

Maddie crossed the floor. "How many years have you been doing this?" she asked. "Taking in vampires, taking out vampires?"

He shook his head. "Many."

She sat on the couch next to him. When she could find her voice, she asked, "Why did you make me forget?"

He did not look up. Did not look away from the yarn that glowed like fire between his palms.

"Archer?" Maddie put her hand on his arm.

He lifted his head and met her gaze. "You asked me to. You were young. A full life awaited you. Sunlight awaited you." He lifted the yarn ever so slightly. "Not the night."

"Oh." She didn't know what to say. Too many emotions rolled through her. Loss. Regret. Hope.

"What if I don't want to forget any more?"

"Once a memory is taken, it cannot be returned," he said softly.

Maddie nodded. She knew that. "Is there ever a chance to make new memories?

Archer stared at her, silent for so long, Maddie started blushing again.

"I know I'm older," she stammered. "I mean I'm not a college girl any more, not quite as thin as I was, as pretty as I was, but I love knitting, and yarn —"

And then Archer was bending over her, pulling her close, his lips hot, needful, his teeth scraping the edge of her mouth, inviting her to open for him, promising her pleasure, promising her more.

Maddie moaned. She touched him, stroked him, and savored the textures and tastes of him, until her body and soul came alive, and she knew she would never forget this, never forget him again.

One day, I found myself standing at the foot of the Astoria Bridge in Astoria, Oregon, staring up at the metal rungs notched all the way to the wide blue sky above me. I wondered about the people whom those rungs were made for, people who put their lives at risk to do their jobs. I wondered if it would only be our lives we would put at risk to do the jobs of the future.

STRINGING TOMORROW

It felt as if we had begun each of our days here, caught by the violet light of the new rising sun: she, wrapped in a solar blanket against the cold I could not feel, I buckling the last latch on my safety belt.

"Don't go," said Celia, my lovely, childless wife.

"I won't be long. Home tonight. The string break doesn't look too severe." No sound from her. I looked up from the all-go green on my wrist pack. Her eyes were dark, mouth tugged down in a frown.

"I promise, Celia." I extended my hand and gently pushed the dark strands of hair away from her temple. Her skin was warm against the fingertip sensors in my gloves. "I'll be home tonight."

"It will need to be tonight," she said. "The appointment to choose a child is tomorrow. With or without you, Allen."

"Can it wait?"

"It has waited. I've waited," she said. The wind tugged at the edge of her blanket, and I knew it was true. Ten years of hoping. There was no denying I could never father a child of my own blood. My modified body, made to walk the strings, had ensured I would never reproduce.

"I'll be home soon." I'd hoped it sounded positive, but she shook her head. She knew me too well. Knew I hated the idea of picking a baby off a shelf, out of a file, a jar.

I put both hands out and gently squeezed her arms. She drew into my embrace, blanket and all, and I inhaled the sweet copper scent of her. Flesh and bone, so warm and alive in my coldwire and bio-composite arms. Fifteen years we'd been married. Fifteen years I'd watched her go from hope to despair of ever conceiving a child.

The green on my wrist flashed. My shift was on. "Ce, I need to go."

She nodded against my chest. When she stepped back, I was surprised to see her tears. I hadn't felt her crying.

"I promise I'll be home."

She looked up at me, held my gaze, searched for a guarantee in my words.

"I won't wait past tomorrow," she said. She turned back into the house and shut the door behind her.

The wind stirred the lines above my head and I glanced up. Strings a meter thick zigged from horizon to horizon between jutting, jointed metal frames, netting the dawn sky, catching the last light of stars. It was for the song of the strings that I endured the training and the modifications it took to walk the strings, mend the strings, sort and route every possible word and dream into Archives before they were lost.

I slipped my index finger into the slot on my wrist pack. "Allen Bourne. Locate to site."

"Allen Bourne," a soft alto of Archives said in my left ear. "Site Baud 15, Cross at 45. Break approximately one point one mill. Transport requested?"

The upper window of the house flickered with yellow light. Celia at her computer station, activating the lines, digging into Archive's knowledge, browsing for babies.

"Transport requested?" Archives asked again.

"Yes." I walked to the flatpad a few meters — safe distance — away from the house. The sun, deep-lit as an orchid, pulled free from the horizon and scattered maroon light across the sloping hills that surrounded our property. Our house, painted white and modeled after the old farm houses of Earth, glowed pink in the new day. I checked my gear one last time, the familiar ritual — belt, wrist, eyes and ears. All go. All green.

"Transport."

I pulled a quick breath. The world snapped.

cheeks already red. "Cold as a grave today," he said. "Let's hope the lines aren't frozen." He rubbed his gloved hands together and tipped his head back and up. "No luck," he said. "Solid ice up there."

I followed his glance up the spires. They glinted silver, even in shadow.

"I'll lead."

He chuckled. "You're welcome to it." He took the remaining steps between us, and latched his safety line onto my belt.

I latched my line onto his belt hook and gave it a short tug.

"Think we'll get home early?" He was smiling, but worry drew his eyebrows together. "It's just that Vera has a trip planned. We're going to see her folks." His voice trailed off as people's tend to do when I hold eye contact for too long.

I nodded like I understood, though I had no parents to visit. "I told Celia I'd be home tonight."

"Good." He smiled again, but did not look me in the eyes. I rechecked my belt.

He keyed the code into his wrist pack and signaled our ready. All lights blinked blue.

"Team accepted, string mapped, break identified," Archives said in my ear. "Proceed one point one mill."

We walked to the nearest tower, step in step with each other. At the base of the tower, metal steps — snug indentations that scooped up the center of the tower — could be seen. It was a simple, if long, climb to the strings above, this part of the towers not yet having been fitted with a lift.

I took a deep breath and caught the sweet odor of dew and pollen rising from bent grass, then put both hands on the grips. I pulled myself up, boots finding the toeholds with practiced ease.

After a hundred steps, I glanced over my shoulder to make sure Don had taken position. He was below me, setting the safety mags that would support my weight, and his, if I fell. The mags interfered with the dataflow on the strings too much to take them all the way to the top, but a linemen never climbed alone.

"Transport completed," Archives said.

My chest uncollapsed and I waited for inertia to stabilize. Transport is one of the first tests a Lineman takes — an efficient way to discover who recovers quickly from relocated mass, and who doesn't. Constructs can take the snap once a day. It had given me the edge when I first applied to work the Lines. It was, I believed, the main reason I had risen to head position of the quadrant.

The disorientation passed. I looked up.

Archives had gone organic over fifty thousand years ago, yet great juts of jointed metal still thrust up out of the grass and hills, connected by dark strings. The metal bones of Archives skewered the land and jabbed at the sky like the skeleton of a ship that had washed ashore before the sea grasses grew up to claim it.

Metal girders rose to dizzying heights. Data lines stretched from one horizon to the other. All the information from hundreds of inhabited planets, millions of civilizations was sieved through the spindled girders, channeled down the strings — every scrap, every whisper, every plan, every desire, every dream stored deep in the internal honeycomb of Archives.

It was my job to repair the physical breaks in the lines, my job to keep Archives from missing a single word from the stars above.

I looked back to the ground and saw the blocky form of Don Jango coming toward me. Heavy mag blocks swung over the shoulder of his bulky insulated suit, counter-rhythm to his steps. At the sight of another line walker, my hands fell into the familiar routine, pausing over belt, wrist, eyes and ears. Don drew close enough I could see his smile.

"Weren't you just on duty?" he asked.

I paused. No, it had been two days ago, and a day before that, and another before that. I tried to think of when I last spent a full day at home, and was chilled to discover I could not.

"A while ago," I answered.

Don sniffed, his brown eyes violet in the morning light, his

Don tugged my belt line, twice, short. All go.

I climbed.

Mind set, eyes upward, one hand, one step, one push up, again, again, again. I breathed harder, and listened to the snick and shush of my boots in and out of the cups, punctuated by the slight vibration of the mags being placed, lifted, and placed again.

The world fell behind me, the strings above grew. Strings that looked fragile from below became thicker the closer I came to them. I lost myself to the simple rhythm of the climb. Don signaled the halfway with a single tug on my belt. I stopped and shifted my weight from the balls of my feet to back along the sides. I shrugged my shoulders to loosen them, and turned my hip into the tower.

The view was stunning.

Endless organic green stained by the violet sun rolled out to the edge of the sky. The great dark data strings pulled between jointed metal. It didn't matter how many times I made the climb, it still stirred something deep within me. The data towers were harps, bones, looms crossed with thread heavy enough to bind the stars and all the worlds of humanity together.

Archives heard every cry of the human race. I wondered if it heard the dreams of artificial men, of constructs like me. If, perhaps, the strings could hear my hopes, my dreams.

The wind picked up, pressing my harness closer to my insulated shirt and drawing tears to the edge of my eyes. Above me, the strings thrummed. I sensed voices, sounds, signals, tones and rhythm, all the worlds living, being, doing, far above my head.

Almost, I could make out my name drifting on the winds. I closed my eyes for a moment and concentrated. A sharp double tug at my belt broke the moment. Time to be moving.

Up.

Hands and feet found the familiar pace, pushing the tower a step at a time beneath me.

The voices above were louder. I tried to control my breathing to better hear them, but I was too far away to catch anything but snatched words.

". . . Promise . . ."

". . . too late . . . baby . . ."

". . . Override . . . Allen . . ."

I climbed. The tower swayed in fitful winds, and vibrated with each lift and set of the mags.

All the world seemed in rhythm. But my heart beat too fast. I wanted to hear the voices. I knew they were talking about me. I climbed faster.

". . . options . . ."

". . . alternate reality . . ."

". . . baby . . ."

Oxygen deprivation. The thought was suddenly clear. I was suffering auditory hallucinations. There were no voices. I paused my upward climb. One hand automatically fell to the safety line, giving two short tugs so Don would keep the correct distance below me.

I pulled the oxygen tube from my collar and took a few deep breaths. Nothing seemed to change, other than my breathing slowed slightly. I could still hear the voices calling.

". . . Allen . . ."

". . . choose . . . promise . . ."

". . . waiting . . ."

I pressed my forehead against the metal pole, wanting the cold to shock me, wanting the buzz of voices to fade. The voices kept on, ghostly snatches just above my head, at the edge of my hearing.

". . . without you . . ."

". . . without . . ."

". . . without . . ."

I couldn't sense the cold metal against my skin at all.

There were reasons to abort a job, times when weather, illness, equipment failure and other troubles indicate a lineman should call it quits and try again the next day.

This was one of those times. But it would keep me out at this site at least another day. I'd told Celia I'd be home. If I were late, she'd think I didn't want children, didn't want her, didn't want our life together.

"Transport requested?" I jerked at the soft voice of Archives and open my eyes. Don was tugging, three short tugs with a pause. Weather warning. I squinted at the rolling clouds building to the East — a storm rising to catch the sun. We had two or three hours before the storm reached us, but once it did, it would stop our repairs.

Mending a break takes more than an hour. Then there was the slow climb down.

"Transport requested?" Archives asked again.

"No." I tugged my safety line once. "Estimate storm front arrival."

"Two point six hours," Archives replied.

Just enough time if I stayed focused. I climbed.

"Map the break," I said.

Archives flashed a map of thin blue lines — the strings above me — over my eyepiece. The break showed as a red oval, thirty yards out from the metal tower. That meant I'd have to bypass, maybe crawl out and deal with the fusion on the line, patching by hand, swinging with nothing but the fractured wire and the far far below beneath me.

If I were lucky, I could ratchet the line taut from the platform and send a bond-line out to self patch. If I wasn't lucky, the storm would hit while I was dangling by a wire.

I pushed that thought out of my mind.

". . . promise . . ."

". . . Allen choose . . ."

". . . good-bye . . ."

The top was only a few steps away. I glanced down, saw Don swing over to the catch platform and anchor the mags into permanent latch-joints. He got busy rerouting the power on the information pull, down the broken line.

He had family to visit.

I promised Ce I'd be there tonight.

The storm drew closer.

I climbed to the top, slipped up through the hole in the upmost railed platform and stood.

Voices, song, a broken, overwhelming sound churned around

me. I covered my ears and searched for the source. The break in the line shone with yellow light toward the dark sky, the same yellow in the window of our house, but this light hurt my eyes to look at it.

I lowered eye shields and knelt. My fingers knew what to do — link, wrap, ratchet. Activate the bond-line, feed it out, guide it like a wire snake twisting out to cover the break. I did these things, trying not to think of the storm I could feel pushing at my back, trying not to think of the voices, Celia, dreams. The bond-line snaked out around and around the line. Once the bond-line reached the break, I triggered the fusion. My wrist pack blinked red. Patch failure.

I'd told her I'd come home. I glanced up, and wished I hadn't. The storm covered the sky, tendrils reaching out to wrap the sun.

The wind hit.

I held on as the tower swayed, flexible enough to withstand the last thousand years of storms. But it wasn't the tower I was worried about. It was the lines. They whipped in the gusts, snapping, thrumming, throwing the voices louder around me, the split in the line like a yellow eye, glancing off to search the storm.

"Allen. Storm looks pretty bad. Abort?" It was Don's voice in my ear. He'd interfered with Archives' connection, a dangerous action this close to a broken line, where the access to Archives' instructions was critical.

My reply was brief, "No."

The storm whipped. Belt tools slapped my hips. I attached the come-along to the main line. I pumped the ratchet, pulling the heavy main line slowly taut. The break map at the left corner of my eye shield showed a point where two lines intersected above the break. If I could pull the broken line close enough, I should be able to crawl out to that intersection above the break and seal the line below by hand.

When the ratchet couldn't be cranked any farther, I called over to Don. "I'm crawling out. Unhook safety."

"Negative, Allen. Don't unhook. Abort repair. We can take care of this after the storm rolls over."

Which would be too late. Tomorrow, maybe the next day, and I'd promised Ce.

I unlatched his safety hook on my belt. "Unlatch, Don. I'm crawling out."

Don swore once in my ear. I waited, but there was no movement on my belt line, nothing that indicated Don had un-latched my hook from his belt. I tried a different tactic.

"You have family to see, Don. The break's not far, just a few meters out. Let me get this done so we can go home."

Still no response.

"Unhook, Don, or I'll cut my line."

The line at my belt tugged. I could feel the unfamiliar weight of it swaying free in the wind. I triggered the recoil. The line slid up and wound into my harness.

Don's line scooted to the edge of the platform and slipped over. I waited to a count of twenty.

"Safety re-set?" I asked.

"Hooked and solid as a stone. You damn well better latch that safety to the platform, Allen. I am not going to make the climb down alone."

"Affirmative." I slapped the hook over the railing on the far side of the platform and tugged it once. With the safety there, instead of on the side nearest the line break, I'd have more of a chance of missing the main tower if I slipped. Of course, if I slipped, the chances that I'd survive without getting tangled or battered to death by the winds were slimmer than I wanted to admit.

I ducked under the railing and placed both hands on the wire. As slowly and carefully as I could, I wrapped my legs around the line and let the world invert.

Hanging upside down by my calves and hands, I began my backward advance.

The storm howled and spat hail. I tilted my head back once to glance over my shoulder. The line below me was ob-scured by hail. I tipped my head back up and tracked my progress by the map on my eyeshield.

Razor sharp ice bit at the backs of my hands, my exposed

jaw and chin. I scooted palms along the wire, its surface rough enough to give at least some traction in the wind. My legs stayed locked at the ankles. The line pitched and swung in the wind.

The voices were louder, sounding almost as if they were in my earpiece.

". . . Allen . . ."

". . . Choose . . ."

". . . all dreams . . ."

The break was almost in reach. Two more stretches. One. I saw another line cross the one I was suspended from and made my way to the intersection for a better hold. The blueline map across my eyeshield blinked yellow. I didn't need the map to tell me the break was below me. I could smell it, rank as melted steel, feel it, hot as a yellow sun, and hear it. The voices called my name.

"Allen," Celia.

"Allen," Don.

"Allen," Archives — no, that voice was my own.

I twisted and looked down into the break. Yellow as the center of pure fire, yellow as old Sol. Bright enough to bring tears to my eyes, yet I found I couldn't blink, couldn't squint.

The voices rose from the split in the line, a ragged fissure three meters in length. Playing across the bright light were images, ghosts, flashes of colors vaporous as moonlight and mist. The figures were easy to make out, familiar: my wife, Ce, wrapped in the solar blanket waiting for me, Don's bulky form, walking ever closer and yet not moving, and me, staring up at myself.

I looked down into my own eyes, and saw myself smile. The image of me wasn't wearing a safety belt and harness, but rather was bare-chested, bare-footed and wore light, loose pants. I stared. I looked so human, my skin the same color as Celia's, my chest complete with nipples and hair. The way I had once looked. That image was joined by another, smaller image. A child, an impossible daughter, with Celia's smile and my eyes.

The image of me extended a hand. I could see fingernails there, and the creased lines of a palm made of living flesh instead of my own smooth palm, the inhuman palm of a linewalker.

The voices called out.

". . . Allen . . ."

". . . can't wait . . ."

". . . dreams . . ."

I let go of the line with one hand and reached for the yellow light. The image of me drew forward. Our fingers brushed briefly past each other. I stretched further, intent on something else, something more.

". . . Transport home? . . ." Don's voice.

". . . Transport child? . . ." Celia.

". . . Transport reality? . . ." Archives' voice.

I let go of the line with my other hand and triggered the welder, spraying and sealing the break in one motion.

But not before I answered all the voices. "Yes."

"Don't go," said Celia, my lovely wife.

Familiar words. It felt as if we had begun each of our days here, caught by the violet light of the new rising sun: she, wrapped in a solar blanket against the cold, I buckling the last latch on my safety belt.

"I won't be long. The string-break doesn't look too severe." No sound from her. I looked up from the all-go green on my wrist pack. Her eyes were dark, mouth tugged down in a frown. That was familiar too.

"I promise, Celia." I extended my hand and gently pushed the strands of her hair away from her temple.

"I know." She turned in the doorway.

Just before the door closed, I saw a small figure looking out at me. She had her mother's smile and my eyes.

A chill ran down my spine.

I slipped my index finger into the slot on my wrist pack. "Allen Bourne."

"Transport requested?" the soft voice of Archives asked.

"Negative," I said. "Request off-duty status."

There was a pause, and I realized my heart was pounding too hard. My fingers fell in their familiar ritual, belt, wrist, eyes and ears. I was surprised to feel ice on my shoulders.

"Acknowledged," Archives said. "Off-duty status granted."

I shook my head and studied the ice melting in my bare, lined hand. For a moment, I remembered something more, a hand like mine, but smooth as plastic. There had been a choice. I had chosen a life, this life, this reality . . . then the memory was gone. I shook my head again. A man only had one life, didn't he?

The light flicked on in the house, and I glimpsed the shadow of Celia and our little girl. She was three now, I remembered. Memory tugged, of Celia's pregnancy, of the hard work it took to become a lineman, choosing not to have the modifications. The relief we both had in that choice when years after I took the job here on Archives, they discovered the sterilizing side-effects of modification.

I took a deep breath, filling my lungs with cold air. It felt like a storm was coming. Better to be home than up on the lines today.

I smiled and walked back to the house, the familiar thrum of wind through the lines singing out in choices and dreams far above my head.

I have a real love for this odd, dark world. This sprang from a read-out-loud challenge with the theme: "Christmas Lights."

X‗DAY

Jenny sat by their X-Day tree and clutched her favorite doll, Claire, against her chest. There was no use hiding how much she loved Claire. Ever since the doll with the matching can of pretend spider spray showed up beneath their tree last year, she hadn't wanted to let her go. But tonight was X-Day Eve, and soon Santa Claus would come down the chimney and take her favorite toy away.

"Bedtime," Mom said from the kitchen. "Leave Claire under the tree with your soldering set."

Jenny glared at the soldering set she'd gotten two years ago. She'd tried to like it. Had spent hours singeing her fingertips while soldering together scraps of metal, wire and broken gears from her dad's work shelves. She wasn't good at soldering, but her dad said mechanics was in her blood.

Jenny thought that was because her father was a mechanic for the northern city machines. He never told her what the machines that ran the world looked like nor what they did, but when he came home at night, it took hours before his hands stopped shaking and he could smile again.

She bent Claire's plastic legs, straightened her skirt and placed her under the tree.

Jenny felt heavy like she was made out of metal and gears herself. Her chest hurt like rusted things scraping together without any oil inside her. She stood and walked behind the wall that separated their sleeping area from the main room. She crawled beneath her blankets on the floor. Dad snored softly in the blankets he and Mom shared.

Jenny felt empty without Claire, and her chest hurt worse.

She listened to Mom roll the flat bread then seal it in a warm-box to keep the spiders out of the dough overnight. Mom came in and turned on the spider strip that glowed red and green along the edge of their sleeping room. She knelt next to Jenny. "Don't worry honey. Santa might not take Claire."

Jenny watched her mom's face for hope and didn't find it. Santa always took the good toys.

"Goodnight, Mom," she said.

Mom kissed her then slipped beneath the blankets with Dad.

Jenny stared at the ceiling that reflected the red and green from the spider strip. Tears slipped down her cheeks, hot as oil, but didn't loosen the grinding hurt in her chest.

The spider strip snapped and sizzled as night creepers died trying to cross it. She had counted thirty-one deaths when she realized she'd forgotten to put Claire's can of spider spray under the tree with her. She sat and pulled her big can of spray, and Claire's miniature one, out from beneath her pillow.

Squirting the floor ahead of her, Claire crossed the living room, the fist-sized spiders scattering.

The doll was still under the tree. Except for the spiders that covered her, one hanging from the back of her head so that only one eye and her lips showed between hairy legs, Claire looked okay. Jenny sprayed her doll and the spiders scuttled away to the edges of the room like angry whispers.

Jenny put the tiny can of spider spray in Claire's lap and was trying to decide if she should take Claire back to bed with her when a scuffling echoed from the roof. Santa! She could ask him to leave Claire behind. But good little girls weren't supposed to catch Santa taking gifts.

The scuffling turned into a coordinated ringing that grew louder, like the drumming of fingers, or fast footsteps down the metal chimney. A green and red glow poured out from the fireplace and filled the room. Then the floor no longer moved with shadows. Every spider in the house had fled.

Jenny hid behind a chair and watched, wide-eyed. Santa came down the chimney.

The tip of his black boot poked out of the fireplace, and his leg, though skinnier than she'd imagined, was red. His other black tipped leg dangled down. And then a third. And a fourth. Santa crawled out of the fireplace, eight thin legs, bulbous hairy red body, and a round head with white hairs between his mandibles. Green and red light the same colors as the spider strip poured out of his multiple eyes.

Jenny felt a scream in her throat, and pressed her hand hard over her mouth. Santa undulated to the tree, each leg working in mechanical unison. He poked at the soldering set with his spiked front foot, and she had a wild, crazy hope he'd take it. Then he pushed it away and snatched up Claire. His mandibles spread wide and he stuffed Claire down his throat. She got stuck for a moment or two, then Santa shoved her the rest of the way down.

Jenny moaned.

Santa's head swivelled. Red and green light poured over her. His eyes were not like the house spiders. They were glassy and flashed red and green like the ticking of a clock. Jenny held very still.

Santa looked away. His bulbous body jiggled and he spat out a toy, covered in silver and gold tinsel, and left it beneath the tree. Then Santa scurried to the fireplace, gripped the edge with six legs, and up the chimney he crawled.

Jenny was too frightened to move. Claire was gone. And Santa was not a jolly old elf. He was a machine and a spider and had eaten her doll! Had he eaten all her other toys? Her bear, her books, her jacks? Or had he swallowed them, and wrapped them in sticky web for some other child?

When her hands stopped shaking, she walked to the tree and looked at her gift. A ratchet set — the kind of gift she usually hated — with a matching hammer. She picked them up. The silver and gold webbing that wrapped them was warm and smelled like the city machine oil her father kept on his shelves.

X-Day was about giving and taking. She was old enough to understand that. She was old enough to understand other things too.

Jenny opened the door, letting the cool air in. She tucked the ratchet set under her arm, glanced out at the red and green lights that wobbled and skittered along another roof, and down another chimney. She picked up the hammer and big can of bug spray, figuring she could move faster on the ground than he could picking his way across rooftops.

Not that it mattered. Jenny would follow the red and green lights all the way to the northern city if that's what it took to get Claire back. She smiled as she stepped outside, the hammer heavy in her hand. She decided this X-Day, she would give Santa a gift he'd never forget.

This dark, yet hopeful story was written in response to articles I had read about modern-day slavery and generational indentured service. It made me angry to think that in our current world, slavery and suffering still exists. I put that anger into words here.

MENDERS

There are certain things that can't be done unless the mind is shut off and the body is left to its own accord. Things that if I think about them even a little too much, will make me realize what I have done, and what it makes me. Boiling a baby is one of those things.

The fire beneath the copper pot smokes. I smell of salt, steam and wood in our close, damp work room. The other menders who weave and spin thread for the lord are in the room, quiet, working, waiting for me to drop the birthing cocoon into the pot. I want my mate, Bind, to be here, but then I remember why he is not.

Follow touches my shoulder, her fingers as dry as old wool. "Soon, Favor," she says.

The fire at my feet is growing hot, and I can smell the burnt-hair singe of my skirts.

Spin's needles scrape and click in the shadows, knotting old thread into cloth. Beyond that sound, I hear Work, steady, efficient, as he bends to the loom near the darkening window.

Only Bind is not here.

I look at my baby in my hands, wrapped in its cocoon, not yet breathing. The thread that pours from my fingertip and connects to the cocoon is gold in the late light, and will be silver in the dawn. I make the last loop of thread around my baby's head to finish the cocoon. The pulse of my life flows to my child, once, just once, in both greeting and farewell. Then I lift my baby over the pot. I drop the baby into the water. The string between us snaps.

I can't see anything after that. The first time, I couldn't look away. I saw the cocoon bob, turn in the boiling water. Watched as Follow stirred the pot, her old arms strong and steady on the long handled paddle. Saw Spin insert her needles into the cocoon, gently prying the strands apart, discarding the baby in search of the real treasure, the threads of the cocoon, which she caught first on one needle, then on a slender stick, turning, until the thread pulled around itself, the stick growing fat with my baby's death.

There will be enough thread that I can rest from birthing for a week. One cocoon each week fills our lord's pockets with coin, and the lands beyond with the finest fabric ever made: birthing fabric, soft and strong as silk and steel.

"Rest now, Favor." Follow touches my arm again and brings me back into the now. I am standing with my back turned to the pot. I don't hear the roll of the water, don't hear Spin's needles click like pebbles against the side of the pot, don't hear Work stride out of the room. I don't imagine my baby's eyes looking up for me.

The lord doesn't allow a birthing ceremony for our children. No sweet honey to grace a baby's lips, no prayers to bless its soul. But he does want to know when the cocoon is in the pot.

I walk to the small console set in the wall by the door and press my hand against the glass pad. The pad is cool, then warms with the hum of electricity as it takes information from me. I know the lord will now trigger sensors in the pot to weigh and measure the cocoon while it bobs in the water. He will know exactly how much thread it will yield.

It takes all my strength and Follow's hand beneath my elbow to walk through the wooden blind that separates our sleeping chamber from the work room. I fall onto my cot, feeling thin enough the light of the sun could pour through me and I'd give no shadow. There is no blanket to cover me, but Follow's hand strokes my arm, her fingers strong enough they could dig through me and sew me together at my core if I needed.

I wish Bind were here.

"Honey and blessings," Follow says. "No birthing tomorrow, Favor, no plucking or spinning. Tomorrow's for mending. Mending you'll do. Mending you'll be."

Old words. Words that held us, kept us, made us.

I absorb the words, and let them remake what I have undone in myself. I listen to Follow and absorb her strength and begin to think again, to know. But deep within me there is a hollowness growing. Something is not the way it used to be. Change is coming, and change is only another word for pain.

In the night, when Follow and Spin have gone to their own cots and Work has left to serve the lord, I lie awake. The hollow feeling of change is growing. I can taste it in the air, can smell it in the sweet vines that release pollen for the night moths.

I hear babies crying in the wind. I do not sleep.

Morning comes on hot and quick. Like a snap of fingers, darkness is gone and the burning heat of the sun steals away the cool air. We are at the end of summer, the last of the heat. Soon the rains will fall.

"You need to drink." I am surprised to see Work standing next to my cot. He holds out a tall blue mug and smiles. His face is round, but not soft, each feature: green eyes, hook nose, angled cheeks, square chin, are hard. His shoulders are thick and his hair is pulled back in a fall of brown silk down his back.

"Drink, Favor. You've gone too thin now." His voice is soft.

I think of saying no, but Work is strong and can make me rise even if I don't want to.

"Have you seen Bind?" I ask as I sit. Work hands me the cup and shakes his head. Work is always at the lord's call, always at the estate. I hope he would have caught a glimpse of Bind while attending the lord before sunrise.

"Bind is in the cell, I think."

I shudder at the knowledge — fleeting knowledge Bind has shared with me — of the cell. The cell is empty of the world. No light. No sound. No texture. Nothing to touch. Nothing to learn.

Work sees me shudder and sits at the foot of my cot. His thick fingers lace together. "Bind tried to leave again through the gate, Favor."

"I know." I sip the thick, bitter water that will make me whole again, that will make me strong enough to bear another child.

"The lord was enraged." Work nods, as if approving his choice of words. "He found Bind beyond the gate. Well into the woods. They dragged him back by the hair."

I sip the water and taste papery bits of Mulberry leaves on my tongue. I try not to show Work my pain.

Work is silent, lets me drink. I wonder why Work has not left me, why he sits on the end of my cot, why he waits. He puts his hand on my foot. I look away from my cup and into his green eyes.

"The lord wants me to mate you, Favor."

"No," I say, my voice a whisper of shock. Then stronger, the image of Bind's death whirling through my mind, "No. Only Bind. Tell the lord, I will only mate Bind. Please," I reach out for him, touch the hard ropes of his arm and draw back immediately. "Tell him I will not mate you."

Work is so still, his face so calm and blank, I begin to worry. There is something in his face I should recognize, something I should know. I want to touch him and learn, but he takes his hand from my foot, and leans away.

Work stands. "I will tell him, Favor. I do not know if he will listen." He turns. His back stiffens and his fingers clench into fists. He touches nothing as he walks out of the room.

I finish the water and go out into the other room. The pot is cold, the fires beneath it dead. Spin and Follow sit close to the windows, already bent to their tasks. Spin's small hands are filled with wooden bobbins strung with precious threads so incredibly thin they are invisible to even the lords before we bind them together, twist them into strands a hundred thick, that only then the lords regard with wonder and greed.

Follow sits on a stool and pulls a shuttle through a warp and weft, loosely weaving the fabric that the lords will sell, the priceless birthing fabric.

"Should I weave today?" I ask. My own fingers want to be busy, to be filled with forgetting through doing.

Follow looks up at me, her plain face crinkles in thought. I wonder if she touched Work when he left, and understands him better than I.

"Today you mend." She waves one hand at me, at my empty belly. "Rest and drink. Walk in the shade. Today, even the lord won't mind." She holds up one end of the fabric that lays like a river of silver moonlight on the hard wood floor.

"So fine, Favor." She smiles, proud. "I've never seen better."

It should make me happy, should please me to be serving the lords in such a fine way, but all I can think of is Bind being drug by the hair through the undergrowth of the thick woods, and Work's strong hands balled into fists.

I murmur a thank you to Follow and walk out onto the estate grounds. The brace of air from the northern sea clears my thoughts, but cannot soothe the tangle of my fears. I need to touch something that does not hurt. I need to learn, to feel something new.

I walk toward the estate, wanting to somehow find Bind in the white marbled halls and grand rooms. The lord may allow me into the hall, but never deeper than that, never into the rooms I have only imaged through Work's descriptions of them.

Still, I walk toward the estate, the sun warming the top of my head and my back. I begin to feel a little dizzy, and know I should have drunk more than a cup of water. I look up at the estate, glowing white on the slight rise ahead where trees from the deep forest have been brought in and shaped to the lord's pleasure, offering shade and sweet fragrances near the estate itself. I look up at the glass windows, bright as chips of steel against the blue sky day.

I could ask for a cup of water there. I could say I am confused, turned around in my walking and fatigued from birthing.

And if the lord thinks me confused, too tired to breed again, will he send Work to mate with Follow? Will he be rid of both me and Bind?

No, there is no gain in showing weakness to the lord.

Still, I need water and touching. There is a creek that flows through the southern-most edge of the grounds even in the driest heat of summer. I turn and retrace my steps, walking past the squat brown square of our house. I do not go inside. I do not want to hear the weaving of thread, the clack of wooden bobbins.

My stride grows stronger once I have passed the house and I have an urge to run, to let the burnt grasses rush by beneath my feet, to blindly find a gate in the fence and push through to the other side. To touch every leaf, every tree, every stone, and to learn and know more than any of my kind should know.

I place my fingers against my mouth, then my throat. I am shaking from the wild thought of it, vibrating with the hunger for knowledge. These thoughts are insane and yet I want them. They will get me killed, dragged, locked away in the cell like Bind.

I shake my head and push the wildness away, keeping my eyes on my feet. The creek is near. It will give me some taste of difference, will trickle with water that has touched rocks and hills and far away mountains. I hear the creek's liquid voice just ahead. And I hear something else — breathing. I look up and see a man on the other side of the fence.

The world seems suddenly to fold the wrong way, as if all the corners no longer match.

I have never seen this man before. He is tall and lean, his hair a shock of white, straying out from beneath a hat. His clothes are as brown as tree bark and fit tightly to his frame. Straps over his shoulder speak of a weight he carries there — a pack — and he has a silver box in one hand, a walking stick in the other. His skin is the lightest brown I have ever seen and creased around his eyes, across his forehead and down his cheeks in such a fascinating way, my fingers itch to touch them, to trace, to know.

He holds very still. Except for his breathing and the blinking of his eyes, I would not know that he was there.

"Hello," he says. "May I enter this gate?"

He speaks to me and his voice is edged with delicious difference. I feel a warmth grow in me, a need to touch, learn, absorb the knowledge of him.

"Please," he says. "I am a traveler and mean no harm. Is there shelter I can find here? Is there food?"

I nod, his voice lighting my hunger. I savor the strangeness of his speech, absorb the nuances of a voice unlike the others I have heard since my birth. He does not move, and I realize he is waiting for me to open the gate he stands behind.

I look at the gate, made of wood and iron, no higher than my waist, yet stronger than any wall to keep me in. I have never touched the gates before. That touch, that knowing, is forbidden.

But today I will learn this thing. This one thing: gate.

I reach out and touch the top rail of the gate with my fingertips. It is warm with the day's heat. It fills me with the knowledge of hinge and latch and swing. I absorb balance, and understand tension of fence and post, strength of post rooted deep in the earth. The knowing is good, but is not enough to ease my hunger.

I push the gate outward and it swings easily, silently. The open space between the fence and the world on the other side is shocking as winter wind. I step back hastily, moving away from the open space, moving away before I fall out into the forest beyond, into a world I both want and fear.

Then the man is there, filling the space, solid, whole. He swings the gate shut behind himself and waits. I look up at him, at the curious humor in his eyes. There is so much I could know if I touched him.

I fold my hands together in front of me and look down at my feet. "Please," I say, "I will take you to the lord."

The man makes a sound of such delight, I cannot help but look up at him again. I am caught by his smile, and feel myself returning it.

"Yes," he says, his pleasure sending joy through me. "I would like to meet the lord of this place."

We walk, me in front and he behind. His footsteps are heavy, booted. His walking stick taps lightly. We walk up the slight rise. Just ahead is the square of our house.

"What is your name?" he asks me.

"Favor." I am surprised at the quickness of my answer. Everything within me is clamoring to reveal itself to him. The need to talk to him, to tell, to share my knowledge, this place, my life, is overwhelming. I want him to know all of me, want him to let me know him in return. I have never experienced such a need to spill everything I have known out at a stranger's feet. But I do not think the lord will approve. I put my teeth against my bottom lip, tucking my words away tight. I walk.

"Is this where the lord lives, Favor?" the man asks as we approach our house.

"No. We live here. The menders," I say.

We walk past the house and I have to slow because the man has turned to better see it. I wait, and wish he would ask me another question so that I can hear his voice, so that I can tell him more of what I know, of all the things I have learned. So I can learn in turn, from him.

He glances at me. "Menders." It is not a question, so I do not answer. We begin walking again. It is only a short while before the hill rises enough and the estate comes into view. White and smooth, with roofs made of glittering copper, jade and gold, it is beautiful.

"Ah," he exhales. "The lord's house."

And even though it is not a question, I speak. "Yes. The lord has lived here for hundreds of years."

"The same lord?" His surprise sends a thrill through my body. He does not have this knowledge. I trip over my thoughts in my haste to give it to him.

"No. There are many lords. Each a son of a son of the first lord. All have lived in this estate. Menders have served them all."

"And how have the menders served?"

My thrill at speaking to him chills into fear. We are not to speak of our work. Not to speak of the thread, the spinning, the fabric. Not to speak of the babies in the cocoons.

"We do as he asks," I finally say.

"I see," the man says. He does not say more, and I fight with fear and hope that he will.

Finally, we are at the door to the estate. It is much like the gate, and I know how to open it, and do so, the smooth metal latch fitting easily in my hand, the door swinging inward at the lightest touch.

We step into the estate. It is cool here, and clever lights tucked away in hollows of the wall, give the illusion of warmth. I do not walk farther than the entry hall, but the man steps past me, over to the curtains that hang at the large windows to our right. He holds the silver box near the curtain, pressing a button upon it, and I feel a strange tingle tighten my belly. It is as if another mender is touching me, whispering my name, asking to know me. Then the sensation is gone and the man gently rubs the edge of the curtain between his fingers. He lets the curtain drop, and looks over at the rug that stretches from the doorway to the end of the hallway.

"Lovely," he says.

I look at the rug and agree. The colors variegate from deep orange to pale peach. It is like a sunset spilled upon the floor.

The man kneels with his back toward me and holds his box to the rug. The tingle comes over me again, stronger, and I cannot help but take a step toward him, toward the call from the box in his hand. Then the tingle is gone, and I am left confused. The man runs his fingers over the rug's fine, but common, fibers.

"Ah," he says, and I can feel his disappointment.

As he stands, I hear two sets of footsteps approaching. For a moment, I pray it is Bind. Bind who will touch me, who will share in my knowing. I fasten my gaze on my feet, fold my hands. The lord and Work walk into the room.

"Favor," the lord says in his soft, lilting voice. "What have you done?"

It is a question. I am compelled to answer. "This is a traveler who asked if there were food and shelter. He walked through the south gate. I brought him here." At each word I wait for the lord to strike. The silence in the room is so heavy, it hurts. I wonder if this is what Bind endures in the cell.

"A traveler," the lord says. "Where do you hail from?"

The man steps up, and holds his hand out in a curious manner. I can not resist looking, watching as his hand and the lord's hand meet. The world feels folded wrong again. In all my years, in all the lords I have served, I have never seen them touch or be touched.

I dart a look to Work, who stands stolidly behind the lord. Work gives me a steady, flat gaze, and I wonder how he can not show his shock at the event.

"Jonathan Alceste, my lord. It is an honor to finally meet one of the esteemed Ceive family," the man, Jonathan, says.

"Why are you in my private estate, Mr. Alceste?"

"I beg your indulgence." He bows his head. "I come with what may be of great news to you."

"I do not care to hear news from a stranger."

"Please, Lord Ceive. If you would give me even one night. I have traveled the deep forest for three weeks on foot. The nearest navigable waterway was more than the research craft could endure, even with the technology at the Interplanetary Historical Institution's disposal."

"Enough." The lord's voice is quiet, cold as night.

The man silences. Work and I wait, though I can barely contain these new words: research, technology, institution, interplanetary. I can only taste the barest hint of what they may mean, and they seem familiar to me, like a pattern in fabric I once knew, long ago. The need for more of these words is overpowering. I lean toward the man to touch him.

Work's eyes flash in warning, and I fight my need, staying my hand.

"Work," the lord says, "take Favor to where she belongs.

Finish the task I have set you to. Mr. Alceste," he says with obvious anger, "follow me silently."

As is the way, we obey the words of the lord. But the other words, the words from Jonathan the stranger are gestating inside me. I ache to know their meaning. My fingers rub and rub again against the pattern of my own palm that I know too well. I walk behind Work, and see the anger in his back. It is only once we reach the door to the house that Work speaks.

"Drink, Favor. You will need your strength." It is all he says before he walks away, off to the east, toward the holding house where fabric is stored before it is shipped into the world.

I duck into the house and am struck with the smallness of it, the salted mulberry scent of it, the darkness, the sameness.

Follow and Spin are where I left them. They are too consumed by the rhythms of their tasks to look up. I walk through the wooden blinds and fill a cup with salty water and boiled mulberry leaves from the kettle that rests above the small fire pit in our sleeping chamber. I drink slowly, refill my cup and refill it again, thinking I will never fill myself.

I set the cup on the floor and walk to my cot, my belly distended with the weight of the water. I lie down, and though I do not want to sleep, the water and mulberry lull me and I doze.

Follow's voice wakes me: "Put him here, Work. We will need the space to mend."

I am up from my cot and moving across the floor. Vaguely, I realize it is now dark outside and our lanterns have been lit to ease the blackness within the house.

Something is wrong. Work is here, here at night, when he should be at the estate tending the lord. Then I see who Work is laying gently on the wooden floor: Bind.

I walk over and kneel beside him, my lover, my mate. Bind is thin, all his color drained. His long hair, once smooth and gold as birthing thread, is tangled and ripped twine. The wetness from the wounds in his scalp pours down his thin face. His eyes are open, but I know he can not see me.

"Where was he, Work?" I ask. Follow, always sensible, is

pouring more water into the kettle, brewing the restorative mulberry leaf.

Work shifts his weight. He is uncomfortable with my question. I look up at him.

"Tell me you did not do this," I say.

Even in the low light I can see the anger that colors his face. "If you knew, Favor, what I have done. What I do every night so that this —" he points at Bind's stilled form, "— would never happen, you would not accuse me so."

Work's anger, so strong in the room, clears my thoughts. "Was he in the cell?"

Work nods. "Keep him here, Favor. Mend him. If you want him to stay alive, don't let him out of this house until that which you have seen is gone. The lord told me it will be gone in the morning." Work pauses. "There is much I must do tonight." He walks out the door, and across the yard to the estate and the night duties I have never understood.

I cradle Bind's head in my lap and gently brush my fingertips through his hair, over his scalp, his face, his eyes and lips. I have no honey and blessings for him. But I don't need either for a mending. The threads of me flow from my fingertips, healing his wounds. It is a slow, dream-like process. I mend while Follow helps Bind sip, then drink the water. I know Spin is there too, touching Bind to give him comfort, safety, and the knowing of us beside him. We can learn of his pain, absorb the knowledge of it, but we do not. It is the one privacy we can give to each other. We alone choose who to share our pain with.

Bind shifts his feet, moves his fingers, then his arms. He rolls his head to one side and blinks. When he looks up at me, I know he can see me again.

"Favor?"

"Who else?" I smile. Between Follow, Spin, and I, we help Bind to his feet and then to the bed chambers. We bring him to my cot so that I can lay with him and further heal his wounds.

Bind says nothing during this. He allows us to take him where we will, as if we are his lords and he our mender.

The other women go to their cots and I lay on my side next to Bind. My cot is narrow and we rest, pressed body to body, against each other.

He looks at my face for a long, long moment, and his hand slides down to my flat belly. He does not ask of the baby. He does not have to. This close, just Bind and I, there is nothing I can hide.

"What have you seen, Favor?" he asks, his voice soft and safe. "What have you known that has brought a change in you?"

"There is a stranger. Jonathan. A man. Tall, thin, old. His voice —" I pause, remembering. I touch Bind's lips with my own and feel Bind fill with the knowledge of my experience. He wraps his arms around me, holds me closer. And in exchange for my knowledge, I share his pain.

It is this way between us, between mates. We join for babies, but I do not want to carry another child so soon. Bind pulls the knowledge from me in a sweet rising desire and I do not want to turn him away. We share the stranger's words, his voice, the wild taste of freedom, the certain knowledge of something beyond our gate. Something we both want. A world. Freedom.

Bind stays tangled with me, and I with him. Thread by thread, I feel the chrysalis of the child begin within me, sweet as honey and blessings. This child, I do not want to lose. This child I want to keep safe from the lord's needs.

It is not yet morning when Bind whispers, "I will find the man. Speak with him. Perhaps he will take us. Both of us," his hand slips down to my belly and the child who grows there, "all of us, away."

"I will go with you."

He looks surprised at this, his brown eyes wide. "You do not understand, Favor —"

"What do I not understand? Pain? I have birthed a thousand babies, and never seen one live. I understand pain. Do you think I can not feel your wild hope? The wanting to run through the gates and never stop?" I touch his face gently even though I am still angry. "We will find the stranger. We will ask for knowledge together."

Bind leans into the soothing touch of my hand and I realize how tired he is, how thin. He does not have enough strength even to fight me.

We rise, silently. Favor and Spin open their eyes and watch us walk from the room. They do not care where we are going, do not ask, though the fear of our decision is so thick on the air, they can not ignore what we are planning. I hear them turn in their cots, feel them draw their awareness away.

We step outside the house.

"Where are you going in the night?" Work's voice is so close, I jump and press my hands over my belly.

Work shifts his weight, and behind him I see the tall pale form of the stranger. "Favor, Bind," Jonathan says, "come with Work and me. Quickly, before dawn."

"Work?" I ask. I do not understand. The world is folding again, turning inside out. Where is the lord? Why is Work not tending him?

Bind backs away, his hand on my arm, ready to run. But where can we run? What gate is left open for menders?

I tug out of Bind's hold and walk up to Work. "Explain this to me." I stretch my fingers toward his lips. "Let me know."

Work's eyes narrow and his hard features flush with guilt. "You do not want to know it all, Favor."

"I have lived it all. Let me touch you Work, or I will go to the lord and let him decide my actions tonight." Even that small declaration of my own will is as frightening as when the gate swung open. But I stand strong.

Work looks over my shoulder at Bind. I do not look back, do not want to see if my mate agrees with my choice.

Finally, Work nods.

I lean toward Work and press my fingers against his lips. I ease closer to him, slowly. My fingers slide down to his chest. The images Work carries, his knowledge, is so foreign I wonder that I did not sense it in him before. Work trembles at my touch. I lean fully against him, my lips pressing against his so that we can know, can experience each other's knowledge.

I see a strange room that can only be within the estate, feel Work's fear of it, then his hunger to understand it. In the room are words, recorded words. More words than I can understand, concepts that leave me dizzy. Of planets, of technology. First contact.

Work tries to pull away from me when I cross that concept, and I dig my fingers deeper into him, needing to know and drawing the knowledge from him with my lips.

First contact. Interspecies integration. Cultural impact. The creations were simple, safe. Blankets. Blankets woven of threads that held information. Threads programmed to adapt, to self-repair, to absorb a culture and send that information back to the givers.

Hundreds of years ago, just blankets. Hundreds of years ago, contact was lost. But the threads adapted, absorbed the new culture, and became more than just blankets. The threads became us.

I pull away from Work so quickly it hurts.

"How long have you known?" My voice is rough.

Work rubs his hand over his face, as if trying to ease what he too has seen from me, the birthing again and again of babies, the pots, the fires.

"Years. I did not understand. None of it made sense. The historian was the missing piece."

Historian. I now know what Jonathan is.

"You were never meant to be slaves," Jonathan says. "The institution has tried for years to find a way to release you from the Ceive family. But we thought you were fabric. Valuable, priceless blankets. Stolen technology. If we had known you had become self-aware —"

He has no chance to finish. A crack of sound, louder than spring thunder splits the air. Jonathan jerks and crumples to the ground. Something red seeps through to soak his clothing. He is wounded. Dying.

From out of the darkness, we hear the lord's voice. "Step away from him and go into your house."

"Understand him, quickly, Favor," Work says. "Before he is dead." Work steps between the lord and Jonathan's fallen body.

I drop to my knees and place my hands on Jonathan's chest, even though I hear the lord's footsteps coming nearer.

I hiss at the acid feel of his blood, so different than ours. Images, more vivid than any I have seen, fill me. Skies, stars, books and languages. A woman's face, red hair, gray eyes, like no one I have ever seen, the laugh of a red-haired child.

Thunder cracks in the air again, and I hear Work grunt, know that he falls.

Behind me, Bind makes a sound I have only heard from a wounded animal. I glance up and see him rush past me and into the darkness toward the lord, to stop him from wounding again. To stop him from killing again. From killing me and our child.

"No!" I scream.

There is more thunder. I shudder as the thread of Bind's life snaps.

My mate. Dead. Hatred pours through me, over me. I tear through all that Jonathan has known, hungry for knowledge, consuming what I find in his fading mind. The blankets, the threads. We have been taught to mend and birth and spin. We can learn more.

We can learn to kill.

The press of warm metal against my chest brings me back to myself. I sense in the metal the workings of energy, of molecular implosion, of pain. I look past the gun and up at the lord.

"Go back to your cot, Favor. Now."

I do not think he expects me to stand and step over the dead historian's body so quickly. I do not think he expects me to shove the gun aside and wrap my arms around him, and hold him close.

I know he does not expect me to dig fingers into his flesh and send the threads, finer than a needle, sharper than glass, into him. His body is not exactly like Jonathan's but it is close enough. I find his heart and wrap it, bind it, tight and tighter, until it can no longer move. His finger spasms on the gun's trigger, sending balls of raw energy streaking into the night.

I hold him close. Until he no longer breathes. Then, I push the lord away.

When Work can move again, stand again, he finds me beside Bind's body, my fingers tangled in his hair.

"Favor?" Work says. His voice is filled with ache. I know he is injured — his shoulder — and know how to fix it. But I can not take my hands away from Bind. I can not bear to know I have lost him.

"Favor, do you know how we can leave?" I look up, and see he has gathered Follow and Spin. None of them have supplies, but I don't suppose we will need any. There is plenty of water in the forest for the three week journey to the ship that awaits Jonathan's return. Still, I do not know how I can leave Bind behind, and choose instead, the new world.

Work goes on one knee, and puts his hand down into Bind's long hair. He tangles his fingers with mine, holds my fingers in the warmth of his. "Do you want to come, Favor?"

His touch, strong, steady, pulls me from the pain. Just far enough I can nod. There is one other I must live for. There is my child, Bind's child who I will not let die.

Work patiently draws Bind's hair away from my fingers, slowly taking away the last connection between us. Then he plucks a single strand. With that strand in his hand, he draws me up to my feet.

I look into Work's face, tired and lined with pain. I take the strand of Bind's hair and tie it around my neck. There is knowledge in that single strand of hair. I hope I will find a way to reweave Bind from that strand — a technology I glimpsed in the historian's mind.

But now there is more I need do. I place my hand on Work's shoulder and send threads from my fingers to mend his body. It is not as hard as it once was. I have learned so much.

I take Work's hand and lead him and Follow and Spin to the gate nearest Jonathan's craft. Within me, Bind's child stirs.

My footsteps fall fast, and faster. I run and run, and whisper promises like beads of hope hung on fragile strings.

Sweet honey for my baby's lips. Prayers to bless its soul. I will know, see, touch, learn. Anything. Everything. To keep his child safe. To watch our child grow.

Then the fence is there, in my reach. I stretch out my hand, touch the gate. Work and Follow and Spin are beside me, waiting, watching as I work the latch, and open the world.

I'd been given the advice to stop writing such lyrical, descriptive short stories. Taking that advice to heart, I tried writing several "bare-bones" stories to no avail. Eventually, I gave up and threw myself headfirst into this lyrical, rhythmic original fairytale.

LEEWARD TO THE SKY

Crouched beneath the wet stone doorframes in the old town of Brinkofsea, sits Stigin Niddle, fingers too bent to make the magic, build the magic, push the magic, flying, driving the night into morn.

Some see her, bent Stigin Niddle, making the finest sails the fleets have worn. Sails so thin a child's smile shines through them, so strong, the storms of black winter can't tear them. Sails over her bony legs, like a wedding dress about a corpse, sails flowing like honey and sunlight to the edge, but never beyond the stony-arch of the doorway where Stigin Niddle sits, pushing magic.

Boat captains treat her like queen-goddess-nymph ruler of luck and weather. Buy her sails with never a haggle. Pour gold at her feet, bow away, and adorn their great hulled ships with fabric richer than their finest tales.

Crewmen treat her like mother's own yes-lady, as-you-say lady and tip their hats as they go by to find less respectable women leaning from up-above windows with perfume and bright dresses promising moist warm evenings.

Fish-hawkers treat her like ugly girl odd-out sister and keep her fed, fish and crab and sleek, pungent eel.

Magic under foot, ugly, happy Stigin, spinning sails in the damp doorways of Brinkofsea.

Until the landman came, from high mountain stone and thunder, pushed by a wind that smelled of change, looking for magic caught by the small sea town, hungry for something brief and sweet, like the last wine of summer on a lover's lips.

He didn't know he wanted Stigin Niddle. He didn't know magic was an ugly thing.

Twelve days he walked the cobbled town, twelve days striding, bootheels against wood dock, eyes taking in slate sky and jade-tipped waves. Looking for the taste, the song, the filling for a hunger that pushed at his skin and bone, the need that only quieted at night in the amber embrace of ale.

Met a man, a shipman-boatwright of strong, long-fingered, building hands. A man whose hands bent plank, carved ships from mind to solid, breathing creatures of tall mast and rig.

Lovely Ladies, he called them, Grand Dames of tomorrow's horizon. The shipman-boatwright made his own kind of magic, and gave it to the vessels he created.

The man from the mountain almost found what he searched for there, his own hands pressed against sea-soaked teak, the lift and fall of ship rocking his hips like a languid lover.

Eyes closed, mouth open he breathed in the wild call of the sea, of the ship straining against the tethered hold of land, thirsty for the sky's edge and knew this was as close to magic as ever he had come.

But the birds above called out, the wind drew against his skin, reminding him of land, of his mountains, of the hollow hunger deep within.

A false love, this ship. The man opened his eyes and shook his head. No, to the shipman-boatwright whose eyes were so caught by the beauty of his own creations, he did not notice the man leave — did not know he was once again alone with the great mahogany lady. No.

Yet something about the ship called to the man from the mountains, lingered even as his boot touched the cob-solid gangplank. Something here, a part of this ship, was that which he sought.

The man from the mountains turned, looked over shoulders wide and strong from life between the stone and wind of cliffs.

Something there, in the ship, a half-heard song, caught between gull cry. Soft as a feather shaving sky. A snap of sail.

The man from the mountains smiled. Yes. The woven strands, gossamer as diamond-spun spider silk, caught by wind to snap in short brilliant laughter, like a voice caught singing.

Magic.

He walked back to the deck, boots beating rhythm to his heart and pushed both hands into the unfurled sail. He felt the shock of need roll down his spine to pool, heavy and warm between his thighs. Never closer than this, than his hands against a sail too fragile to exist in a world of hook and lashings. Never closer had he been to ending his search. To finally know magic.

He shook the shipman-boatwright until his eyes cleared of rapt fascination for the vessel. Sail, he asked. Where?

Lips bowed in a smile, the shipman pointed. Stigin Niddle. Weaver, maker, doorstoop croucher. In the heart of Brinkofsea, perfect, magic Stigin.

The man from the mountains ran. Boots fell in cobbled tones, singing his need, pounding with haste. So close. Would that which he sought slide away like cloud to sun, before he could glimpse it, know it finally, fully?

If he were in his mountain's hold, his feet would have known the way to go, but here in the shack and alley town of Brinkofsea, his feet followed street after street, coming no closer to the center, the call, the thing called Stigin Niddle.

Night came, bringing a cold wet cloak from the ocean's depth. Brinkofsea huddled in the cold, doors closed, windows drawn. Lantern light pushed out from the cracks between cedar shakes, throwing gold rods of light into the slick cobble streets. Smoke slipped up stone chimneys, mingled, mixed with fog and cold.

The man from the mountains stopped, changing his breath, until it rose and fell in rhythm with the ocean. Magic was here, wrapped in the fog, he could taste it like honey on his tongue, feel it like the cold heat of mint against his skin.

But magic is elusive, hidden, the sound of madness creeping. Though the man followed the call, careful to keep his footfalls soft, his breathing in rhythm with fog-muted waves, magic was ho-ho, and you won't see, in the dark wet streets of Brinkofsea.

On the cusping break of night to dawn, the man walked the last alley, the last street, morning cry of bird and hard smell of baked salt-bread filling the air where fog had once lay, fog which pulled away without the man feeling its loss.

Shipmen called while feet of runners pattered across cobble. Tide is turning, night is turning, life is turning. Up now, men and boys, up now rope and sail, up upon the crashing waves, before the chance is gone.

With each step, the man from the mountains wondered if fate was turning, if he too should shoulder against the wind, find his way home, taking defeat at his side.

And there, near the end of the alley, in the shadows of a doorway, leeward to the sky, blind to the wind, a woman sat sewing. Sails the color of dawn-painted clouds billowed and shimmered, laying like maidens of gossamer, fae beauty, bare to the pale sun, calling, calling, magic here beneath the stone, in the cold dark shadows.

So drawn to the sails, the man did not see the woman behind them for several moments. When he did look, his eyes, dazzled by gossamer beauty, could not believe the vision before them.

Thin to nothing, hair long and wild, Stigin Niddle sat, her sharp face tipped to the side, as if she heard a song no mortal could follow, her fingers lithe and long, spinning magic beneath her palms into cloth. Eyes lost in the gray of the stone which surrounded her, she rocked slowly, her mouth pulled in a smile only babes, or the mad can wear.

And despite the hollows of her cheeks, the pale skin covered with thin silver tracks of snails gone by, despite the cast of blue about her lips and eyes, as if she were long adrift in the cold, cold sea, the man from the mountain knew that magic, the filling, the need that had called him from snug and warm mountain holding was here, before him, in the lifeless eyes and flying hands of Stigin Niddle.

A fish hawker came, tossed yesterday's carp at her feet,

stared at the man of the mountain, the stranger who could not take his eyes off the woman beneath the sails and knew, with pity, that the man had never seen the ugly side of magic.

The fish hawker put a strong calloused hand on the arm of the man — wet and cold — his skin running with droplets of last night's fog, his breath oddly in time with the ocean caressing the edge of Brinkofsea, in time with Stigin's fingers pushing, coaxing cloth to spring, full and sewn from nothing but her hands.

The fish hawker pulled on the man's arm, intent to take him somewhere warm, a fire, a hot mug of tea, away from the ugly odd woman, spinning magic for a world she could no longer see.

But the man from the mountain pushed aside the fish hawker's hand, and before he could think again, before the fall of one wave curled into another, he bent, and caught Stigin Niddle's hands between his own.

You are bound no longer to this town, bound no longer to stone and shadow, no longer to magic's call. Come with me, lady Stigin, and the mountains themselves will bow down to you, hold you dear, precious, love you — but less even than I shall love you.

The hawker laughed. Could the man from the mountain think a woman such as that, a creature such as that would hear his words, bide his call? Magic has fed upon her humanity, sails have replaced her soul. She is but an empty shell, lost and singing, mad, and happy among the drift of sea and swell.

Ugly Stigin, perfect odd, sister Stigin. Not a creature that can be captured, not a woman to hear the heart of a man.

The man listened not to the hawker's words, listened not to the gulls crying fool, fool, listened not to the slow drip of fog and morning sliding down the stone, down Stigin's shoulders, her hair, her face. He listened instead to his heart, pounding with the strength of the mountain, the land come to claim that which the sea had taken, his lady, his love.

Fool, fool, the gulls cried from above, poor mistaken fool, the hawker echoed.

But Stigin did not hear the words of the hawker or the gulls. She did not hear the crash of the waves. Slowly, slowly, like sand sliding down stone, Stigin's hands rested, her fingers lying still and white as folded wings against sails that no longer spun.

The man from the mountains laughed out full, and plucked her up, the nearly nothing of her left, and pulled her against his chest. Love I will give you, love shall you know. No longer the dampness of doorway, no longer the endless skein of sails to be spun.

At the moment the man held her, cradled her face against his own, the hawker cried out, the townsfolk cried out, the captains who had called her queen-nymph-goddess, the crewmen who had called her yes-lady, as-you-wish lady, called out as one, for then the spell was broken, and Stigin Niddle was no longer the heart of gray Brinkofsea, no longer the single, simple vessel for the magic of sail, the taming of the sea to pour through.

Lost it all when Stigin Niddle smiled and breathed again, her first breath.

They speak of her still, of Stigin Niddle, of the ugly, magical creature born of the sea, through whose hands the finest of sails were woven. They speak of the day magic was lost to the town of Brinkofsea, and they speak of the man, whose hands were not afraid to touch, and heart was not afraid to love the ugly beauty of magic.

I wrote this during a class at the Oregon coast. The assignment was to incorporate the setting of the ocean into a story. Somehow life and death got mixed in there too, and the meaning of family, love, and loss.

FISHING THE EDGE OF THE WORLD

Morning came over the hills of Devil's Bay like a long exhale, the pale light caught gold by shore pines. Sadie was already on her side of the beach, the heavy fish bucket sloshing water down her clamming boots and staining the sand pewter.

Salt air came into her nostrils cool, chilled the back of her throat and made her mouth fill with the taste of tears. Ocean air always tasted like tears, though most people never noticed.

Sadie grunted and trudged up to the edge of the drainage stream, a glassy ribbon of water that rippled from the bank and widened out to the ocean's reach.

George was late again.

She put her bucket of fish water down on the sand, the metal rim of the pail sinking like a cookie cutter into dough. She squinted down the length of the beach. There weren't any people on the beach yet, nothing to block her view of the sand, the green-tarnished waves and the curve of land that hooked out and caught the edge of the horizon.

When she looked away from the horizon, George was on the beach walking toward her.

He wore the same black jacket he always wore, his gray hair lifting in the breeze, his tall form getting taller as he neared. His kept his hands in his pockets.

Sadie had been married to George, and working with him for more years than she remembered. She could tell by his slow-swinging stride and the skull-splitting grin that he had something to say to her, something he liked and she wouldn't.

"Hallo, Sadie." George sauntered up, but did not cross over the narrow stream between them. There were rules, and he followed them. "Any new fish last night?"

"A few. I was by the hospital." Tiny fish in the bucket splashed in the water. "Did you and Troy work things out?"

George's grin faded and a crow called out, the sound of it as black as wings, as sudden as death.

"No, no." He glanced off over her shoulder, his gaze sharp with old pain as he stared at the cottages that lined the cliffs above the beach, then away, to the ocean. "Haven't seen Troy since yesterday when he went into town."

"You let him go?" Her voice came out too sharp, and she licked her lips before adding, "Do you know where he is?"

"Easy, easy. I found him and called. He was still in town, about three miles away and walking north."

North. Closer to where Katie lived with her mother.

"He should be here any minute," George said.

The sound of trees and brush being pushed apart drew Sadie's gaze up the stream bank, past a half-buried gray log, and up to the land's edge.

Troy pushed the last branch of shore pine blocking his way between the land and sand. The branch flashed bright in sunlight, then swung back into shadow, swallowing the sound of commuter traffic that buzzed north and south on Highway 101.

There was no sound between them except the breath of the waves.

Troy hesitated, one hand behind his back as if the trees were a life line and he were falling fast. He wore faded denim and a plain white t-shirt. His feet, of course, were bare. Sadie felt a familiar pang of regret when his eyes narrowed into accusing slits.

They had done what they could for him — been the only mother and father he had known — tried to show him how to make the best out of this existence.

He hadn't listened.

Troy strode toward them through the ankle-deep sand at

the land's edge. "Glad to see you, son." George did not turn to look at Troy, but his voice was warm.

Troy walked right past him, leaving the smell of crushed leaves and broken twigs to mingle and die in the salt air. Troy was young enough he could have been their real son, his hair a shaved crop of black like George's had once been, his eyes deep-set above a broody mouth.

Sadie's heart beat harder as he stepped into the surf. The bucket in her hand rang out with a low bell-tone, as if it had just been rapped by a rock and the fish splashed and swam harder. She closed her eyes. This, then was the day she had dreaded.

Troy walked until he was ankle deep in the ocean. He faced the dark line of the horizon where a troller stood up, tipped out of view, stood up again. He didn't look down at the froth that curled up and around his feet, and lapped darkly at the cuffs of his jeans.

Sadie glanced at George, who was still looking at his own horizon, over her shoulder. Waiting for her to invite him over the stream, and give him the bucket. Following the rules.

"Help with the bucket, will you George?" she asked. "It's a heavy load today."

"Sure. Sure thing." George sucked on his bottom lip and glanced at Troy, then back at Sadie. "Going to be a good day for fish, I think."

He didn't sound happy about it.

But then, neither was she.

George took a step, two, both white sneakers forming damns in the stream, footprints pressing, then gone beneath the shallow water.

Three steps, and George was on her side of the beach.

The wind whipped, hard, as if it had been waiting for George to reach the other side of the stream before rushing from the iced edge of the Pacific. Waves flicked up, turned pointed and dark farther out, wind-whipped and white closer in. Wind strained through trees, stirred brown grasses that rattled like dry bones.

Sadie shivered as the wind gusted by.

She touched George's arm, his coat cold and slick beneath her fingertips. He paused and looked down. She caught a whiff of cherry tobacco, and the sweet warmth of rum as he brushed at her short, gray curls, his thick fingers tracing the lines of old sorrows across her cheek.

"Maybe the fish will all swim away," he said, his words soft. But his eyes held the knowledge that his words were false. "The three of us could just go home. Leave the bucket where it is."

It was the same thing he had said last fall. The same hope both of them knew could never come true. They had their jobs now. They had chosen them. Even if they didn't always like them.

Sadie smiled anyway, acknowledging the sentiment.

"How about we take the bucket down the beach a ways and sit?" she said. "Watch the children play."

"The log, maybe?" George bent and curled his fingers around the bucket's metal handle.

In the hollow space where George had been, Sadie once again saw Troy. He had turned to face her. Both hands were at his sides, curled tight as stone fists. His lips were moving around words lost to the shush and crackle of waves.

His words drew the wind. Loose dry sand snapped at her boots, her coat, and finally, stung her face. Sadie tasted lightning, copper-cold on the air.

Sadie lifted two fingers of her left hand and cancelled Troy's commands to the wind and sand. The wind stopped, the sand dropped, and the morning was still.

George straightened, blocking her view of Troy again.

"Easy now, Sadie. There's a long day left. Let's find the log before the living wake up," George said.

Sadie nodded, and followed George back across the stream to his side of the beach.

The agate lickers came down to the beach to walk the wet strip of sand where the ocean slipped in, rolled stones, covered and uncovered gems. Agate lickers usually traveled alone, strolling slowly, heads hung as if a heavy weight pulled at their necks, their gaze on the sand. They looked old and slow no matter their age, and only paused for the glint of a mossy, a milky or a blood amber chunk of the earth's castoff bones.

Sadie had always liked the agate lickers, but today, they moved too slowly, like harbingers of a world mourning its own life/death rhythm.

Families spilled out of hotels and summer cottages set along the cliffs. More people poured from parked cars. People with blankets, baskets, backpacks and coffee cups. Tiny children with floppy hats rode on shoulders, older children bounced and careened down steep stairways that were clamped against the banks like braces of concrete, steel, and wood. The children stopped five steps above the sand, tugged their shoes off and flung themselves out and out, thrilling in a moment of flight before they landed with a soft thud on the beach beneath them.

George and Sadie had chosen their favorite spot, and sat with their legs straight in front of them and a log that looked like the bleached rib of a whale at their backs.

Sadie's fish bucket sat between them, a cool metal pool that reflected no light.

Troy was pacing. Twelve steps north, twelve steps left in front of them, close enough Sadie could hear the sugar-crunch of his strides. He stared forward, and turned toward the ocean to change direction. He never looked their way.

"Might be sunny all day," George said. His head swivelled from side to side as he watched Troy pace.

"Good day for the children to play," Sadie said.

Troy stopped, turned, glared.

"Why did you make me come back?" They were the first words he had spoken since he came back from the land, and his voice sounded raw from the salt air.

"It was your choice," Sadie said. A squabbling flight of seagulls passed above them, and a dog yipped by, chasing a tennis ball down the sand.

"I chose to leave you," Troy said.

"You chose to stay with us three years ago. Not at the top of the cliff when you took your last step, but halfway down, many moments before you hit the surf and stones." Sadie said.

George slipped his hand around the back of the bucket, searching and finding her hand. His hand was cold, bone hard, and rough as a winter stone. Sadie shivered, but held his hand, drawing what strength from it she could.

"You came back to us again today when we called," Sadie said. "You are a part of the sand and the wind and the stone now. You cannot take back your first step in life. Nor your last."

"But my Katie —"

"Your daughter is gone. Three years ago. You let her go, when you stepped into air." Sadie said this softer, for she had said these words so many times, they were faded and thinned.

"Holding on to Katie will only bring sorrow to you. And to her."

George squeezed her hand, and his grip hurt, but it was a reminder of how strong they were, together.

"But I can't just —" he waved his hand, at the families, the bright sky. "How can I watch this? How can you?"

Three children, two girls and a boy, laughed and raced down to the ocean, where they splashed and squealed in the waves.

The bucket hummed, as if a wooden spoon had been rapped against it once, twice, three fresh, sweet notes as each child, as each soul, touched the waves.

A fourth child, younger and slower under the burden of a bright yellow beach ball rambled down to the water. She stopped a short distance from the smooth, shallow wave, and waited for the foam to trickle over her bare toes.

The bucket hummed again, sour and sharp.

Troy gasped. "Katie?"

The little girl tipped her face toward the sky and smiled.

"Don't go to her, Son." George's voice was grave and cool. "She wouldn't see you."

Troy paused, his entire body looking like a wire that had been stretched too tight.

A breeze lapped up off of the waves, carrying the smell of kelp, fish, and cool, deep minerals. A young couple walked past, hand-in-hand. They stepped around Troy as if a rock, or bit of seaweed were in their path.

"I can go back once," Troy said. "You told me that, when I . . . at the cliff, three years ago, when you found me. You told me I could go back one time."

"Listen to yourself, Troy," Sadie said. "If you go back, it will be the last time. And it will only last for a moment. No one escapes death. You made your choice to die, and you chose to spend your days with us helping souls find their way to death. We love you. You'll see Katie some day. When she's older."

"When she's dead!" Troy spun, and faced them. "I will not have my daughter grow up without me." His shoulders were angled as if he were facing down a cold wind. His feet were braced, one behind and one in front. "Please, let me go," he said.

Sadie nodded. George nodded.

The bucket between them swirled, water lapping to the edge, but never quite lifting beyond. Thousands of fish now swam in the water, impossibly tiny, but perfect, souls.

The children on the beach laughed and the waves slapped and turned, teasing, gently pushing, like a mother to a child.

Sadie squeezed George's bone-cold hand, tucked her legs, and pushed up onto her feet. She brushed sand off the back of her pants and walked three steps, her boots *thucking* at her knees. She stood next to Troy.

She placed her hand on his shoulder. He was trembling.

"I don't know if you understand this, Troy," she said.

His eyes were red-rimmed, salt-sore, and his white t-shirt was damp with the spray off the waves that hung in the air even though the sun poured down. She watched as his face became pale, his lips the blue-white of a broken mussel shell.

"Please." He swallowed. "I just can't watch her anymore. Please let me go."

Sadie held her arms out to him, to her almost-son who was taller than she, but came into her embrace like a lost child seeking shelter. Her arms surrounded him, and she heard George's coat swish as he stood.

George placed his long-fingered hand, the skin of it so thin Sadie could see the bones beneath, on top of Troy's head.

"Close your eyes, Sadie," George said from over her shoulder.

Sadie closed her eyes. "Be gentle with him, George."

"Sadie." A soft reprimand. "You know better."

Sadie breathed in, and waited for the feeling, the hollowness within her heart that would tell her another child, another soul had been taken by death's cool hands. It was all part of the dance, she knew, all part of the world living and dying. All part of their job.

But this child, this man, had been their son, had learned how to laugh with them, how to accept his own fate. In a way, how to live.

Perhaps they had taught him too well.

George drew his fingers lightly through the close-crop of Troy's hair. He was being gentle, Sadie knew he was, but Troy stiffened against her, his arms clamping at her waist like hard pincers. It was hard to die. And harder to have your death taken away.

One more second, she thought to herself, and tried to convey to Troy. One more second and it will be done.

"I love you, Troy," she whispered.

A beach ball thumped into her leg.

Sadie jerked and dislodged George's hand.

Troy relaxed in her arms as a spark of life deep within him woke and bloomed.

Sadie did not let go of him, even as his bones broke and folded against her, even as his muscles bled again from injuries he had long avoided.

Troy whimpered, a dying puppy sound.

"Okay, now, Troy," she said. "I'm going to help you walk out to the ocean. The pain won't be so bad there."

She helped him walk, he still backward in her arms.

George, she knew, would not follow. The temptation to snatch away his soul, an impulse only avoided once, and by her interference, would soon come over him. For now, the bucket would satisfy his hunger. Soon that would not be enough.

But Sadie had promised Troy a moment with his daughter.

The water swirled cold around her boots. Out in the rolling stack of waves, she saw a sea-lion's head poke up, then dip under again. Sunlight glinted emerald-sharp off the waves.

Sadie stopped and kissed Troy on his bloody temple. "I love you. So much, that I will give you this."

Sadie stepped back, turned her back, walked up the beach to where George stood. His hand was clenched, the knuckles white around the bucket's handle. His expression was cunning and hungry on a face she had seen hold great kindness.

"He's still standing, Sadie," George said, low, and loving, but unable to hide the pleasure.

Sadie stopped next to George, and put her right hand on the bucket, over his bony knuckles. She faced the living, the land, the Douglas fir, telephone lines and blank-windowed hotels that framed reflections of sky and cloud. She stared at the road, a black smooth stretch that led away from the beach, away from the ocean, away from herself. She understood why Troy had wanted to leave, to walk among the living, even if only once.

She also understood why he could not.

"I can't watch, George. Just tell me if he smiles."

"She hasn't seen him yet," George said. Tight words. Hungry.

"She will."

"Ah. Yes. Soon."

"Tell me," Sadie whispered.

"She's running. Chasing her ball. She's in the waves. Splashing. The ball is rolling away from her fingers. She is looking up, out."

"Yes," she said in exhale.

"He's there for her, Sadie. She can see him."

"And?"

"She's running again."

Sadie nodded, and watched a flight of crows lift and caw, strangled and strident, into the sky. "She ran away?"

"No, Sadie. She's running to him. Watch him, Sadie. Watch our son."

Sadie kept her hand on the bucket handle and turned in toward George so that she stood half behind his right arm, and twisted to look at the ocean. She did not want to let George hold the bucket alone.

Katie had indeed run out into the water. Her yellow ball bobbed farther out than she could reach, was almost as far gone as the sea lion had been.

Troy stood — still stood — though every brush of the wind, every shift of the sand caused him to sway, to totter.

He was bloody. Broken. One arm hung uselessly at his side. But his eyes burned with a determined light. He held his good arm out for her. She ran to him. Ran deeper into the surf, the water sucking at her short legs.

Nothing in the world mattered but the man before her. Children her age often forget the world is a dangerous place.

"Quickly, George," Sadie said, though she knew she didn't have to.

At the moment Katie reached Troy's side, when her fingers pressed and caught at his wet denim pants leg, when Troy looked down at her, Sadie said, "Good-bye."

George lifted his fingers, and the ocean pulled out, faster and farther, as if low tide had come too soon.

Troy and Katie embraced on the damp sand, the clicking popping sound of tiny creatures beneath the sand louder than the wave pulling away.

Troy smiled.

George's fingers dipped down.

The wave powered in like a clap of thunder, crashing against black stones, faster than a shark, churning with the rotted green stink of kelp and sea grass, jelly fish, crab and stones.

Troy teetered as the wave hit him on the back of the thighs, then he was down, broken arm flailing a loose circle behind his head, body swallowed in the surf.

A yellow beach ball rode the wave merrily up to shore. But there was no child left to chase it.

The wave licked up to where Sadie and George stood, foam fizzing atop the water that had gone brown and heavy with sand. As one, they lifted the bucket a bit higher, and watched the water run up the beach past them.

When the wave withdrew, taking with it sandals, plastic shovels and a lawn chair, George cleared his throat.

"Good day for fishing."

Sadie nodded, her gaze on the sky, the horizon, and the deep, cold sea. "They all are. For you."

She patted his arm to take the sting out of her words. "I think I want to walk awhile."

"Want me to take the bucket?" George asked.

"No." Sadie shifted her hold on the handle, and George slipped his fingers out from beneath hers. The bucket was even heavier than this morning, heavier than the world. Within it, tiny fish swam.

"Then I'll see you tonight, Sadie."

"At the stream's edge," Sadie agreed.

She turned north, and trudged along the beach, the water from her fish bucket slopping at first, and then steady with the sway of her steps.

Night feathered across the sky, damping the last fire — orange and pink from the sun. Stars pricked like chips of broken agates thrown up to the heavens.

Sadie stood on the edge of the little river, the warm, living sounds of cars and laughter, of people coming and going, reaching out from the small coastal town.

The honey and hickory smell of barbeque chicken lingered in the rare, windless night, and beneath that, the charcoal snap of smokey bonfires.

Someone was burning marshmallows and melting chocolate.

George stepped beside her, looking as she did past the pools of light from the hotel lamps at the houses, the windows and living beyond.

"Did you think it would last?" he asked.

"No," she said.

"He was a good son," George said, "I think you did well for him, Sadie."

Sadie said nothing. A rowdy high school fighting song rose from a nearby bonfire and behind her, the ocean breathed in and out, lending a damp cool blanket to the night. She didn't think she had done much good for anyone today.

"Have you emptied the bucket?"

The bucket. Sadie glanced at George. He was tall, and gray-haired, his smile warm and kind. The man she had loved, had always loved, from the day they both stepped hand-in-hand off the cliff to fall to the sands below.

"I was waiting for you," she said.

George nodded. "It's time to let them go, Sadie."

She bent and lifted the bucket, heavy, and so thick with the tiny flickering fish, that she knew if she waited any longer, they would have jumped out of the water themselves. It was hard, but she was used to this part of the job too, and wrestled the bucket over to the edge of the glassy stream without George's help.

She tipped the bucket on its side and the water whooshed into the river, filling with the wild, undulation of a hundred thousand fish, swimming to the embrace of the deep, cold sea. But two fish, one larger, one smaller, struggled against the stream, fighting upriver, to the land, to the living. They held their ground for a moment, and then were swept away, side-by-side to the sea.

An editor was looking for an ogre and pixie story with the theme of "Fantasy Gone Wrong." Having never written about an ogre or pixie, I immediately volunteered. This story is a light take on cultural expectations, rules, and how we define our happiness. Did I mention there are ogres and pixies in it?

MOONLIGHTING

T himble Jack crept out of the broom closet and surveyed the tidy stone kitchen. Watery beams of moonlight flowed through the windows and pooled in the sink, giving Thimble plenty of light to work by. Pixies were creatures of the night, and did their best work when the sun had gone to the soft side of dreaming. He put his hands on his naked hips and strolled around the kitchen looking for dirt. Floors nicely swept, stove turned off for the night, and a small bowl of water left out for him. Everything perfectly in place, everything perfectly clean. Thimble frowned. The mistress of the house was a compulsive housekeeper. He hadn't had any real work to do for months.

Thimble stretched his dragonfly wings and flitted into the tidy living room, dining room and small den. All clean. Thimble scowled. He'd been replaced by vacuum cleaners, spray bottles and scrubbing bubbles! With nothing to clean and no one to punish for being lazy, he was doomed to a life of tedium, with nothing but a bowl of water for his trouble. He was going to go crazy as an ogre.

Wait! The child slept upstairs in the nursery. Surely there would be a misplaced toy, an unstacked book. Thimble felt the heat of wicked hope warm his pixie bones. If he were lucky, he might even have time to tie the child's hair in knots for not picking up her toys. Joy!

Fast as snow melt beneath a unicorn hoof, Thimble danced up the stairs, his bare feet making the sound of distant bells.

He didn't bother looking in the parent's bedroom — the

woman didn't even allow a wrinkle in a raisin. But the little girl's room would be gold.

He shoved at the door and walked into the nursery. A single open window at the far side of the room poured silver moonlight across the floor, bookcase, toy chest and bed.

Thimble pulled at his ears in frustration. Nothing was out of place. Not good. Not good. He flitted to the girl's bed, his wings clicking softly. Maybe she had smuggled a cookie under the covers, forgotten to brush her hair, wash her face — something naughty, anything at all.

He landed on the freshly laundered linens and strode up to inspect her face.

"Dolly!" she screeched.

Thimble jumped and quick-footed it backward. He tripped over her pile of extra pillows.

"Go to sleep," he whispered. It had been decades since he'd been spotted by a human and even longer than that since any creature had spoken to him. He was getting slow, losing his edge. This too-clean house was dulling his pixie reflexes. He pushed up to his feet and gathered a fist full of magic, ready to send her sleeping if he had to.

The little girl frowned and pulled her dolly out from beneath her covers. She looked at the doll, looked at him and held the doll out for him. "Dolly," she said again.

Thimble shuddered. It was one of those stiff, plastic, yellow-haired, painted-faced things. They gave him the creeps.

"Yes, yes. Lovely. Go to sleep now."

"All gone." The girl tugged the pink ruffled dress and shoes off the doll, wadded them up in her sweaty fist and shoved them at him. "You."

Clothes! The one thing pixies longed for above all others. But these weren't the clothes he'd spent three hundred years dreaming about: a nice set of trousers, soft jacket and maybe a jaunty hat. This was a cheap, sparkly dress and strappy purple heels. He refused to take them. He would not wear them. He wouldn't be caught dead looking like a fairy tarted up on a twenty year bender.

But there were rules about clothes. Pixie rules. Rules Thimble could not break. One: take the clothes. Two: put them on. Three: dance and taunt. Four: leave the house forever.

The girl made a grab for him, which he lithely side stepped. She stuck out her lower lip and glared. "You!" She dumped the clothes at his feet.

By the wands, she was not going to back down. Maybe it was time to knock the little whelp out. Thimble drew back a palm full of magic.

"Mommy, Mommy!" the girl yelled.

Thimble heard a deep click as the light turned on in the parent's bedroom. This would be bad — very bad. If he used his magic to put her to sleep, he wouldn't have time to turn invisible before her parents arrived. But if he went invisible instead, he would be breaking rule number one: take the clothes.

"Hush, now, hush," Thimble said. "See? I have the dress." He picked it up and reluctantly wiggled into it. The dress was a sleeveless number and had a stiff, scratchy skirt that itched his nether regions. The shoes were no better — they pinched and rubbed and made his ankles feel like they were made out of marbles. He took a couple steps and had to throw out his arms and wings to keep from falling flat.

The little girl clapped her hands and smiled.

Having clothes was horrible. But they *were* clothes, and they were *his* clothes. He laughed and pointed at the girl — as good a taunt as he could manage without falling off the high heels and breaking his neck.

He hated these clothes! He loved these clothes! He wanted to hide under a hill so no one could see him! He wanted to dance with joy! The clash of emotions that filled him was staggering. But no matter what he wanted, the only thing he could do was follow rule number four: leave the house. Forever. No more cleaning. No more teasing. No more of anything that Thimble loved. He definitely hated these clothes.

Thimble took to the air. The dress had an opening in the back that his wings fit through, which was good. He didn't think he'd make it very far on heels alone.

"Wait," the little girl said.

But Thimble could not wait. Just as the girl's mother opened the door, he dove into moonlight and flew out the window. The little girl cried, but he did not look back.

A knot of sorrow settled in Thimble's chest as he flew over the land. Being out of the house seemed as strange to him as going to work in the cottage had three hundred years ago. He felt uprooted, alone, and the dress was riding up his rear.

He took a deep breath. He had made a new life for himself three hundred years ago, he could do so again. All he needed was a new house to clean. That thought brought a smile to his lips. Surely, not all humans were as fastidious as his last mistress. There had to be humans who still left acorns on their window sills and bowls of milk by the door, inviting pixies into the house. And he knew how to find out: check the pixie stick.

Thimble flew to the magic lands of his childhood and straight into the forest where the pixie stick stood. He angled down and landed neatly next to the stick. The magic stick rang with a sweet constant bell tone, and a shaft of moonlight always found a way through the tree branches to illuminate the oldest pixie artifact. Here, every wish in the world could be heard, sorted, and distributed to the creature who could best grant them. Magical notes would cling to the stick until a pixie pulled it off. But there was not a single note on the stick. That couldn't be right. Thimble put his hands behind his back and took a couple steps. His heels sunk in the moss. He lurched and fell.

He hated shoes! He pulled the shoes off and rubbed at his blistered feet, trying to think of a rule that didn't include shoes. Ah, yes. Shoes weren't clothing, they were accessories. He was sure of it. And the rules did not state that pixies must accessorize their new clothes. Thimble threw both shoes into the surrounding brush, and grinned when the plastic hit mud.

Now he could find that new house. He stood, brushed off his dress, and walked around the pixie stick again. Empty. Not a wish or a hope or a request visible. No wonder it was so quiet here. There were no wishes left. With nothing to clean, and no one to tease, he would be crazy as an ogre.

Thimble scowled and kicked the stick. The stick rang like a gong and a single scrap of paper fluttered down and landed in front of Thimble's feet.

Thimble laughed. Thimble danced a quick jig, which wasn't easy in a skirt. Thimble picked up the paper and read the address. He had a wish, a house, a home!

The address wasn't hard to find. Even though it had been three hundred years since Thimble lived in the places of magic, he still knew his way around. Sure the trees had grown, fallen, and grown again, and mountains had studded their feet with new human towns. He had grown up here, and would know his way as well today as in another three hundred years.

Still, when he reached the house, he was confused. The place was right — set deep within a forest and tucked up against an imposing rock wall, with a small, spring-fed creek burbling by. But the house did not resemble any of the human houses he had ever seen. This place was made of trees torn out by their roots, packed with mud and clumps of moss and weeds.

Thimble looked at the address written in indelible magic on the note, then looked above the door. It was the right place. Someone inside that house had wished for help keeping the house. Thimble could do that.

He strode up to the door. There was no inviting acorn on the window sill, which was no surprise since there were no windows. But he couldn't sense a bowl of water by the door, either. He brushed away his worry with a short laugh. He'd pinch the owner black and blue until he or she remembered to put the bowl of water out for him every night. He'd clean and tease and make mischief like no human had ever seen. His heart pounded beetle-quick with excitement, his palms sweated magic. His thighs itched, but that was from the dress. Yes, this was going to work out just fine.

Thimble straightened the straps of his dress. He gave his leg a good scratch, then knocked on the door.

The heavy footsteps of something big, much bigger than a human, so big, the ground shook and shale trickled like dry bones down the cliffside answered his knock. Maybe this was a bad idea.

The door groaned on rusted hinges and swung inward.

A brute of a creature filled the doorway, glowering out over the forest while scratching at his hairy armpit.

This thing was not human. This thing was something Thimble had lived his life avoiding, a dangerous, stupid, pixie-smashing creature. This thing was an ogre.

It was still night, and ogres were creatures of the day. This one yawned, showing rows of pixie-grinding teeth and a curved set of yellowed tusks. Thimble had just woken a sleeping ogre. He held very still. The ogre would never notice him unless he looked down.

The ogre looked down. "Here for the job?" The ogre's voice rumbled like low thunder and sent more loose rocks tumbling off the cliff.

"I am a pixie," Thimble said. "I will keep the house for you, so long as you leave a bowl of water out for me every night."

The ogre scratched his other arm pit. "Aren't you a little pink for a pixie?"

"Aren't you a little talkative for an ogre?"

The ogre sneered, his thick lip curling back over lumpy teeth.

This was it, Thimble thought. He was going to be smashed into pixie paste and buried in a horrible pink frock.

But instead of smashing and bashing, the ogre grunted a couple times and stepped back into the house.

Thimble swallowed until his heart stopped kicking at his chest. He lifted his chin high and entered the ogre's abode.

He had never seen such a mess in all his years! There was only one room to the house, but it looked like a garbage pit. Broken chairs, cracked dishes and unrecognizable mounds of things he could only guess at cluttered the misshapen room. The sink in the corner dripped, sending out a trail of mud that smelled like old cabbage across the floor. No living creature in its right mind would want to live here.

The only thing standing was a tattered curtain separating the main room from a cave-like sleeping hollow.

"What do you expect me to do with this?" Thimble asked.

The ogre waved a meaty hand toward the room. "You're the pixie. Take care of it." Then he lumbered into his cave and tugged the curtain into place.

Thimble was left alone with nothing but the broken tuba snores from the ogre. What was he going to do? There wasn't any way he could clean this mess by morning. But the thought of going back to the empty pixie stick, or worse, to a meticulously kept home gave him chills. Better to have something impossible to do than nothing at all. He cracked his knuckles, hiked up his skirts and got to work.

The morning sun rose over the forest and sent bursts of light and bird song into the mud hut. Thimble yawned and wiped the filthy rag over the last stubborn spot on the wall. He couldn't believe how much he'd gotten done. He'd repaired the table and chairs, mopped the floor that turned out to be stone, and fixed the sink. He'd washed the dishes, mended the ogres' big smelly socks, and even dusted the two mammoth boots he had found under a pile of dry leaves and sticks.

Not bad for a night's work. No, better than that — it was amazing for a night's work. There wasn't a pixie alive who could have done as much as well. The ogre was sure to be pleased. Thimble would get his water, and maybe after a nice day's sleep, he would feel up to pinching the big beast for making such a mess in the first place.

Thimble's smile turned into a yawn. Later. All he wanted now was sleep. He padded over to the cleanest, driest corner by the door, ready to bed down.

The ogre stirred, snorted, and pulled the ratty curtain aside. The ogre took one look at the room and rubbed his blood shot eyes. He took a second look at the room and roared.

"What have you done?" The ogre stomped across the clean room until he towered over Thimble.

Thimble was tired. Bone tired. His day had started with a three-year-old pushing him around and now this big brute had thought he could bully him. Well, Thimble Jack was not a pixie to be intimidated.

"I cleaned your house," Thimble shouted over the ogre's heavy breathing.

"I didn't want you to clean it," the ogre growled. "I wanted it to be worse!"

"Then why did you let a pixie in your house?"

"So you would mess things up."

Thimble pulled at his ears. "We make mischief, not messes, you ignorant clod." And even as the words were out of Thimble's mouth, he knew he had gone too far.

The ogre snarled and spit and raised his fists. But instead of crushing Thimble, the big oaf looked Thimble in the eye and picked up a chair. He smashed it against the table top.

"Wait — " Thimble said.

The ogre picked up the other chair and smashed it.

"Don't —"

The ogre clomped over to the wall, and chunks of dirt bigger than Thimble fell to the floor.

"Stop —"

But Thimble's protests only seemed to fuel the ogre's tantrum. He stomped over to the sink and picked up a plate. He threw the plate in the sink and bits of clay shattered onto the floor.

"That's it!" Thimble gathered his magic in both hands and threw it at the ogre.

The ogre reeled like someone had just whacked him across the head, but that wasn't enough to stop the raging brute. He glared at Thimble and picked up a cup.

Thimble flew at the ogre. "If you smash that cup, I will patch it so fast, you won't know what hit you."

The ogre bared his teeth and threw the cup in the sink. Thimble dashed down after it. Just before the mug hit the sink, he threw a handful of magic at it, and the cup bounced safely, and landed whole.

The ogre grunted and picked up the bucket in the sink. He heaved it against one wall. Water spilled across the floor.

Thimble flew over the spill. With a flick of his wrist, the water was gone, and so was the dirt beneath it.

The ogre grunted again and kicked the leaf pile around. Thimble sent a breeze to push the leaves back into a pile in the corner.

The ogre grunted several times, a sound strangely like laughter, and picked up the table.

"Oh, for the love of wands, you wouldn't." Thimble braced himself. The table was too big for him to catch when it fell, and it would probably explode into a million messy splinters.

Still holding the table over his head, the ogre stopped, tipped his head to the side and shrugged one shoulder. "Too hard to fix?"

And that's when Thimble noticed it. The ogre wasn't scowling, he was smiling.

"Uh, yes. That's a bit much."

The ogre nodded and put the table back down. He stomped over to the trunk that held his clean, folded clothes and looked over his shoulder at Thimble. When Thimble didn't say anything, the ogre cleared his throat.

"Right," Thimble said, more confused than angry. "Don't you dare."

The ogre grunted and busied himself wadding up shirts and breeches and throwing them around the house.

Thimble tried to stay out of the way and do some thinking. The ogre liked making messes, and he liked cleaning. And from the wicked glint in the ogre's eyes, he knew the old boy had other tricks up his sleeve. Staying here would be madness.

But it certainly wouldn't be boring.

Thimble grinned and scratched at the itchy dress. Maybe this wasn't so bad.

"Fine," Thimble said, trying to sound angry. "You mess everything up, but I will clean it. Every night while you sleep, I will wake and make your house fresh as a spring day."

The ogre grunted. "You'll never be able to clean everything before I start wreaking havoc."

"And you'll never be able to ruin everything before I start wreaking order."

They glared at each other, then Thimble nodded. The deal was set.

"Good then, I'm off to sleep. See that you don't keep me awake with your smashing and bashing, or I'll pinch you so hard, you'll be black and blue until your birthday."

The ogre grunted several times. "You don't scare me, Pinkie."

"You don't know me very well, Ugly."

The ogre chuckled again.

Thimble scratched at his thigh and trundled over to the corner by the door.

"See you in the evening," Thimble yawned.

But the ogre followed Thimble to the corner and held his hand out.

"What?" Thimble asked, hoping the big behemoth didn't want him to shake on the deal.

"Give me that ridiculous dress."

"Make me," Thimble said. Bad move. The ogre plucked him up by the wings and stripped the pink frock off him quicker than skinning a grape.

Thimble kicked and bit and pounded on the ogre's hand to no avail.

The ogre put Thimble back down on his feet and patted his head. "When you want it back, you let me know." The ogre pulled at a key on a string out from beneath his coarse tunic, and unlocked the only cabinet in the house. Thimble saw a flash of gold, a wink of jewels, then the ogre tossed his dress in there and locked the door.

"Monster," Thimble grumbled without much heat.

The ogre shrugged and went about crushing sticks into sawdust.

The truth was, now that he was out of that dress he felt much better. More like his old self. Free to make his own choices and to come or go as he pleased. And besides, now he could go back to dreaming about a proper set of clothes, maybe with a hat and matching shoes — comfortable shoes. He felt better than he had in years. Thimble curled up, with nothing but dry leaves for a bed, and chuckled. "Crazy as an ogre," he muttered.

The ogre just grunted in reply.

Written to the read-out-loud challenge theme "Christmas Gifts," this story takes a look at what gifts we truly cherish and the bravery it takes to give with all our heart.

CHRISTMAS CARD

Tommy inched across the carpet on his belly and elbows, coming ever closer to the wrapped packages under the tree. He had stared at those gifts for so long, his Mom had said there ought to be eye holes in the wrapping. He'd checked. No holes. Even though he wasn't allowed to touch the gifts, he had found another way to make the packages move. The dog, Pufferbelly, worked like magic.

"Here, kitta, kitty," he whispered at the neighbor's orange tabby who had just stuck her head in the empty window pane beside the front door. The cat's eyes were gold as old coins, and wide with curiosity. The cat wasn't purring, but she slid her head side to side, then slipped through the empty pane. She cautiously approached him.

Right on time, Pufferbelly came through the open back door, barking with all his might. One loud dash past the tree — the cat screeched out the window — the dog pushed the front door open on its loose hinges, leaving packages scattered in his wake.

Tommy grinned and swallowed down the evil laughter he'd been using since Halloween. This was working perfectly this time.

He crawled the rest of the way to the tree, careful to follow Mom's "don't touch the gifts or so help me you'll be grounded" rule.

The green box was for Dad — the one that looked like it held a shirt or sweater. Tommy had found this same present under the tree two years ago, and last year too.

On top of the green box was a weird little gift wrapped in red. It frightened him a little because he didn't recognize it. It was round on one end, like a ball, then long and looped on the other, but the whole thing was only as big as his hand. He paused, breathing quietly against the carpet as the unfamiliarity of that gift came over him cold, like a silver thaw. He must know what that gift was. He always knew what they were.

The package tipped off of dad's gift and hit the floor with a sweet jingle. Tommy smiled. Baby Elli's rattle, of course.

He glanced around to make sure Mom wasn't looking. The house was dim. The fireplace full of wood that had gotten dusty from never being lit. Even the tree was no longer green. But that didn't matter. What mattered was that Mom hadn't come out of the kitchen to see what all the commotion was yet.

Tommy scooted over to the package for Mom. He knew what was in this one even without looking. He'd been there to help Dad pick it out for her. It was a bathrobe, with red and blue stripes. Tommy had liked it best, even better than the pink one, because it was soft as a brand-new teddy bear before the new gets rubbed off of it.

One last gift to find. It had landed close to the door. Tommy moved between dusty tree ornaments. The gift was almost in reach and yes! there was a tear right down the front of the wrapping. Perfect!

Forget scooting, forget the warnings he knew by heart. Tommy sat on his knees in front of the gift, concentrated, and picked up his present. It was a medium-sized box with snowmen wrapping paper. Tommy pulled the lid off the box. A blue hat, matching mittens and scarf were inside. Pretty dull stuff. But the thing he'd been hoping for, wishing for, was nestled right in the middle of the scarf and hat. Doppelganger-Swapper cards. Rare version with an Extralife card!

Tommy grabbed the cards and looked through them quickly. They were smeared, like someone had taken a big eraser and rubbed them blank. But one card was still good — the one he hadn't tried yet — the Extralife card.

Tommy carefully placed the Extralife card on top of the

deck and set the deck on his knees. Then he put on his hat, gloves and scarf.

It was magic. As soon as the hat was settled on his head, and the cards were in his hands again, the room lit up. The fire crackled to life behind him. The ornaments were off the floor and on the tree, sparkling like they had just been hung.

"Couldn't wait?"

Tommy tried to look guilty, but couldn't hold back his smile. He stood and ran to his mom. "Thank you! This is the coolest Christmas ever!"

Mom smiled. A car horn honked outside and Mom tucked his hat closer over his ears. "Daddy and Elli are waiting for us," she said, and Tommy felt sad. That was familiar, too. He'd been sad today before.

"We need to be on the highway before the storm hits," Mom said. She zipped up her coat and Tommy was sure he saw dust puff out from it.

He shook his head. "I don't want to go to Grandma's, Mom."

Mom knelt and helped him put on his coat. He slid his arms into it, and it was cold, damp. She zipped it tight around his body. He shivered.

"I know, honey, but Grandma's getting pretty old. This might be the last Christmas we can see her. And besides, someone already got his gift." She raised an eyebrow, but he knew she wasn't really mad.

"I still don't want to go." He waited, hoping Mom would do something different this time, maybe listen to him and say they could all stay.

Mom took his hand and opened the door. "The ice will be here in a couple hours. We don't want to be on the road when the storm hits."

Nothing. Nothing different. Tommy felt the cards in his hand grow warm. One Doppleganger-Swapper card left. His last chance to change tonight.

"Tommy," his mom said, "don't worry. We'll come home in time for Santa to fill our stockings tomorrow night."

For a moment, Mom's hand felt warm in his and she smiled.

Maybe everything was already okay. Maybe just finding the cards, and putting the Extralife on top fixed everything.

Tommy looked over his shoulder at the stockings on the mantle. They had holes in them and were covered with spider webs. The living room was dim again, dusty. The tree was brown and brittle.

Soon the storm would bring screeching tires, Mom's scream, Dad's yell and the awful sound of crushed metal. Then cold and silence. He had already used Reset, Swaptime and Slowplay.

Nothing left but one Extralife.

Tommy pulled the deck out of his pocket and glanced at the top card. If he held real tight to it, he might get to live a real life again. Maybe the emergency team would pull him out first, and he would still be breathing.

And what about the rest of his family?

"Mom," he said, "Merry Christmas." He handed her the card.

She smiled a puzzled smile, but took the card and put it in her pocket.

"Merry Christmas. Now, stop worrying, honey, everything's going to be okay."

Tommy nodded and walked with her out the door. Maybe this year, Mom would be right.

Back when I was experimenting with how to write quickly, a friend issued a challenge: write three stories in six days. This very short story was one of the tales that fell off my fingertips. Even though it's short, it hints at a much bigger magical world. I've often found myself wondering what happens next with this boy.

DUCKS IN A ROW

I didn't have the gun in my hand yet. Another boy, about twelve years old like me, walked away from the carnival booth and a little kid, maybe six, put down his nickel. There was room for three people to play but the other two guns were gone, leaving empty chains swinging over the booth's edge.

I'd never been to the carnival before, never seen a real shooting gallery. But I was real good with a gun, or at least that's what my dad would say if he were alive. So I waited my turn even though my ankles hurt, the blisters on my hands were sore, and a storm was brewing in the hot August sky.

The stuffed toy prizes, hanging in a drift of blue and pink and green on a rod above the booth, whispered to the kid with the gun, but I don't think he heard them the way I did.

"Low," they said, "slow."

The kid aimed high, missed twice, and winged one duck, which made a funny quacking sound, but didn't tip over like it should. The boy looked pretty disappointed and dug in his pockets, but didn't have any money left. He looked up once at the toys, then walked away.

My turn. The guy behind the booth held out greasy hands.

"Nickel for three shots, Sonny," he said.

"Say we make it an even four?"

The man shook his head. "Rules say three, or go try another game. There are folks waiting their turn."

But there wasn't anyone behind me. The wind picked up and the stuffed toys swayed a little more. There was anger and storm in that breeze, coming up big and soon.

If I wanted my shots, I'd best take them now.

So I put down my nickel and the man flipped the lever beneath the lip of the booth to set my gun up for three shots. The gun wasn't much more than a toy rifle, slick and light with a sight on it that was shiny on the top edge and bent pretty bad. I held the rifle up and tucked the stock in tight against my bruised shoulder. I sighted down the barrel to get a feel for the thing even though holding it made the broken blisters on my palms sting.

All the while the ducks clicked by, dragged by a chain wrapped round their feet that clattered over hidden spokes. I shifted how I stood, taking some of the weight off my worst foot.

Painted yellow squares filled the spaces between the ducks. When I looked at them real close, I realized they were shaped like headstones.

"Gonna shoot, or you gonna look at them all day?" the man said.

I thought about flicking the barrel over at the man, pop a BB in his cheek, but this gun didn't have no BB's in it, only air. I put my finger against the trigger and sighted the ducks. Once I squeezed the trigger, air would pop out. If I missed my shot the ducks would play a tape recorded ping or ricochet sound.

If I hit just the right point on the duck at just the right time, the duck would tip over and I'd win myself some respect. And a little justice for all.

I waited, took a deep breath, squeezed, readied for the recoil. My dad would have thought I did a real good job. The one thing he told me I was good at was handling guns. Taught me all he knew himself.

The ping rang out and a sharp ricochet echoed. I'd had the heart of the duck clear in my sights but I didn't even graze the wooden bird.

That wasn't right. If there was one thing I did well, it was shoot.

The wind blew harder until the toys above me rocked, creaked.

"Aim low," the toys whispered to me as inanimate objects often did. "Wait for the last moment. The man, the man slows the chain."

I thought it was right kind of the dead toys to give me advice and all, but I wasn't sure I should take advice from something that had been hanging by its neck since the carnival opened six days ago. Still, I sighted again, waited for the ducks to rock up over the edge of the shooting gallery like a locomotive cranking up a switchback, and started counting.

I had good rhythm. It meant the difference between getting a fist in the eye or the chin and knowing how to dodge the worst of my dad's whip at my back. When I counted out the duck's pace and put the sight where the duck's heart — in just three beats — should be, I knew I was gonna hit it dead on.

Out of the side of my eye, I watched the guy behind the booth. He looked bored, like he was watching the rest of the carnival: the snake girls, and balloon clowns and folks with half eaten corn dogs and ice cones.

But I knew he was looking at me out of the corner of his eyes, just like I was corner-looking him. I took a deep breath, squeezed the trigger, and saw the fella's hand twitch beneath the lip of the booth.

Ping! Ka-zing! The duck quacked, but damn-sure didn't fall over.

I made an exasperated sound. The wind was building up right along with my anger.

"It's a challenge," the man said, "but you look like a fine strapping boy with a good eye and a steady hand. Last shot, you'll have it sighted. For another nickel, I'll load you up three more shots."

The air smelled like hot iron and the clouds rumbled like bellows feeding fire. There'd be a hard rain soon. Another whopper of a storm to clean away my sin. Something hot and loud. Something big as the one that came up yesterday while I was pulling the gun out of the attic. Thunder roaring so loud it covered the shots of the .30-06. Something that would bring rain to soften the dirt and make for good grave digging all night long even if all you had was one shovel and your bare hands.

I hunched my bruised shoulder against the stock and tipped my head a bit to see if I could hear any of the toys talking again. They all just swung there uncommonly quiet as dead things should be, the way I wished my dad had been. I nodded at the man.

"Keep your finger off the lever, and I'll take my last shot."

"Oh no," the toys gurgled.

The man tipped back on his heels, then up again, looking like my dad used to — smiling like the dickens and still mad enough to hit my face into the back of my head.

"This game ain't fixed, boy. Nothing but the lever to load the gun back here. I'd show you so, but you're not allowed to lean over this edge. Now take your shot and get on out of here."

"Low," said the toys above me.

"Quack, click," said the ducks being dragged by the chain.

"You saying you're an honest man?" I asked. "That this is an honest game and I could bring me a sheriff, or lawman back here and they'd see there was no wrong doings?"

"Sure thing, Sonny. Bring all the law you want."

I nodded again, real slow, like my daddy used to when he talked to the law and told them there wasn't nothing strange about my bruises, wasn't nothing wrong about my broken ankles.

"Just so long as we have a reckoning of things."

"Fire your shot, Sonny, and get your britches home to your mamma."

"Low," said the toys, "slow."

I licked my lips and sighted the ducks.

Click, click, click, the ducks rounded the edge, dragged by the chain around their ankles, cutting their flesh and bone with every step as they stumbled behind their daddy's pickup. The ducks staggered forward, ready to get shot, maybe even thinking it would be a relief. I counted, took a deep breath.

The fella flicked his finger under the counter. The ducks slowed. I pivoted so the gun was aimed at the middle of the man's forehead. His eyes opened so wide his eyebrows got hung up under his greasy hair. I squeezed the trigger. Thunder boomed.

He jerked.

Ping! Ka-zing! The ducks quacked. And all fell over.

I held the rifle there at the man's head, feeling the long straight line of power that poured from the end of the gun to the bone in my cheek and right on back to where the stock was tucked up against my heart. It felt warm. Powerful. Strong. Like a man should feel, my dad would say. Except I wasn't sure I wanted to feel like that kind of man.

The gun went heavy and cold in my hands.

"What the hell do you think you're doing?" the man asked.

I tipped the rifle down a notch, so the barrel was pointed at his mouth and crooked teeth. Truth was, I suddenly didn't like the gun in my hands at all. Thunder rumbled again and I knew the storm was coming to me.

"You owe me four prizes."

"Bull crap."

I motioned to the ducks with the gun.

He looked over. Sure enough, all four of the wooden ducks were tipped over, flat as a widow's heart.

"You didn't hit those with your shot, boy. You cheated."

"Not likely. This here's a fair game. We agreed on that. I'll take my prizes now."

He glared at me. "The wind blew them over."

"I aim to take what I've earned."

"Get out of here," he said. "You're not getting anything from me."

I raised the rifle again, swallowed hard so my voice came out even and strong.

"Mister," I said, "you know you cheated. You know I shot those first two ducks clean just like the kid in front of me did, and the kid in front of him did. And you know I knocked down those four ducks while this rifle was aimed at your head. I'm a good shot, that's what I'm saying. And if I'm good with a toy gun, you better believe I'm good with anything I put my hands on."

I don't think he understood what I was saying, but he got enough of my drift to snarl at me and pull two toys down by their haunches. "Take your damn toys, but don't ever play this booth again, hear?"

I put the rifle down with full gratefulness and rubbed the feel of it off my palms before taking the two dogs from him. "These are fine, and I'll take them to the kids you cheated in front of me. But I want the ducks too."

"Get the hell out of here, boy."

The wind kicked up and got the booth rocking so hard, all the toys fell off the bar and went rolling like cotton candy tumbleweeds down the dirt and sawdust lane, bouncing into tents and booths along the midway. The man made a grab for the toys, but none of them blew his way, happier, I suppose, to take their chances on the wind. The plywood bolster board of the booth above him fell and darn near crushed his fingers, except he jumped back fast and howled, so I think he mostly got scraped.

Off his footing, he flailed back into the ducks. The chain broke. Ducks and wooden headstones fell to the ground.

Which was all right with me. Every living thing deserves to be free. My daddy never said that, but I know it's true — now that he's dead.

Me, I just turned away, leaned into the wind, and started walking. I planned on finding those boys and giving them the prizes they'd earned. I planned on handing out a little justice for all, and then leaving this town to try being good at something else. Maybe try being someone else. Someone free.

The four ducks waddled up behind me, like inanimate objects sometimes do, wooden feet making clack, clack, clack sounds against the dirt, wooden wings flapping as the thunderstorm finally rang out and pulled a good strong rain out of the hot August sky.

I love origin myths and wanted to write a myth about the origin of music. After finishing the story, I knew it was missing something. Finally, it dawned on me that I needed another character. I added Sath, the snake to the story, and then the myth felt complete.

SINGING DOWN THE SUN

I t wasn't the music that changed, bell-sweet and delicate as a moth's wing. Jai always heard the music no matter where she had hidden it. But the silence within the melody was different, the pauses between each note too long, then too short. Jai tightened her grip on the handle of her hoe and glanced up at Black Ridge where a forest of yellow pine stood dark in shadow. She knew what the changes in the song meant. It meant Wind and Shadow had found a new child to do their bidding.

"What will you do about the music?" a soft voice asked.

Jai startled at the sound of the ancient corn snake, Sath, who sunned on the flat stone at the corner of her garden. He was her forever-companion, the one creature who had promised to never leave her. But he had been gone for nearly a year and had returned this morning as if he had never left. As if she had not spent long days and nights worrying that Wind or Shadow had found him, killed him.

His sinuous body looked like a rope of sunlight, his scales jewels of orange and yellow with deep black outlining the patterns down the length of him. She had forgotten how beautiful he was, but had not forgotten how afraid and betrayed she had felt when he left.

"There's nothing I can do," Jai answered.

Sath lifted his head, black tongue flicking out to taste the air, the wind, the song. "The song has changed."

Jai didn't answer.

"Wind and Shadow will take the child," he whispered.

Jai blinked sweat from her eyes. "You have been gone for a year. Did you come back to tell me what I already know? I won't teach another child. The gods can fight without me this time." Jai went back to hoeing the dirt between the summer-green shoots at her feet.

"But I am home now," Sath said.

"That is not enough."

Sath rocked his head from side to side, his black eyes never moving from her. "I am sorry you were alone. But the child is —"

"— the child is not my problem."

"Even if he dies?"

The wind carried the song to her, melody and pauses chilling the sweat on her back and neck, tugging her faded cotton dress and the handkerchief covering her thick black hair.

Jai did not answer the snake. She pulled the hoe through weeds knowing that Sath was right. When Moon discovered Wind and Shadow had caught a child, there would be a battle for the music, and the child would die.

It'd happened before. She had found the first child who played the music many years ago. He was a fine strong boy named Julian. Julian had been a quick student. He'd learned how music had come into the world. He'd learned that Wind and Shadow wanted it, and that Moon wanted it more. He had fought to keep the music hidden in the world, like she had, like it was meant to be. Maybe he'd been too strong. Like an oak cracking down under a storm.

He had been only six years old.

And that slip of a girl, pretty and bright as the sunrise, Margaret Ann. Jai had taught her too. Tried to teach her to ignore Wind and Shadow. But Margaret Ann had gone walking in the night and was swallowed up by moonlight. Poor little bird, Jai thought, poor sweet child.

"I've buried enough children," Jai said. "Teaching them didn't help." She struck the dirt, broke clumps, uprooted weeds, but the memory of the children would not go away.

Sath drew into a tighter coil, resting his fiery head upon

circles of scales. "Not teaching helps less," he said. He gave a slow, gentle hiss. "Please, forever-companion?"

"Forever-companions don't leave each other." Jai finished weeding the row and the next, following the curve of the land. All the day Sath watched her with dark unblinking eyes. And all the day the music drifted down to her, sweeter than she'd ever heard it before.

There was power in that song and there was power in the player. But she had made up her mind.

At the last of the last row, Jai straightened her back. The shawl of night would soon come down. Time to fix a meal, boil water for tea, soak her feet.

"Are you coming?" she asked Sath.

The snake uncoiled and slipped off the edge of the stone like a ribbon of orange and umber and gold. He crossed the rich tilled soil and stopped at her foot.

"Will you teach the child?" he whispered.

"No."

"Ahh," Sath said sadly.

The sound of his disappointment made Jai wish she could take the words back, but she did not want to teach another child, could not bear to see the gods tear a soul apart again. Jai ignored the snake and made her way to her house: a sturdy square cabin with two windows and a pitched shake roof shaded by a gnarled hickory that combed the wind in leafy exhale. Perhaps the child's ignorance would also be his saving.

Just as she reached the edge of her yard, just as she looked up at her doorstep and saw the small silent figure standing there — that very moment — she realized the music had stopped, leaving nothing but the warble of the night bird and the whisper of the old hickory tree.

The child was small, dusky-skinned and red-haired. A boy. Long in the leg, and serious of eye. He looked to be ten, still dream-slight, as if not yet anchored to this living world.

Oh, please no, Jai thought. "What are you doing out this late, child? Don't you have no mama calling you in for supper?"

The child blinked, shook his head. He pressed his back

against her front door. He held a wooden bowl-shaped instrument tightly against his chest — string and wood and magic itself. There. On her doorstep. In his arms.

No one had ever pulled it down from the mountains. No one, not one adult who had no chance of it really, nor one child who could still hold magic bare and true in their hands, had ever gone up to the mountains and brought the music down to her.

"Please help him," Sath said from the grass at her feet.

Jai put one hand on her hip and tried hard not to show her fear. She did not want to fight the gods again.

"There's no place for you here, child," she said. "No place for that music. You should go on to your mama now."

"I don't have a mama," the boy said, and his voice was honey and starlight, the sound of a barefoot angel begging on her doorstep. "I don't have a daddy, neither."

Jai shook her head. None of the children who were taken by Wind and Shadow had kin.

"There's no room for you," she said again.

"Jai," Sath whispered, "please don't turn him away."

The boy looked down at the snake.

"He told me," the boy said. "Told me I should find you. Said you would help me. Please. I don't have another place to stay."

Jai was surprised the boy could understand the snake — Sath had never spoken to anyone but her. She was even more surprised that Sath would tell the child to come to her, that he would expect her to help again.

"Maybe you should have stayed gone," she said to Sath. "Maybe you should go now."

Sath lifted up, high enough the blunt tip of his mouth could touch her fingertips. His whisper was so soft, she could feel it on her fingers more than she could hear it. "We are — we were forever-companions. You trusted me for many years. Trust me now. Then I will go."

Jai opened her mouth to tell the boy to leave but a gust of wind whipped by. The wood and string bowl in the boy's hands hummed a sweet, low, soul-tugging tone. Even at half the yard away, Jai could see the child sway beneath the music's power.

"Please don't be mad at the snake," the boy said. "It's not his fault. I will try to pay you back any way you want if you'll help me."

Holy, holy, always the sweetest children. How could she turn her back on him now? Jai glared again at the snake. Sath arched back down to the ground and slipped through the grass toward the house, toward the boy.

Jai stepped forward with a heavy sigh.

"I'll do what I can, child. Don't expect miracles. You are tied to this thing," she pointed at the instrument, "until the end of time." *Your time,* she thought. "But that doesn't mean you have to fear. You are the one who plays the music. It doesn't play you."

As if to prove her wrong, the wind snatched at the strings again, and the boy's fingers found their place on the strings. His eyes glazed and two strong notes rang out.

Jai put her hand on the boy's shoulder, breaking the spell. "First rule is you keep your hands off the strings if you want into my house."

The boy's eyes cleared. He swallowed. "Yes, Ma'am."

"Second rule is to listen to me. This is not an easy thing." *For either of us,* she thought.

The boy nodded. "I'll try to do right."

Jai stepped past him, avoiding even a casual brush with the instrument. She did not want to feel its power in her hands again.

"Come inside, and I'll get us some food. We have some time yet before night thickens and Moon wakes."

The boy followed her into the house and stood in the middle of the small living room, a shadow in the uncertain light. Jai moved around the room and lit the kerosene lamps. The light revealed a wood rocking chair and padded couch, a braided rug and a rough stone fireplace with a mantel made of a lightning rod. Sath was no where to be seen, though she was sure he had slipped into the house ahead of them.

Once all the lanterns were lit, the boy gasped.

The stronger light showed walls covered by hundreds of musical instruments. Hung by cords, hung by nails, hung by strings, every conceivable musical instrument rested against the walls, repeating the sounds of Jai's footsteps in gentle harmony.

"Do you play them?" the boy asked.

Jai raised an eyebrow. "Didn't think I spent all my days hoeing the field, did you? I've been a few places in my long life, boy — what *is* your name, child?"

"Julian Jones," he said.

"Julian?" Jai's heart caught. Her first. Her oak-strong boy. Buried so many years ago beneath the moss and loam of a continent far and an ocean away. But this boy was different than her first Julian. This boy was built like a supple willow and had a voice as sweet as a afternoon dream.

"I haven't heard that name in a long, long time." Jai walked into the small clean kitchen and lit the lamps. There were no windows here to let in sun or moon light. Sath might be here, but she did not see him.

"That name has strength, child," she said.

"Will it help?" his voice was almost lost to the wind blowing outside.

"Every little bit helps when Wind and Shadow want you to serve them. Do you know the old stories, Julian? About how music first came to the land?"

Julian shook his head and took a step toward the kitchen, then stopped.

"Come on, child. Sit at the table."

Julian came into the room and a long streak of orange followed at his side. The boy eased into the chair, keeping the instrument cradled in his lap. Once he was settled, Sath slipped up the wooden rungs of the chair until his wide diamond head rested just above the boy's shoulder.

Jai wondered why Sath was so protective of the child, wondered if he had promised the boy to be his forever-companion. That thought made her heart ache. She turned to the sink and pumped water into the kettle, putting the hurt aside. They had only an hour before Moon woke.

Jai had told the story of music to every child. She had tried every way she could think of to defeat Moon and Shadow and Wind. But no matter what she taught the children, no matter what they tried, the gods always won, always drank the music down, and with it the child's life.

Wind scraped across her rooftop, clawing to get in.

She rekindled the wood stove and pulled the morning's bread out of the warmer. Her thoughts raced. What way to destroy the instrument? What way to stop the gods?

"In long ago days," Jai said, "Sun would walk over the edge of the horizon to the dreaming world each night. Sun's dreams were beautiful and terrible, frightening and foolish. They were so filled with wonder, the sound of them caused the stars to blink in awe and all the world to tremble."

She put the kettle on the stove and turned to place a plate of bread in front of the boy. Outside, Wind rattled in the hickory tree.

"Every night sister Moon listened to Sun's dreams and grew jealous of the beauty she would never see in her dark world. She wanted those dreams, wanted what her brother, the Sun, had.

"So Moon sent Wind to catch Sun's dreams and bring them into the night. But Wind had no hands, and the dreams slipped away before he could reach Moon. Then Moon sent Shadow into the dreaming land. But even in dream, Sun shone too brightly for Shadow to touch."

Julian was perched on the edge of his chair, looking as if at any moment he would fly away. Jai hurried.

"Moon was crazy with want. A greedy, selfish want. She shone that hard cold eye of hers down across all the lands, across the seas, and into the hearts of every soul until she found herself a brave child. A girl with more curiosity than good sense."

"A brave girl," Sath whispered.

Jai shook her head.

"A foolish girl that listened to Moon's call and let her feet follow. She found her way over the edge of the world and into the dreaming land.

"There, the girl scooped up armfuls of dreams that glittered like jewels. She put the dreams into the wooden bowl she carried and ran back to the waking world.

"But Moon was waiting for her at the edge of the horizon. Waiting with Wind and Shadow. All three of them so greedy, they tussled for the bowl of dreams.

"The girl tripped and the bowl flew. Moon tried to save the dreams by sealing the bowl with silver light, but Shadow and Wind wanted it too and tore at the bowl, shredding Moon's light into strings.

"The bowl up-ended and dreams poured out between the moonlight strings, crying a sweet music as never a soul on earth had heard.

"The music of Sun's dreams soaked into the land and was caught in every river, every stone, every tree, bird, beast and all the souls between."

Wind buffeted the roof. Shadow crept down the walls, leaching light from nooks and corners. But Julian watched only Jai.

"What about the girl?" he asked.

He didn't ask about the bowl. Didn't wonder where the magical instrument had gotten off to. Of course, he shouldn't wonder. He held it against his heart.

"A snake who had been resting on the edge of the world whispered for her to get up just as the Sun came into the waking world and discovered the spilled dreams. Sun was angry, but the snake told Sun it was not the girl's fault. Instead of killing the girl, Sun bound her to guard the moon-strung bowl, to keep it hidden from Wind and Shadow, and most of all, from Moon.

"The girl did this for a long, long time. She hid the bowl in all parts of the world, but always, always, Wind and Shadow found it. Always, always, they lured a child to play the music for them and jealous Moon."

"They still want the Sun's dreams," Julian breathed. His hands clutched the bowl so tight, his knuckles were white.

Jai did not want to tell him the rest — the worst. "No mortal can endure playing the instrument for long. Maybe a day, maybe a week. But Sun's dreams are so pure, so strong, they burn flesh and bone to dust."

"I won't play for them," he said.

Jai's skin chilled.

"I'll break the bowl, cut the strings, or, or throw it back over the horizon."

"No mortal power can break that bowl, boy. No answer as simple as that." Poor, sweet bird, she thought, what more could she give him? What words to guide him?

"Teach him," Sath whispered.

Jai knelt at the boy's feet and placed one hand on his knee. He was trembling. "I can teach you how to survive this night," she said.

"What should I do?"

"Don't say no to the wind, child. Don't refuse the shadow. Play the music for them, let them have their song through you. Bend like a blade of grass, and they'll let you free for at least a little while."

Dark eyes searched hers. "That's never worked before, has it?"

Wind tore at the shakes. Shadows spread like spilled ink across the ceiling.

"We'll make it work," Jai said. "You are strong enough to bend."

Julian closed his eyes, his mouth tugged down. When he opened his eyes, Jai could see his fear, fresh and sharp. A fear she shared.

Shadows licked out. A lamp dimmed.

"Did you try to break it?" he asked.

"A hundred, hundred times." Beyond the living room, the front door bucked beneath pounding gusts. Instruments within the room rang out in answer.

Julian stood and walked into the living room, facing the door, his back to Jai.

"Did you play the music for them?"

"For a thousand, thousand years." She stepped up behind him and placed her hand on his thin shoulder. Sath had wrapped around Julian's waist and rested his head on the boy's other shoulder.

Hinges groaned, darkness swallowed lamp light.

"Did you try to play it wrong?" Julian asked.

"There is no wrong way to play a dream, child. There is only your way."

The door burst open. Wind stood beyond the doorway, larger than the room could hold. His arms and legs were ragged tornados of dust and dead grasses, his face the flat cold mask of storm. Only his eyes seemed solid, and those were bottomless swirling vortices that drank thought and emptied minds.

Behind him skulked his brother, Shadow. Against the dark of the night, Jai could only see Shadow if he moved, a nightmare shaped like a great cat or monstrous dog, with only the razored glint of fangs and claw to show his passing.

Wind and Shadow strode toward the house.

"Bend child," Jai said, wanting to close her eyes and run from here, but unable to do either beneath the hold of Wind and Shadow. "Play for them."

"Your way," Sath whispered beside the boy's ear.

"My way," Julian said.

He placed his fingers against the strings. But instead of plucking, his fingers lay flat, muting the music, denying the gods.

Wind howled. Shadow swelled and grew, filling the air, until it felt the house would crush beneath the weight of the night.

Jai squeezed Julian's shoulder, hoping to hold him steady against the gods while Sath whispered to him.

"Play," she said again.

Music, soft as a sigh, rose to fill the room. It was not the burning power of Sun's dreams pouring through moonlight strings. It was a softer song, a child's melody. A lullaby.

Julian was singing, his voice sweet and clear, like river against stone, like time against the world.

Please, no, Jai thought, *don't fight the gods.* But Julian did not stop singing. This was his way, his denial of the music, his choice to stand strong and not bend. Just like her other oak-strong boy.

And Sath was singing with him.

Jai could not let them fight alone. She added her warm, low voice to their song. The instruments on the walls echoed the lullaby. Note by note, they stood against the gods. Wind tore at the room trying to stop them. Shadow crushed down.

Still, they sang.

In a moment of song, in a beat of three hearts, Wind and Shadow pulled away from the house.

Julian swayed. "Are they gone?" he asked.

But Jai knew that in only a moment, a beat of three hearts . . .

Wind struck the house. The door exploded. Splinters of wood knifed through the room. Julian cried out, turned toward Jai.

Shadow leapt through the doorway, so hard and cold, it was as if the air was made of claw and ice.

Blinded, deafened, Jai pulled Julian behind her and reached for the bowl in his hands. Her palm touched the strings and moonlight left blistering burns. Wind snatched the bowl from her fingertips and hurled it against the wall. Wind struck her and Jai fell to her knees, holding Julian close to protect him from Wind and Shadow.

Julian struggled free of her grip.

No! she tried to say, but shadow clogged her mouth and the wind stole her words.

One step, two, and Julian was gone. She could not see him, lost to Wind and Shadow, but she could hear him, his halting voice, his soft song.

Wind and Shadow saw him too. They tore out of the house so quickly, the natural darkness brought tears of pain to Jai's eyes. In that light, she saw Julian. He stood in front of the open the door, his clothes tattered, his thin body straight, bloody, Sath wrapped around his chest like braided armor.

In his hands was the moon-strung bowl. He lifted the bowl up above his head and called out.

"I have them! I have all of Sun's dreams and all of the songs."

From the black sky, Moon woke. Moonlight poured over him like platinum fire, the cold cruel eye of a jealous god.

"Julian!" Jai called. "Come back."

He glanced over his shoulder, his dark eyes filled with fear, his mouth set in a thin line. Sath lifted his head and whispered, "Good-bye, forever-companion. I am sorry."

Then the boy turned back to the door and held the bowl out in his hands.

"I won't play for you," he said. "They aren't your dreams to hear." Julian softly sang the lullaby.

Moon's anger was like sharp fingers pressing into Jai's ears. A snap, a flash of pain, and her ears popped and bled. Beyond the door, Wind roared like a great ocean, and the air filled with Shadow, choking out all light except that single beam of ice surrounding Julian and Sath.

Jai pushed up to her feet. She had to pull Julian and Sath away from the moonlight. She couldn't let them die.

Wind and Shadow and Moon pulled back to strike.

"Now!" Sath hissed.

Julian yelled and held the bowl before him like a shield. Wind and Shadow struck. Moonstrings snapped. The bowl shattered. A thousand, thousand glittering dreams fell from between the splinters of wood. All at once, beautiful notes cried out, the pure, the last song of Sun's dreams.

Wood and moonlight sliced through the room, whipped by the wind that battered Julian down to his knees. Jai stumbled toward Julian, but could not reach him through the flying debris.

The walls groaned. Instruments fell and shattered against the floor.

Wind and Shadow clawed into the room, snatching at the remaining bits of the bowl — wood and broken strings that would never sing again — then screamed away to the distant face of Moon. As if released from a spell, clouds crowded the night sky and smothered the moonlight.

When Jai could hear again, when she could see, she found a lamp and match and brought both back to find Julian lying dazed in the middle of the destroyed room.

He was covered in dust and splinters of wood and reed, Sath still wrapped around his thin chest and waist. A trickle of blood ran tracks down his arm and hand, too dark to be his own.

"Sath?" Jai said. Her hands shook as she ran fingers against Sath's cool glossy scales trying to find the source of the bleeding. Not a fast flow, she realized. Just scratches, no deep wounds.

Sath shifted, his head appearing from near the boy's neck. "The child?"

Jai brushed dirt and wood from Julian's hair and felt for his pulse.

"Fine," she said, her voice trembling with relief. "He's fine."

Julian looked up at her, his eyes wide with shock. "Should I go now?"

Jai brushed the dust from his cheek. "No. I think you should stay right here."

"You said there was no place for me here, and your house, the instruments, Sun's dreams. I broke them. I ruined them all," he whispered.

"Hush, child," Jai said, "you didn't ruin anything. You made it right again. Something I'd never been strong enough to do."

"But the music, your music . . ."

"The music wasn't mine. It was Sun's."

She drew him into her arms.

"So I can stay?" Julian asked softly.

"Yes," Jai said.

"And so can the snake?"

Jai brushed her fingers across the top of Sath's head, remembering the hurtful things she had said to him. "If he wants to stay with such a foolish girl."

Sath tipped his head to one side, his dark eyes warm and deep. "I promised a brave girl I would be her forever-companion. My home is here with her."

"Thank you," Jai whispered. And she held the boy and the snake in her arms until Sun walked to the edge of the waking world and brought with him the warmth of day.

The heart of this story came from the concept that life often forces us to change and grow, and sometimes, so does death.

HERE AFTER LIFE

It took the four of them half the day to convince Jim he was them, they were him, and they were all dead. It finally hit home when the twenty-four-year-old guy in cut-offs and no shirt shoved the baby in Jim's hands and said, "You can fucking argue all you want, but I am not looking after this kid anymore."

Jim blinked at the cold familiarity of those words. God, he had been a dick at that age. Luckily, the baby wasn't very heavy, and Jim managed not to drop him. "What am I supposed to do with him?"

"You're the oldest now — you figure it out." Twenty-four-year-old patted the pockets of his cutoffs and fished out a lighter and a crushed pack of cigarettes.

"Hey, I quit," Jim said, nodding toward the cigarette.

Twenty-four-year-old flicked, puffed, and took a long, deep breath. "When you were thirty." The cigarette bobbed between his lips as he spoke. "Too bad for you."

Jim could have strangled him then, if he wasn't, if they weren't, well, if things were different.

Jim looked over at the thirteen-year-old boy who paced at their maximum distance from each other — about four feet. He was mohawked and studded, chains connecting distant body parts. One look brought back the pain, the itch — worse — the snags and embarrassing rips.

Six-year-old Jimmy stood next to Jim and stared at him with a thoughtful expression.

"So this is me — I mean us?" Jim asked Twenty-four-year-old. Talking made his head hurt. They'd said something about a car, but Jim couldn't remember anything before the last few hours when he'd opened his eyes and realized he was sitting out here on the grass median in front of the hospital, surrounded by the four of them.

"That's right," Twenty-four-year-old said around the cigarette. "You catch on quick for an old guy." He walked a short distance away and sat on the fake boulder in front of the Mercy General sign.

The baby in Jim's hands squirmed. Jim looked down at him. Man, he was an ugly kid. Yellow skin, yellow eyes and a head shaped like a number two potato. Jaundice — that's what it was called, a failing of the liver that's usually taken care of with sun lamps and fluids. Had he had a serious case of it when he was born? Jim tried to remember if his mom had ever mentioned it. His thoughts hit a slick wall, and he gave up trying.

Baby made a sour face. He looked like he was going to cry or puke, but instead stared, glassy-eyed, over Jim's shoulder. He seemed awfully calm. Maybe being dead did that to a kid.

"You okay?" Jim jiggled him, but the baby just stared.

"Of course he's not okay, he's dead," the thirteen-year-old said.

Jim managed to tuck the baby up against one shoulder. "Hey, Kid. Since you know so much, how about giving me a hand with the baby?"

Thirteen-year-old stopped pacing. His shoulders hunched in the loose black t-shirt, then he slowly turned, all attitude and hypo-allergenic steel. Black streaks ran down his cheeks from the inmost corner of his eyes, and Jim tried to remember why he'd done the Alice Cooper look. "The name's Fly," he said.

Jim laughed. He'd forgotten about that.

Fly flipped him off and went back to pacing.

Which left six-year-old Jimmy.

"He's okay," Jimmy said. "I watched baby before Fly came, and he watched him until he," he nodded toward Twenty-

four-year-old, "got here. It's not hard. You just have to carry
him. He doesn't eat or mess his diapers, you know."

Jim didn't know, but it made sense, if any of this did. "So
you're the smart guy, huh? Do you have any idea why we're
here, all of us — I mean me — broken apart like this, or what
we're waiting around for?"

Jimmy's brown eyes lost their shine, and his mouth turned
down. Six. The year Dad had flown to London and stayed
there. The year he'd caught pneumonia so bad he passed out
when he tried to stand. His first ambulance ride, his first breathing tube. Six came rushing back to Jim in a way he hadn't
wanted to feel, taste, or remember in years.

"We're not dead enough. Part of us is still alive in there."
Jimmy pointed toward the hospital, and the room Jim vaguely
remembered. Surgery? Had his heart cashed in on its choles-
terol count? No, an accident. Car. Head on. Fifty miles an
hour around the curve from the airport bar. Driving hard. Driving away from Lucy.

"Jeezus," Jim said.

"It's pretty boring most of the time," Jimmy said. "I kinda
hoped we'd die in the car wreck, but we got you instead."

"Thanks," Jim drawled.

Fly scoffed.

Jimmy tipped his head to the side. "Sorry," he said. "It hurt
a lot, didn't it?"

God, Jim thought, how did a sweet little kid like that turn
into thirteen-year-old rivet-face over there? That thought made
Jim think Twenty-four-year-old probably wondered how come
he had to end up forty pounds overweight and saddled to a go-
nowhere mail-clerk job.

"I don't remember the pain much," Jim said to Jimmy. Not
the pain from the accident. Strangely, the pain he remembered
was Lucy's handshake, her tears, her good-bye that ended a
five year relationship. A relationship he'd hoped would last
forever.

Jimmy nodded, an ancient six-year-old pro at all this.

"She was neat," he said softly.

"Lucy?" Jim asked, surprised Jimmy knew what he was thinking.

"Yeah. Why didn't you just give her the ring?"

"People change," Jim said, done talking to the sweet little kid now.

"Hey, Smokes," Jim called to Twenty-four-year old. "What are we doing here?"

Twenty-four-year-old got to his feet with a smooth motion Jim had given up thirty pounds ago. "Let me go through this once." He walked close enough that Jim should be able to smell the cigarette smoke, but no matter how hard he inhaled, he couldn't smell anything.

"We're dead. Can't eat, piss or bleed. We can't get any farther away than about four feet from each other, and have to stay within a couple blocks of our real body — the living us — him." He nodded toward the hospital and took a drag off the cigarette. "My guess is we're stuck this way until the living us — him — dies for good."

"So why aren't we in there?" Jim asked.

"I hate hospitals," Twenty-four-year-old said. He gave Jim a look that said you should know, you should remember.

"I don't care," Jim said, "I'm not just going to wait out here until I — we — die. I want to go in. I want to see me — us — him with my own eyes."

"Weren't you listening? We can't go anywhere unless we go together, and I'm not going in there."

Jim opened his mouth to tell him exactly where he could stick his attitude when Jimmy spoke up.

"Something's wrong with Baby."

"What?" Jim shifted the baby down from his shoulder and held him out along his hand and arm again.

Baby was still yellow, but his eyes were shut, and he seemed even more still than he had been. Jim shook him gently.

"Hey, guy. Wake up."

Baby jiggled, but his eyes stayed shut, his chest still. Jim felt a chill wash over his skin. Baby wasn't breathing.

"Oh man," Fly said, his voice cracking.

"Jeezus," Twenty-four-year-old exhaled.

"Is he . . .are we . . .?" Fly said.

Jim took a breath, held it a minute, trying hard to feel Baby's heartbeat, and not sure that he'd had one before.

Baby began to fade, the edges first, wisping away like fog before a wind, fingers, arms, feet and legs.

"This hasn't happened before," Twenty-four-year-old told Jim, eye to eye, man to man. He tried to look like he could handle it, but he was scared out of his skin and Jim knew it.

"What are we going to do? What's happening to us?" Fly had worked himself up into a scream, and his eyes were suddenly as young as Jimmy's.

Thirteen. The year he'd found Mom's body. The year he'd realized how little justice was in the justice system. The year he'd washed a bottle of Sleepeeze down with two bottles of Nyquil and woke up for the stomach pump.

Jim could taste the charcoal in his throat, the greasy grit against the back of his lips, coating his tongue. He suddenly realized the charcoal streaks down Fly's cheeks weren't mascara.

Fly's hands shook, the chain between his eyebrow and bottom lip trembled. It looked like he was ready to run. Fact was, Jim wanted to run too. Turn his back on all this, on all of them, and just get the hell away from here.

Jimmy's small hand touched Jim's free hand. "Are we dying now?"

The last bit of Baby, his chest and stomach, faded from Jim's left hand and forearm. Jim stared at where Baby had been only a moment before, and felt the dull ping of something deep within himself falling away. Emotional vertigo. He shook his head to clear it, to deny reality, then gave up and let his arm drop.

"Maybe this is the way it works." Jim used his calm voice for Fly and Jimmy, the voice even Lucy believed. "Maybe we'll go one at a time, and that's okay. I mean, Baby lasted thirty-eight years, right?"

"Or there can only be four of us at a time," Twenty-four-year-old said. "Maximum spirit capacity, or some such shit."

Jim voiced a much darker thought. "Maybe something is happening to the living us. A stroke, brain damage, heart attack."

"Fuck," Fly said. He really looked like he needed a smoke.

"Smokes," Jim said, but Twenty-four-year-old was already handing Fly his cigarette. Fly took a couple deep puffs and tried to pull himself together.

"Thanks," Jim said.

Twenty-four-year-old nodded. "Now what?"

Jim could feel Fly glance over at him. Jimmy squeezed Jim's hand.

Twenty-four-year-old didn't break eye contact. He tipped his head toward the hospital. He looked calm and together about it on the outside, even though Jim had a pretty good idea what he felt on the inside.

Jim looked away from him and forced a cheerful note in his voice. "Time to pay ourself a visit, boys." He could tell not even Jimmy bought it.

The three stayed close to Jim. They crossed the thin grassy strip between the parking lot and ER driveway. Their feet made no noise over the grass or the pavement. At the door to ER, Jim put his free hand out to push the door open.

"You don't —" Jimmy said, and then he realized he didn't — didn't have to put his hand out, didn't have to brace for anything — because he was through the glass doors without opening them. He looked over his shoulder and shook his head. Zero sensation. No heat, cold, or anything that indicated they'd just passed through something solid.

"Is it always like that?" Jim asked.

Fly shrugged. "What did you expect?"

They walked through the hospital, and Jim had the strange feeling that the building moved around them more than they moved through it. After a few floors, he got used to the way it worked, and then it felt predictable, if not exactly normal. Except for having no need to open doors, they navigated the hospital like living people, hallways and doors, white signs with arrows and names. Jim took his time, trying to think.

Why hadn't he just died like he'd always thought he would — in one piece, at one time — at least as one person for Godsake. Was he afraid to die? Despite Fly's reaction, he'd never really been afraid of death, had long ago accepted its inevitability. What then? Why was he becoming ghosts of himself?

Fifth floor. Jim could feel a difference here, and knew without looking at the sign-in board that his living self must be close. He made his way down the hall, and took the turn to the left. Outside a plain blonde wood door, he paused.

His heart, which he hadn't noticed during the walk, the stairs, or any other time, suddenly squeezed tight, like the stress-attacks he used to get.

"Damn," he whispered.

Fly nodded, and Twenty-four-year-old said, "Did I mention it hurts?"

Jimmy's hand seemed lighter all of a sudden.

Jim looked down at him, and Jimmy tipped his head up and smiled. Jim swore he could see the shine of the floor through his face.

"I'm okay," Jimmy said.

Did he seem more pale than he had been moments before, his skin translucent? Jim hesitated.

"Listen," Twenty-four-year-old said, "Either get this over with now, or we're getting the hell out of here."

Jim suddenly remembered Twenty-four. The year he'd gone fishing with the guys on the North Santiam. The year the air was filled with a mother's scream and a little girl slipped through the rapids. He had jumped. A face flashed by, then the orange of a life jacket. Jim grabbed. The girl slipped from his grip, and he was pulled under into cold blackness. Two months later he woke up in the hospital. He'd missed the girl's funeral, and spent his last year of college learning to walk again.

Twenty-four-year-old exhaled, long and slow, like he didn't know what Jim was remembering. "Well?" Twenty-four-year-old asked.

Jim took a deep breath. This was like that jump, except

there was no way he could guess at the dangers beyond the door. He tightened his grip on Jimmy's hand and walked through.

All the things he'd expected to be in the room were there. The bland wallpaper, the dull glossed floor, the I.V. stand, the bed. And in the bed, a man.

Jim stared across the room at himself. The pain in his chest tightened. He felt too hot, too cold, and sick enough to puke. He had accepted that he wasn't alive, but to see himself lying there, bandaged, tubed, but breathing, and so utterly alive — it all seemed wrong.

This, this . . . imposter was going to finish his life, make his decisions, do the things he'd put off for later, or worse, never do them at all.

Screw that.

Shock gave way to anger.

Jim strode forward. The pain in his chest tightened the nearer he came to his living self.

He leaned over the bed, his hands extended. He didn't know exactly what he was planning to do — maybe shake him, maybe choke the life out of him.

Just before his fingers touched his living flesh he heard Twenty-four-year-old say, "Do it."

Fly said, "Shit," and Jimmy whispered, "Oh, no."

Jim did it anyway. His hands sank into his living chest. A hot electric wave crashed down over him. There was a slippery moment of vertigo while he fell and fell, too far, out to the edge of a shocking coldness. Then he turned and willed himself up, to the heat, to the electric pulse and buzz of blood and cell, to the cluttered, noisy thoughts, the pain, the breath. To living.

Jim took a breath. It was harsh, dry. He coughed and tasted the stale breeze from the oxygen tube. The machine beep was suddenly loud, the bed beneath him hard, the stiff sheets rough against his skin, skin that felt wrong, too heavy, too hot.

Was he alive? He opened his eyes. The ghosts were there, Fly and Twenty-four-year-old and Jimmy, leaning down over him. They were real enough he could see the surprise in Jimmy's eyes.

"Wow," Jimmy mouthed.

Jim tried to speak. Don't leave, he tried to say, to think, to make them understand, but his throat was raw, his tongue swollen. Exhaustion tugged at his mind, and he felt sleep sliding inexorably closer.

Twenty-four-year-old raised an eyebrow and looked at Fly.

Did they hear him? Jim tried again to speak, but not even a moan made it past his lips.

The ghosts leaned down over him, so close they seemed to blend into one person, a mix of piercing and innocence and calm eyes.

Don't go, Jim tried to say, but his mouth filled with the taste of charcoal and the oxygen tube smelled like smoke. He thought he heard a baby cry and Jimmy laugh, then sleep welled over him and took him down into darkness.

"So, can I go home yet?" Jim asked. He'd already spent a week sleeping and recovering. Today he felt more whole than he had in a long time.

The doctor looked up from the clipboard and smiled. "Not yet, but sooner than you think. How does day after tomorrow sound to you?"

"Couldn't be better," Jim said.

"Good." The doctor turned to the door. "Just call the nurses if you need anything — and Jim, stick to the speed limit from now on." The doctor stepped out of the room.

Jim nodded. There were a lot of things he planned on doing better. He picked up the pen and pad of paper next to his bed and wrote the numbers one through twenty down one side of the page. He penned: "Call Lucy" after number five.

He still had the ring at home on his dresser. He would ask her. Not this week, but not never either. First they would have to really get to know each other again. He had a feeling she'd be surprised at how much he'd changed.

Before that though, he wanted to try for a better position at work, or maybe do a little traveling.

Jim moved the pen between one and five, letting his thoughts wander. Should he start his own business? Buy a house?

He rested the pen against his lips, and re-read his list.

A chill washed over his skin. Written neatly after number one, two and three were the words: Finish college, Pierce ear, Eat ice cream.

Jim glanced up at the mirror across the room. He saw four much younger versions of himself, layered within his reflection.

"How about ice cream first?" he said. And all of Jim grinned.

The Wordos writers group occasionally threw down the gauntlet and challenged each other to write to a specific theme. One such challenge was themed "junkyard planet." That was the spark for this story of freedom, hope, and love thriving in a world filled with ugliness and danger.

FALLING WITH WINGS

My eldest uncle, Setham, said he usually had to dig for the babies, but when he found me I was mostly on top of the muck and staring up at the sky from where I'd fallen. He said I never cried.

Before he turned me over to the raising girls — aunties and sisters and nieces — he stopped by the pipe that stuck out of the piles of broken concrete and washed me off. Then he slathered a thick coat of grease over me from the plastic jug he keeps in his pack. Blessed me and tucked me in a sling against his chest while he took me back to the blocks. Walked the whole way because, even then, Setham didn't have wings.

The raising girls thought it beyond thoughtful of him to bring me in clean and greased thick enough the flies wouldn't bite my tender skin.

"Anointed," they'd said, "one of us now." They named me Dawn.

So caught with my cleanliness and Setham's thoughtfulness, the raising girls didn't bless me as women bless women, as girls bless girls, fingers between fingers, breathing each other's exhales with heads bent in close, giving that sure feeling of being accepted, safe, sistered.

Maybe that was how the difference inside of me started. The difference I couldn't push away, sing away, nor carry up Mount Discard and heave over the side to watch it fall into the heaps of junk below.

When I was old enough, I asked Setham why he cleaned me up like that, and he said with a face so straight you wouldn't think it could hold his quick smile, "Did it to get an extra scoop of sweetberries for dessert."

His smile flashed, was gone again. "Got it, too."

Then he went off to the birthing soils, walking all day through the fields of garbage, clambering up rotted hills and wading waist deep through oil, sewage and the burning mix of chemicals that bleed out of the walls of garbage. Dead things, broken things, rust and filth bob in the muck and sewage, stare with tumored eyes, cut, sting, bite. Setham leaves the home blocks every day to dig sky babies out of that muck.

Finds them, too. Enough babies that each of us girls had to become a raising girl, so all the babies got fed and cleaned and watched and taught. The boys, the uncles, brothers, nephews, take care of hunting and trapping rats and bringing in the buckets of drinking water from the copper pipes that stick out of concrete. We all scrounge for things needed for living: squares of clear plastic, heavy blankets scrubbed and cleaned until they don't move on their own any more, shoes with good strong soles, steel marbles, and strange things of twisted metal and plastic that became chairs, walls, and more.

Doesn't always go that way. Sometimes the boys get into the raising, and the girls get into the hunting. Sometimes the boys fall into scorpion holes, or rats chew them apart. Sometimes the girls die of the fever that comes from handling the babes and not staying clean enough.

I am fifteen now, and I raise the babes and teach the old songs. Not the songs that drift down on a good wind from the sky above the brown clouds. I teach the old songs, songs whispered from lips to ears by uncles and aunts who long ago climbed Mount Discard, spread their shuddering new wings, and vaulted up to the skyworld to see if the sky was any different on the other side.

I teach songs of patience of pain. Of mud and toxweed milk and hunger and sharp things waiting just below the soft of the world.

Songs about the summer flower you ache to smell but burns you blind if you get too close, the spring and autumn thorns and the wild winter dogs that tear out baby hearts and crush bone and skull.

I teach the real songs. Dirt songs.

Sometimes, I imagine that my aunts and uncles, gone to wing, sing down to me in the night to call me up. It is a childish thought, to wish those with wings would remember their birthing soil, would remember the songs they taught, or the babes they raised.

Fifteen, and I am the oldest girl.

Bell who was three years older than me, walked to Mount Discard today. We waited at the flat beyond the blocks, the babies at our feet fussing some, playing some, while Bell walked to the mountain. Took her most of an hour to get there, and another hour to scramble up to the flat wedge of metal that crowns the mountain top. She didn't wait, didn't wave. She just ran and jumped off the mountain. Fell so fast, my heart stopped beating to see her drop. Setham was next to me, and I saw his wingless back stiffen, his hands curl into fists, as if it was his fault she hadn't lifted up to the sky.

Ten-year-old Jarn, who was Bell's favorite nephew, said, "No."

I took Jarn's hand in my own, felt how little and cold it was.

We waited while our hearts beat. No flutter of wings. No stir in the distant air. Bell had fallen below our line of sight. Had broken herself, was probably dead.

Reez, who is nearly fifteen, spat. "Stupid. She should have practiced more." Reez never smiled unless he was killing rats. He smiled now. "I get her wings."

"No!" Jarn screamed.

"Wait," Setham said, his gaze still locked on the foot of Mount Discard.

Reez scowled. We waited. The babies sitting at our feet or tied to our chests made baby sounds — oblivious to Reez's anger, Setham's focus, or Bell's fall.

"Stupid," Reez said again, this time looking straight at Setham who would not look away from Mount Discard.

"There," Setham said.

Bell beat her way up from the hold of the earth, her wings crooked and out of rhythm, her head bent down to her chest, her arms tight against her ribs, as if every ounce of thought, every bit of her strength was in her wings — pumping her up the slippery sky.

"Go," Jarn said. "Fly!"

We watched until she was swallowed by the greasy brown clouds.

"Patience," Setham said, leveling such a look at Reez, "isn't stupid."

"You should know," Reez said.

"If I had not been patient, you would not be here," Setham's voice was low and quiet, and stronger than a yell.

And Reez knew that. He'd asked Setham to tell him the story of his birth-find over and over again. How Reez had landed deep in the muck. How Setham dug harder and faster than ever before. How the muck was so wet, the hole kept filling in. How finally, he had pulled Reez out, bruised and cut, his baby eyes swollen shut and blood coming out of his ears. That Reez survived because he was strong.

Usually the story put Reez in his place, reminded him who he was in our family. Not today. Reez started pacing, like he couldn't hold still, like he didn't want either foot to be on the ground for too long.

I let Jarn lean against me and put my arm over his thin shoulders.

"You know what I saw today?" Reez said.

The other children, most just babies except for Iya, who was seven, shook their heads.

"A little bitty baby rat. Didn't have no front feet." He pulled his arms into his shirt so the sleeves flapped loose. The babies smiled.

"Do you think his feet are going to grow? Maybe catch up with him while he's crawling, face in the muck?"

The babies shook their heads. The aunts and uncles, ten other girls and six boys, all younger than me by a year and more, smiled at Reez's story.

"No? Not even if he's patient?"

The babies shook their heads.

Setham stiffened at that, his wingless back straight.

"You're right," Reez said. "And his litter mates knew his feet wouldn't ever grow too. So they ate him." He sprang forward, all teeth and hard smile, bent over the babies, sleeves flapping.

The older babies squealed in terrified delight. Some started crying. The uncles and aunts laughed.

"Reez," I said, "stop that."

Reez looked up at me, bent so that his shirt was tight against his back and I could see his wing buds, like two angry fists between his shoulder blades. He would be a man soon, would take to the sky.

Setham could see them too. Which was Reez's point.

"Just telling a story, Dawn," Reez said. "Patience doesn't make feet."

"And stories don't make brains." I regretted the words immediately.

Reez's eyes hardened until they matched his killing smile. He straightened, looked at me, then looked at Setham.

"What have I missed lately?" he asked. "Did you crawl into her blanket, Setham?"

"Enough!" I said, hot-faced at the insult. "You know the rules. I'd stab him if he tried." Wouldn't I? Wouldn't I stab my favorite uncle if he touched my cheek softly, traced his hands down my back?

"Napping time now, babies," I said, before Reez could come up with more nonsense. The other raising girls plucked up their babies or held onto the children's hands. Jarn pulled away from me and looked up. He was ten, too old to be treated as a babe. I took his hand anyway. It wasn't easy to watch your favorite aunt or uncle fly away. He squeezed my fingers and was silent as we started back to the blocks. I crooned to him about to-morrow skies, hellos and good-byes.

Neither Reez nor Setham followed us. When I looked back, Reez was walking the other way, his shirt off, his budding wings red and sore at the base of his shoulders and curled like new thistle leaves reaching up toward his neck.

Setham just stood there, like he was rooted to the ground, his face tipped to the mountain, to the sky where Bell had just been.

The babies went to sleep easily and the other boys coaxed Jarn into a game of sticks and marbles. Melda said she'd watch the babies while the other raising girls strained the greens for dinner. I went for Bell's things. She hadn't left much behind, but tradition says all left-behinds go to the big room where anybody can take what they wanted.

I picked up the basket of her stuff: a square of soft red cloth, a perfectly round silver disk, a piece of charcoal, four cups, and a string of metal bars so thin they rang out when the wind touched them. I wondered if Jarn had had a chance to look through her things. I took out the red cloth and put it on Jarn's blanket, then I walked through the low-ceiling maze of plastic walls to the center of our home.

I had not expected Setham to be looking at his naked body in the broken mirrors that covered the wall from ceiling to floor. He was turned so he could look at his own back. He had strong, straight limbs, a wide-shouldered torso and a flat, muscled stomach.

He caught sight of my reflection. His look was angry, then ashamed, and he picked up his breeches from the floor and covered his groin. I could still see his butt and his long, lean, wingless back in the mirror.

"Didn't know you'd come in," I said, trying to make my voice normal.

He must have bathed recently because I could see the color of his blush. His hair brushed over his eyebrows, long enough to hood his eyes when he tipped his head down.

I felt a curious, quick heat below my stomach, and knew I was blushing too. Was this the lust that drew the wings to the sky, to mate, to join, to drop their babies here in the compost and let them be raised by aunties and uncles with no wings of their own?

"Dawn, please don't tell," he said.

I nodded, unable to keep from snatching glances of his back, so odd and beautiful, with all the muscles of a man, but no wings. His thighs and calves were spread just enough, and bunched tight enough, it looked like they alone could carry him into flight.

I shrugged. "I don't have any wings."

"Yet," he said.

"Yet."

"But you still have time."

"So do you." I didn't remind him that he was older than me, older than the oldest girl who hadn't thrown herself off Mount Discard.

"Do you know how many aunts and uncles I have seen take wing?"

I shook my head.

"Thirty." He said it again, softer, as if it were a number he'd never heard before: "Thirty. And all of them were your age, Dawn. Not old, like me."

I put the basket down and stepped closer to him, to my brother-uncle, older than me all my life, strong and patient as he scoured the earth for pieces of the sky.

"You are not old, Sethem. Maybe twenty-one?"

"Twenty-five."

"You will fly. You have wings here." I pressed my fingertips against his chest, over his heart. I could feel the heat from his skin and the rhythm of his blood pumping. He took a small, quick breath. His eyes closed. He placed the fingers of his left hand over mine — his other hand still holding breeches against him.

"Dawn," he whispered.

"Found a new nest of rats," a voice called out from the door.

I jerked, and Setham's head snapped up to look over my shoulder at who had just walked in.

Reez's scowl shifted to a hard, wide smile. I saw him in the mirror behind Setham, and knew he saw Setham's naked back.

I turned, and stepped to block Reez's view of the mirror. "Enough for dinner?" I asked.

"Killed them all," he said, gaze still on Setham. "Worked up a hard hunger." Reez's hands, dirty with rat blood, clenched and unclenched.

"I'll help you clean them and start the fire," I said.

"You got babies to watch?" he asked.

"Not right now, they're sleeping."

I walked over to him, caught my fingers around his hard wrist. The rat blood stank like burnt hair. I slid my hand into his hand. There was a change in his face then, a hunger that was frightening and hot. I'd seen it before, from the men on the edge of wings. It was a look only the sky cured.

"Leave us, Dawn," Setham said. "Reez and I need to talk."

I looked over at Setham, and he was the uncle I had always known, patient and strong. He was taller than Reez, and stronger, I now realized. But the smell of blood and Reez's fists made me hesitate.

There was nothing in tradition about this, nothing in the old songs that talked of men hating men, of wings and no wings. I felt outside this, alone. Scared.

"Dawn," Setham said again in a tone I had obeyed since birth, "go start the fire. We'll be out soon enough."

I walked out. But I went around to the back halls behind the big room and pressed into the little space between two walls, where the plastic and cardboard weren't strong enough to keep me out. I pressed my forehead against the wall and listened.

". . . elder," Setham said. "You are not the first to want my place, Reez."

"I don't want your place. I want you dead."

"You want Dawn. Have for years."

That startled me. Reez and I had been babes together. Sibs. I'd never thought of him as a man wanting until today.

"You don't understand," Reez growled.

"Because I don't have wings?" Setham laughed, but it was a hollow sound. "I understand, Reez. Even without wings. And I've made my choices. One of them involves you."

"I don't want any part of you, Setham."

"I'm leaving tonight."

It felt as if all the world shook out from under my feet.

"Dawn will be the eldest instead of me. You will listen to her and obey her as your elder. She will now make the rules and the decisions. You will not touch her. It is forbidden." Then his voice changed to the familiar, kind uncle.

"I know you can wait for that knowing, that touching, until you wing," Setham said. "You are strong enough. You belong to the sky. Don't tie yourself to the earth."

It was all I could stand to hear. I pushed away from the wall and walked away. I heard the babies crying, and the raising girls' voices shushing. I wanted to walk and keep on walking, away from the blocks where suddenly I was the oldest, to a place, a somewhere no one could take away, leave or change. But I had a fire to start and rats to clean.

By the time night came on, all the brothers and sisters and babies had gathered around the cooking pit while the sky above brooded red and orange.

The smell of cooked rat and stewed toxweed filled the air. I held Shida in my arms. She was two years old already, and loved to run. I could usually make her hold still for meals, but she was wriggling to get free tonight, and I wasn't doing much to keep her still.

Reez turned the rats on the spit. His face was dark as night in the orange of the fire and his eyes looked at me with regret when he thought I didn't see.

I looked for Setham.

Once the meal was cooked, the babies settled down a bit, and even little Shida quieted. We fed them toxweed boiled milky blue. We scooped the soft sweet weed into the babies mouths, and they suckled the juice. The older babies helped themselves to the plate of rat and greens, happy and unaware that something had just changed, something more than another aunt flying away.

Reez knew though. And so did I.

Setham melted in from the shadows, his shirt off, and wearing only breeches and boots. The babies looked up at him and called his name. He was their favorite uncle. He brought them new brothers and sisters, and would lift each of them high in his arms and spin them, laughing, whenever they asked.

Setham smiled as three of the babies ran to him and tugged him over to the fire.

He turned enough that I could see the hard, bare muscles of his back. No wings. Showing all the others his lack and wordlessly telling them he would leave on foot instead of air. My stomach felt cold, and the smell of dinner made me ill.

"Dawn will be the elder now," Setham said. Everyone nodded.

Reez said nothing, though I caught his satisfied smirk.

I ate a little toxweed and drank warm water, but couldn't stomach my worry.

At the end of the meal, Melda and the other raising girls gathered the babies and took them off to tuck under thick blankets. The other boys touched Setham's hand or shoulder, saying their good-byes in the way boys do, with nods and thin smiles. Jarn was the last. He threw his arms around Setham and drew him into a tight hug.

"I'll miss you," Jarn said.

"I'll remember you," Setham replied.

Jarn released him and dashed off after the other boys.

Reez stood and stretched.

"Good-bye, Setham. Enjoy the wilds." He whistled as he walked away, his stride confident, strong.

I shook my head. "I'm sorry, Setham."

"For what? I have no wings. So long as I don't throw myself off Mount Discard, I won't die of it." His smile was quick and warm.

He took the few steps to lower himself next to me, his knees folded criss-cross, facing the coals of the cook fire.

"You're leaving tonight?" I asked.

"I should. Though I worry about Reez."

We were silent a while.

"Has he touched you, Dawn?"

I shook my head. "I'd stab him — any of the girls would — then we'd throw him in a scorpion hole."

Setham chuckled. "You have grown. I'll miss seeing you in wings."

I reached out for his hand, and we twined fingers. His fingers were long and strong, and warmer than mine. They felt fine and right between my own. I felt accepted, blessed, belonged.

"I would go with you," I whispered.

He tilted a look at me. "Did I ever tell you how I came to the blocks?"

I shook my head.

"I wasn't brought here like the babies. No uncle or aunt found me. I walked in on my own."

"That can't be. Only babies come here."

"I remember the skyworld, Dawn. I remember my mother. She said I was five years old — too old to hide in the sky any longer. I remember the day she brought me down to the wilds, and winged away."

"Why would your mother keep you that long?"

Setham shrugged again. "I think if babies are to wing, they must be very young when they come to their birth soil. The wings are in this place somewhere. Maybe in the water, the sun, the toxweed juice. Something about this place has wings in it. But not if you're brought here too late. Not for men like me."

I held his hand and leaned my head so that it rested against the round of his shoulder. We sat there as the fire burned down to darkness.

He turned and helped me up to my feet.

"You never said I couldn't go with you." I searched his eyes. Was I his favorite niece? Could I hope I was more than that?

He brushed one finger over my cheek. "Look down on me when you reach the sky, Dawn. I'll be looking up for you."

He turned and picked up his shirt and pack. Then he walked away.

A baby squalled and another took up the cry. I took a deep breath. There were babies to tend, and food to find. Someone else would have to walk out into the junk and stink to find the babies before the dogs or rats did. I had a lot of decisions to make, people to care for. And I didn't have time to cry because an uncle was walking out of my world instead of flying.

I strode back to the blocks, to the bawling babies, and tried to ignore the strange itch that plucked at my shoulder blades.

When I turned eighteen, and Reez had long taken to the sky, I left the blocks behind me. I gave each of the babies a kiss, and Jarn, who was thirteen and equal to my height, held out a square of red cloth.

"It was Bell's," he said.

"I remember." The cloth was worn, the edges frayed. "Don't you want to keep it?"

He shrugged. "I'll go find her in a couple years." At my look, he grinned sheepishly. "I have her chimes too."

I smiled.

"I'll miss you," I said.

"I'll remember you," he replied. Then, with a smile, "Fly well, Dawn."

I walked away to Mount Discard. My wings had come in slow, but were strong and silky yellow. The wind felt wonderful as it stirred against them, and I stretched them out to unfurl above my head, then tucked them back again, enjoying the pure motion, the inherent promise of flight.

Mount Discard grew larger and larger as I neared it. Once I made it to its base, it took me all afternoon to clamber over the broken bits of metal, wire and chunks of rot and filth until I finally reached the top.

I paused there, all the wilds of my world spread out before me. I clutched the red cloth tight in one fist.

I pushed out, and fell. My wings fanned wide, caught too much air, and I hissed from the jerk of pain that stitched my spine and stomach. I pulled my arms in, and remembered to angle my wings, cutting the air, catching half, just enough, that I could push against it and up. Thermals cupped me, warm like fire, like a hand, and lifted me as I shuddered and sweated, and learned my own body in the wind.

For three days I flew above the wilds, always below the ceiling of brown clouds. It would be easy to slip upward, to see, just once, what color the sky was on the other side. But I kept my gaze on the Earth, looking for something else.

The wilds here were made of stone. Empty stone streets, empty stone houses and stone rivers filled with water that was green and almost clear. Beside the river was a square of bare soil that looked as if it had been dug into rows. And at one end of that soil was a man.

I tucked my wings and landed on my feet a short distance in front of him.

He looked up from his work, rocks in both hands. His eyes narrowed, and then his mouth smiled and he laughed.

I smiled back.

"Dawn?"

"I saw you from above. You weren't looking up."

He tossed the rocks on a pile beyond the dirt and walked closer to me.

"What beautiful wings," he said, his voice as kind and gentle as I had remembered. "You must be the envy of every man in skyworld."

I looked away.

"You have gone to skyworld, haven't you, Dawn?" This now, disapproving.

I looked back at him, my gaze level. "No. Nor do I intend to."

Shetham blinked. "You have wings . . ."

"I love you. I always have. Don't look at me like that. I know what happens in the skyworld. I know I should rise up and find a mate and have a baby and drop it in the birthing soil. And I know the men who have gone there. Reez. Others. Hungry men. Angry men."

"Dawn." He shook his head.

"And I know you." I stepped forward and caught his hands in mine, afraid of his answer and needing him to feel me, to understand me. His hands were stronger than I remembered and he smelled of rich brown dirt that was new to me, and the familiar sweet-sour musk of his own sweat.

"Can you love me even though I have wings?"

Setham gazed at my face. "You'll want more than me someday. You'll want the sky."

"Don't tell me what I want. I know my own heart, Setham. It is not in the sky. It never has been."

"You've given this some thought."

"Years."

He drew me into his arms. He was warm and smooth-muscled, and his fingers over my shirt found the curve of the small of my back, then ventured sweetly up to where the base of my wings pushed through my shirt.

I drew my own hands up from the side of his hips to his back, and savored the long wingless curve of his spine.

"If you decide to go . . ."

"I won't. But I'd take you with me," I said.

Setham pulled back just enough that he could study my face again. Finally, like a slow seep of water through the soil, he smiled. "I believe you would," he said. And the reflection of the sky and earth in his eyes was brown and warm and home.

The women of Nebraska did something heartfelt and remarkable during World War II. Upon hearing their sons would be on the next train through town on the way to deployment overseas, they gathered together and cooked a big meal: cookies, cakes, hot coffee and more to give them before they left. Even though they discovered their sons were not on that train, they invited the soldiers in for the feast. Thus began a tradition. Every time the train stopped in town, the women from miles around were there, offering up a home cooked meal, music, and birthday cake before the soldiers went to war. I found myself thinking about the boys who passed through town on that train and never came home again. This is their story.

WHEN THE TRAIN CALLS LONELY

It's Johnny's words I hear every morning, before the Nebraska night has given up to the pale light of day. His voice draws me out from under my wool blanket and across the wood floor worn down to slivers. I quickly pull into my day stockings and trousers — my night gown's too short now that I've done some growing and spreading — and the cold air snaps welts across my bare skin. Fifteen. A woman. Old enough to be a wife. Old enough to be Johnny's wife. As soon as he comes home.

It's his words that keep me hoping. Hoping for a life better than the one I got dropped into. The McMahons took me in, put me up instead of killing me, like maybe they ought of. They had a big farm, cows and chickens and pigs. The Missus pushed out a baby every spring up until the year I got there. There was a lot of unborn babies that year, too many. If the Missus hadn't been walking the creek grieving, I'd probably still be where my own kin left me, squalling by the tracks.

'Course then maybe I wouldn't have to worry about Johnny. Worry about whether he was coming home in the day or the night. Alive or dying.

A train called out, low and lonely. It would be daylight soon. I pulled on my boots and laced them up.

Talcum didn't do much to cover the color of my skin, not fair enough for most folks' tastes. And my eyes, well, folk looked away from them. I'd taken a hand mirror out to the fields one day and spent time looking at my eyes. Strange color, yellow as river sand with flecks of green. I didn't see the power of them. But when I looked too long at someone, they looked away, and soon as I was gone, they'd whisper about who my kin might be and why I'd been left behind.

Johnny had come into town young, his whole family down to just him and his dad. Some folks said they were drifters, but they took on quick with the elder Smiths up the road and stepped right up to keep Mr. and Mrs. Smith's small farm in shape. Johnny's dad was good with fixing fences, and his drinking didn't mostly get in the way. I'd been taught to mind my manners and elders, so I never brought it up. The other McMahon young waved it in the air like a sweaty rag whenever Johnny came to school, and Johnny, he just kept his head up, and pretended he didn't hear them.

I never said anything when Johnny walked by because he had my breath, and I couldn't get it back when I looked at him. It'd been years like that, Johnny walking by, growing straighter, taller, stronger, and me standing like a shadow, unbreathing, quiet as water stilled at the sight of him.

The summer I turned thirteen, I spent days practicing how I'd say hello to him. I snuck out behind the barn and held my breath until I nearly passed out. Then I made myself say hello. Over and over. None of the McMahon young found me at it. None of them had time to, what with the war needing every able-bodied man and boy.

That year, Mr. McMahon took to his bed, and it was all any of us could do to keep up for him. We stayed by his side every hour of the day, so he wouldn't slip too far into the dreaming lands. Sometimes in the night, Mr. McMahon would look at me, his cloudy eyes going blue, hard and clear, and tell me the dreams he saw. I got to thinking that those dreams might be a fine place to be. Got to thinking that maybe that's where all the townfolk's unborn babies might be, staying in the warm and softness of that world, instead of coming over into the hard light of ours.

On a warm June day, when I should have been minding my chores, I stood out beneath the hackberry tree by the road and waited. Off far and lonely, I could hear the train calling out. Like a wolf who lost its mate, but didn't know any better than to go on keening, looking for a life long spent. Like a soul coming down the living tracks from the dreaming world.

Johnny walked up the road from out of town, his boots kicking up dirt too lazy to lift, a new pitchfork slung across his wide shoulders. I stepped out into the street. My heart rattled my breastbone so hard, my cotton dress trembled. All the rest of me trembled with it. Johnny looked up at me and nodded, and then my breath was gone, caught up in the force of him, like he was hard wind coming down to suck away the sweet summer breezes in me.

But I'd practiced — I'd spent days practicing. I bit the inside of my cheek and exhaled.

"Hello," I said.

"Morning," Johnny said, and that word sang in me.

"I suppose I'd like to be your wife," I said. That was beyond manners. No girl ever asked a man to betroth, but summer was getting on, and soon winter would fall. I didn't know if I'd ever get my breath back to ask him again, to even speak to him, so I'd taken my chance.

Johnny got still. Camped back on one foot and looked at me.

The train called out again and I could hear the engine now, feel it deep under the soles of my feet, moving the world as it came. I thought right then if Johnny said no, I'd find the train and take it out of here, out of this hard living world to a place of dreams.

"You want a man who doesn't have more than the clothes on his back?" He shook his head, slow. "Not much of a husband, Elisabeth. Not enough for a McMahon." He looked off over my shoulder, back at our big two story house, recently painted white, with the clean picket fence around. The Missus liked showing the neighbors we had enough. Enough and some to spare. But it wasn't like that. We got by from the farm okay, but with Mr. McMahon's sickness, and the two oldest boys, Jacob and Matthew, joining the war, and the next two boys soon to go, things had been falling by the side. Too many things.

"When I'm enough," Johnny said in a way that made me think he'd said those words before, maybe enough that he'd worn them in, nice and comfortable. "I'll come back for you. Then I'll marry you, Elisabeth McMahon, and we'll have children of our own." Johnny walked off, a cool wind following him.

All I could think was I wasn't a McMahon, not really a McMahon, but what nerve I'd had was gone, leaving me still as a lake, staring hungry at a sky that would not give up its rain.

It was that night Mr. McMahon left us. I sat in the rocking chair in his room when he pulled free of his bed, free of his covers and his mortal shell. He stood, wearing his Sunday best and stretched his arms out like he'd just had a good long sleep. He turned to look at me, blue eyes hard, clear.

The train called, far off and lonely, and he looked that way, toward the sound.

"I'll be going now, Elisabeth." His voice was stronger than I ever remember hearing it. "You tell them I'll miss them."

"Don't go. Please." I stood and held a hand out for him. He didn't say he was going to miss me, the orphan daughter who did not carry his blood. The girl who saw the dying as well as the living. "Just settle back under the covers and I'll fetch the Missus. She wouldn't like you leaving without saying goodbye."

Mr. McMahon smiled and his eyes were no longer hard. "She'll see me yet. For now, I have a road to be walking, and my boys to see." He touched my hand with his fingers, and it was like winter breathing ice across my palm, burning cold.

Then he wasn't standing there talking to me anymore. When I looked over to his bed, he wasn't breathing either.

I cried myself into the Missus' room. Those of us left, the McMahon women, spent the next few days quiet, or in tears, cooking and cleaning for the funeral. We kept to ourselves, like five strangers in the same house not knowing what to say to each other. Silence took up the space where Mr. McMahon used to be, and none of us had the strength to chase it out.

Johnny did not come to the funeral. It was the next day I found out why. He'd gone off and joined the war.

Seemed like all the men left town over the next few weeks, leaving women and boys and old men behind. The school rooms echoed, and the only voices in the halls, in the churches, were soft and high.

I took to staying home more. Days I worked the farm the way the McMahon men would have, and nights I spent writing letters to Johnny, though I didn't know where to send them.

Johnny's dad took his leaving hard. I went out in the fields to visit him, to bring him rolls, or fresh milk. But he turned those things away, and pulled close to drinking instead.

Each day he drank a little more and worked a little less. So I took to helping him, working the elder Smith's farm every day after I finished my chores at home. I thought maybe I could give Johnny's dad some strength for living, but soon, he just sat and drank, and watched me do his work. The work Johnny used to do.

Last I saw Johnny's dad, was late one night by my bedside. He had his hat in his hands. He stood there though my door had not opened, solemn, shaking his head, dressed in a Sunday best I'd never seen him wear.

"Tell him I love him, Elisabeth," he said.

I nodded. It was the most he'd ever said to me.

"And I'm proud of him. I've always been proud of him."

"Yes sir," I said.

The train called loud, heading out, and he looked that way, just like Mr. McMahon had a month earlier. He put his hat on his head, and while I watched, he wasn't there any more.

They said he'd taken his bottle down to the tracks earlier that night. Passed out. They said the conductor never even saw him.

There wasn't enough of him left for a burial, but we did what we could. The elder Smiths made sure he had a sturdy coffin, likely one of their own they'd been saving. They made sure he had a grave up on the hill too, not down by the creek where it floods every spring.

I stood there after the burial, hurting, for myself, Mr. McMahon, for Johnny. Hurting for Johnny's dad who couldn't believe his son was coming home. I did not know how one heart could hurt so much and still keep on beating.

But the days still came and I found myself mending fences, pitching hay, feeding cattle. I did it for the Smiths who insisted on paying me a small wage. I did it for Johnny's dad who had ran out of strength for living. But more, I did it for Johnny, hoping if I did it good enough, he'd come home to me.

After three months, my hands were strong as any man's, and my height was coming on. I forgot what it was like to wear a skirt, and wore my older brother's trousers, hemmed and taken in at the waist. I cut my hair to keep it out of the way of the men's work we all had to do: fixing and running the farm and equipment, slaughtering and packing, delivering goods, budgeting, planting, and paying the bills. Missus kept a tight hand on our meals. She prided herself on always having something left in the ration books each month, enough sugar she could make up dozens of cookies to mail off to Jacob and Matthew, and the two younger boys, Seth and Roy. She always had enough left to give out at gatherings, at funerals.

She even came upon the idea to meet the train on its stop at the depot each day. She'd take a dozen cookies, some apples, or what extra we had to give to the boys leaving for war. All the other McMahon girls helped her at it, and eventually all the women in town pitched in, bringing what they had to the depot, meeting the men on every train that stopped. All the women helped, except me. I didn't think I could look at those men's faces. Look at them and know they might not make it back home.

I never said so to the Missus, but I already saw the men at night. Lots of men, some young, some old, all of them stopping by my room on their way to dying. They came by when the train rumbled through town. They stood by my bed wearing their Sunday best, and every one of them had things they wanted me to tell their kin. I don't know who told them to stop by and talk to me before they moved on to the dream world. I thought maybe it was Mr. McMahon, and thinking that made me feel good, like it was his way of saying he missed me.

I kept paper and pen under my pillow, and took down names, addresses, and the things that needed to be said. I bought stationery, envelopes, and stamps with the money the elder Smiths paid me. I put the letters in the mail each week. On the envelopes I wrote "Yours, Most Sincerely." I felt like I was doing some small good, doing my part to help with the war.

But when Jacob and Matthew showed up in my room, wearing their Sunday best, I did not want to see them. Jacob's red hair was combed back slick, showing blue eyes like his father's, but older than I remembered, and Matthew's hair was so short, I could see the freckles up high on his forehead. They stood by my bed, Jacob smiling in a sad sort of way, Matthew just looking sad.

"Elisabeth," Jacob said.

I shook my head. "No. Jacob, you shouldn't be here."

He nodded like maybe he thought the same thing and looked off toward the train. I couldn't hear it calling, but he could. Both he and Matthew knew it was coming.

"Tell Mama I love her. Tell all the other girls the same. We fought hard, Elisabeth. We made what difference we could, just like Mama told us to."

"Don't say you're going, Jacob. The Missus can't take any more. I can't take any more."

"Tell her what I said. And remember you're my sister, always have been. Strong as steel, just like Mama." He tousled my short hair and his touch was like snow on the wind.

The train called out, and this time I heard it.

Matthew spoke up, his voice quieter that I ever remembered. "Tell Mama the same — I love her, and tell the girls so too. What you're doing is a good thing, Elisabeth. It means a lot to us all. And tell Mama we got her cookies. That helped too." He leaned down and kissed me on the cheek and I froze inside, not from his touch, but from his pulling away. I couldn't feel my hands, couldn't see the paper. I was too numb to say good-bye. Too numb to write down a word they'd said, even long after they'd left.

I didn't get out of bed that morning. Didn't get up that day. That night I tried to fall asleep in sheets tangled from tossing in them all day. I tried not to hear the train coming. But when more men stopped by to tell me their last words, things they wanted said to the people they loved, I did not know how to turn them away.

So I wrote their words down, all but Jacob's and Matthews's. I got up the next day, mended fences, tended livestock. I mailed letters. All but Jacob's and Matthew's.

Weeks passed, each autumn day drinking a little more life out of the land. I wasn't sleeping much, wasn't eating much. Jacob and Matthew's deaths pulled tight stitches through my heart, so much so, I'd find myself leaning on the fence now and again, crying for no reason. A hundred times I'd tried to tell the Missus what they wanted me to say, but one look at her, and my words were gone. I was left frozen, still as a lake. I wasn't steel, I was water, and too weak to do any good for any of us.

It was Sunday, and raining when the man came to our door. Dressed in a uniform, his chest splattered with medals, he looked dark and somber as a winter grave. He took off his hat and handed the Missus a letter. The letter that told her what I had not been able to, that Jacob and Matthew weren't ever coming home.

When all the rest of them were crying, I felt dry inside, wrung out and hung on a line. There weren't any tears left in me for Jacob and Matthew. I did my part of cooking and cleaning for the funerals. I did my part to let the silence grow big enough to take their place in the house, just like it'd taken Mr. McMahon's place. I wore black and stood sad by their graves.

But the Missus noticed. Noticed me for the first time in a long while.

She opened my door one night.

"Elisabeth?"

"Yes, Missus?"

"May I come in?" She was like that, her manners pressed fine as church linens, no matter how late the hour.

"Yes, Ma'am."

Truth of it was I didn't want her in my room. The train would be coming soon and I didn't know what it would do to have her there. Would the men still stop by, or would another living soul in the room keep them from saying what they needed to say?

She walked across my room, her house shoes making small noises on the old wood floor. She smelled warm as the bread she'd baked for tomorrow's breakfast, and when she sat at the foot of my bed, the springs squeaked.

"You've been writing letters," she said.

I nodded.

"To people we don't know."

I nodded. The train was coming. I knew it, even though I couldn't hear it yet.

"What is in those letters, Elisabeth McMahon?"

I wanted to tell her I wasn't really a McMahon. I was a girl who'd been thrown out by the train track like yesterday's dinner bones. But she was the one who'd taken me in, treated me as well as I could expect. Better, maybe. I had never lied to her. I didn't think I could start doing so now.

I bit the inside of my cheek, exhaled, and tried to say it all in one breath.

"Soldiers stop by on their way through to dying. They tell me things they want their kin to know. Mostly that they love them and miss them. Sometimes they apologize for things. I write it all down and send the letters. That's all. That's all that's in the letters."

The Missus did not look away from my face. Her own eyes were gray and green, the color of old metal. She did not believe me. I supposed I wouldn't believe me either.

Far off, the train called, so distant, it was more feeling than sound.

When she spoke, her voice was stiff as a school teacher reciting numbers. "What did my boys say to you?"

I felt myself freeze up inside, felt my breath stop, my words fade. I tasted blood from biting down so hard. I filled my lungs enough to exhale. I owed her to say this. I pushed the words out past the pain in my chest.

"They said they love you, and they love the girls too. Jacob said they fought hard and made what difference they could, like you told them to. Matthew said your cookies helped." I didn't know if I should say any more. The Missus' face was as frozen as I'd felt, and I was afraid she'd break if I so much as tapped her. But there was more. More I'd been holding inside.

"Jacob said I was made of steel, like you, but I don't see how that's true. And I know you didn't ask, but Mr. McMahon said he'd miss you, but you'd see him yet. And he had a road to walk and he was going to see his boys."

The train called out, closer. I imagined I could feel the engines, barreling through this world, shaking the living.

She nodded. Her eyes were red, but there didn't seem to be any tears left in her.

"Do you think," her voice caught and she swallowed to catch it up again. "Do you think anyone will be by to talk to you tonight?"

"When the train comes."

"I'd like to sit here. If you don't mind." That's when I realized the Missus hadn't always been a McMahon. Before that, she'd had a maiden name, a different people. People with spirits made of steel. Maybe even people who knew how hard it was to sit alone and wait patiently for the dead to come calling.

She put one hand on the covers, her palm resting on my leg. We sat there, looking out my window toward the train we could hear coming, thinking our own thoughts. When the whistle was loud enough, I pulled out my paper and pen and looked at my door instead. The Missus looked that way too.

Three men came walking in, wearing their Sunday best.

I wrote down their words. One man was from Chicago

and wanted to apologize to his father. He said to tell him he was right all along. Another man was from Texas. He gave me the names of all his kin and said to tell them he loved them. The last man said he didn't have any kin. He told me he'd fought bravely, and thrown himself in the way of fire so another man could live. I wrote that down too. I had a box filled with those kinds of letters. Words there wasn't nobody living left to hear, but me.

The train whistled low and lonely and called the men away.

"They're gone," I said to the Missus.

She glanced at the window, then back at my face.

"May I see?"

I handed her the paper, and she read it. She gave it back and patted my leg. "Only once a night?"

I shrugged. "Whenever the train comes through."

"Do you mind if I come sit with you sometimes, some nights?"

"I'd like that," I said. Her asking meant more to me than if she'd come out and said she loved me.

"Good." She stood, and walked across my floor. She stopped at the door. "If the boys, if they come, I'd like to know while they're still here."

I nodded. I didn't have the heart to tell her it happened so fast there wouldn't be time for her to hear me, wouldn't be time for her to walk from her room to mine before they were gone.

Yet, every night, going on two full years now, my mother and I sit together and wait for the train to call the dying to us. Sometimes she sleeps in my room, often enough we put a day bed by the window for her. I write down the words the men tell me, and she addresses the envelopes, never hearing them, never seeing them, but believing just the same. There's a strength in that, a steel I wish I had. I know she is waiting for Seth and Roy to come by my bedside. I know she is praying they won't.

I was praying the same, and more. I was praying the next time I saw Johnny, he'd be on that train, in the daylight, maybe sitting side by side with my brothers, and all of them coming home.

Prayers, even the best of them, don't get answered how you'd expect.

That cold Nebraska morning, when I was fifteen, I went out and did my chores like every day. I was thinking about Johnny's voice like I thought about him most constantly. Before the sun had shouldered over the horizon, I was already headed down the hard packed road to the elder Smith's farm. The frozen mud crunched beneath my boots, and I tucked my chin down closer to my chest to keep my face out of the wind. Even though it was cold enough to see my breath, I was warm inside. Not from doing chores. It seemed the only thing that kept me feeling warm and living anymore was thinking about Johnny. I was remembering how he walked, easy, with a slow swing to his shoulders. I was remembering how he looked at me, his gaze steady, the hope of a smile on his mouth. I imagined he looked at me like something behind glass he was saving up for. Like something he desired.

Before I even reached the Smith's front gate, I heard the thump of an axe hitting wood. It was a comforting morning sound. One thump, followed by the crack of wood splitting, falling. A pause, while another piece of wood was put up on the block, then one thump, followed by the crack of wood falling.

I shook my head. I couldn't believe Mr. Smith had got up so early. Even though he didn't like a girl chopping wood for him, his heart wasn't what it used to be. More than a couple swings of the axe left him winded. Mrs. Smith was still handy with the hatchet, but she didn't chop much more than kindling anymore.

I pushed the gate open and made my way to the woodshed behind the house, intending to take over the chopping for a while. The watery light of dawn played across the yard, veiling lavender across the worn grass, split rail fence, woodshed, and making a ghost of the figure who stood at the chopping block. Even at a distance I knew it was not Mr. Smith. It was Johnny.

Two years had made changes in him. He seemed taller, thicker muscled, but thinner too, so that when he turned sideways, there wasn't as much of him as there used to be. He had on his undershirt, his arms bare. His collared shirt and jacket were folded over the fence rail behind him. He didn't look up, likely didn't see me as I stood there, unbreathing, quiet as water stilled at the sight of him. I wondered if I was seeing him alive or dead.

He took three steps to the shed, picked up piece of wood, took it to the block, set it. He heaved back on the axe, bringing it over his shoulder and driving his weight from the hip to split the wood clean in two.

Johnny had always been strong. He was powerful now. And there was more than strength in his movements. There was anger. Pain.

Three steps, another piece of wood, and anger and pain drove the axe down, shattered the wood into two.

If he'd been on his knees praying, I couldn't have seen the sorrow in his soul better. I was ashamed for seeing him so, and knew I didn't have any right to stand there staring at him, at things he may not want me to see. I turned, quiet as I could, and took a step away.

"Elisabeth."

My heart beat at my breastbone and I trembled. But it had been two years since his words could stop me from speaking. Two hard years.

I pulled my shoulders back and tipped my chin up. I turned to him and nodded.

"Welcome home, Johnny."

He camped back on one foot, the axe laying lazy across his wide shoulders. But the wind did not carry the warmth of summer. When it stirred, it was cold as death. He tipped his head a bit. "Come closer."

Maybe a smart girl would have paused. Maybe a smart girl would have looked at the axe across his shoulder, the power in his body, and made her good-byes. Not me. I walked over to him, strong in my own way, in all I had been and all I had done since he'd left. Strong in what I'd become. He'd seen battles over the blue seas, and I'd seen them too, in the face of every dying man who came to my bed each night.

I stopped in front of him, so close I could feel the heat rising from his sweat. His familiar gaze made my knees weak and my mouth hungry.

I wished I'd run the comb better through my short hair. Wished I'd worn a skirt today, and realized I didn't own any that weren't black.

He waited for me to say something, but I didn't have words for him. There was hurt in his eyes, and a distance I could not cross.

"You cut your hair," he said.

I nodded. "So did you."

That got the ghost of a smile on his lips.

"And the trousers?"

I looked away, feeling the blush heat my cheeks. Not much makings for a wife, me in a man's clothes, doing men's work. I looked back at him, and shrugged.

"Jacob's mostly. No time for frills when there's so much work to be done. I do my own at home, and help out the elder Smiths when I can. Mending fences and such."

That put the thick pain back in his eyes, and something went out of him. He looked down at his boots.

"My dad?" His voice almost wasn't enough to hear in the waking world.

I'd thought he knew his dad was dead, and maybe he did. But maybe he needed a living person to tell him so. I'd written a lot of letters, telling a lot of people I didn't know the last things their loved one had wanted said. It was harder to say it to Johnny, and I wished I could use a pen and paper instead of my own faltering voice.

"Your dad said he loves you." I said it quietly, hoping he'd believe. "He said to tell you he's proud of you. That he's always been proud of you."

Johnny did not look up. "He told you so? When I left? Before then?"

"He told me so." I didn't tell him about his father standing at my bedside, didn't think he'd believe me if the words had come from his father's ghost.

The train whistled, far off. Johnny looked up, looked toward the train, like his father had. Like my father had. Like all the dying had. A shiver of fear ran down my arms. I held my breath and wondered if maybe he would make the same choice. To go to the dying world. My heart pulled tight with pain. I didn't want to do this, didn't want to lose him too.

"Please, Johnny," I whispered. "Don't go."

The train called louder, powering toward the depot. I felt the thrum of its engines like a pressure deep in my ears, building stronger until it filled my head, my chest.

Johnny was so still, I wondered if he was a dream, my dream, standing straight and strong in the pale gold light of dawn. He closed his eyes. The train called out, lonely. Close now. Nearly here.

Johnny took a deep breath. He opened his eyes and turned his face away from the sound, away from the train.

"I don't want to be anywhere but here, Elisabeth. Don't want to be anywhere but home."

I didn't think I had ever heard such sweet words.

He pulled the axe down off his shoulder and set it by his feet. When he held his hand out to me, I took it with my own. We held on tight until the train whistled its leaving sorrow. We held on tight until the engine thundered away. We held on tight.

ABOUT THE AUTHOR

Devon has sold over fifty short stories to fantasy, science fiction, horror, humor, and young adult magazines and anthologies. Her stories have been published in five countries and included in a Year's Best Fantasy collection. Her Allie Beckstrom urban fantasy novels, beginning with **MAGIC TO THE BONE**, are available through Roc books, and her first steampunk novel **DEAD IRON** will be released in July 2011.

Devon has one husband, two sons, and a dog named Mojo. She lives in Oregon and is surrounded by colorful and numerous family members who mostly live within dinner-calling distance of each other. When not writing, Devon is either knitting, remodeling the house-that-was-once-a-barn, or hosting a family celebration.

To contact Devon, or see pictures of her knitting, go to www.devonmonk.com

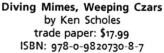
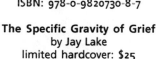

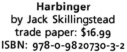

CPSIA information can be obtained at www.ICGtesting.com
Printed in the USA
LVOW111459111011

250049LV00001B/29/P

9 780982 073094